Raoul Whitfield was born in New York in 1898. He spent much of his youth in the Philippines, where his father was a member of the Territorial Government. He returned to the United States in 1916 and began acting in silent films, but soon joined the air service, seeing combat duty in France in 1918. After the war, Whitfield became a reporter for the Pittsburgh *Post*. In 1926 he published his first story in *Black Mask,* where he also published the series that later became his first novel, *Green Ice,* received with high acclaim: Dashiell Hammett praised it as "280 pages of naked action pounded into tough compactness by staccato, hammerlike writing." Whitfield followed *Green Ice* with two more mysteries, *Death in a Bowl* and *The* Virgin *Kills* (all available as Quill Mysterious Classics), as well as several books of aviation adventure fiction. An unhappy second marriage and poor health cut short his writing career.

Otto Penzler, series editor of Quill Mysterious Classics, owns The Mysterious Bookshop in New York City. He is the publisher of The Mysterious Press and *The Armchair Detective* magazine. Mr. Penzler co-authored, with Chris Steinbrunner, the *Encyclopedia of Mystery and Detection,* for which he received the Edgar Allan Poe Award from the Mystery Writers of America.

DEATH IN A BOWL

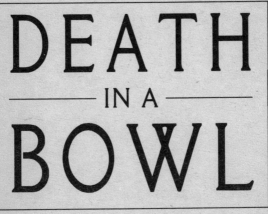

DEATH
— IN A —
BOWL

R A O U L
WHITFIELD

A Quill Mysterious Classic

SERIES EDITOR:
OTTO PENZLER

QUILL
NEW YORK

NOTE: *The characters in this book are imaginary.*

—R. F. W.

Library of Congress Cataloging-in-Publication Data

Whitfield, Raoul.
  Death in a bowl.

  (A Quill mysterious classic)
  I. Title.   II. Series.
PS3545.H656D4   1986   813'.54   85-19237
ISBN 0-688-02864-0 (pbk.)

Printed in the United States of America

First Quill Edition

1 2 3 4 5 6 7 8 9 10

—TO THE THREE VIRGINS
Of Hollywood, sympathetically

CONTENTS

·1·

"I COULD HAVE KILLEDHIM—"

Frey shrugged his broad shoulders, gestured helplessly with spread hands, palms upturned. His face was white and drawn; his eyes, streaked with red, held a weary expression. He said flatly:

"She wouldn't scream like that. She's been shot in the stomach—she wouldn't scream like that."

Ernst Reiner smiled in his superior manner, said something thickly in German, then spoke slowly in English. His tone was low; his words held a precise dignity.

"I use realism to get effects. If she does not scream—I lose an effect. She is shot in the belly, and she screams."

Howard Frey bowed mockingly. "It's your picture," he said. "She gets shot in the stomach, and she screams."

The director nodded, smiled at the mixer seated beside his control board, lifted a French phone. He spoke emphatically to his assistant below, on Set Four.

"Once again, George. The first scream—it is not so sustained. The second, it is high-pitched, sustained. Close to the camera, tell her. She is walking, bent forward, right into it. Terrible pain—that must register. All right, George."

Reiner hung up. He sat in the wicker chair back of the thick glass which made the set below soundproof. He looked down at Maya Rand. She was very beautiful, but very difficult to work with. For that matter all humans were difficult to work with—even Frey, who had written the story.

The action started. Reiner shrugged his shoulders. This was not like the old days—this talking picture business. He could direct only the rehearsals now. He must be close to the mixer when they were shooting. It was the sound he must direct.

Maya was turning now, facing the camera. She was smiling—now she registered fear. She cried out: "No— for God's sake—don't!"

The first shot cracked. She screamed. It was a horrible scream. Three more shots made sound in the silence that followed the scream. Maya was pressing her hands against her stomach now. She was walking toward the camera; her face was twisted. She screamed again. It was good, the way she did that. Reiner pressed a button, lifted the French phone.

"Cut!" he called. "That is good."

Frey swore nastily. "It's damned rotten," he said. "She wouldn't scream that way. And if you can get that piece of business past the Hays office—you're good."

Reiner paid no attention to the man who had practically rewritten the adaptation from the original story. He spoke to the mixer.

"Give her everything—in that last scream. Hold her down—on the first. She doesn't realize what's happened at first, you see. Then, when he keeps on shooting—she realizes—"

The mixer nodded. Frey said bitterly:

"It'll never get by—a woman shot in the stomach. You can do that in a book, but we're making a picture. They'll cut it out—and it'll take the guts out of the picture. It'll be a louse—like the last one you made."

Reiner straightened. He was short, rather heavy. He was a German-American. He stood now, raging, running the palms of his hands, fingers spread stiffly, up and down the material of his coat.

"If the last picture was a louse," he said in a shaken tone, "it was your work, you see? You made it bad, you see?"

Frey was medium in size, well built. He had broad shoulders and good arms. He had hated Reiner for three months, and two days ago he had gone swimming with Maskey, in the Maskey pool. He was bigger than Reiner. He was through with Reiner.

"To hell with you, you fat slob!" he gritted. "You've got to have everything—and still you can't get by. You get the best woman we've got on the lot. You grab off the pick of stories. You shoot every scene a half dozen times, and then need more retakes than any director here. You get the best music, the best lights and sets. Everything. And still you make flops. You don't hand me—"

Reiner was smiling. He said in a cold mocking voice:

"But in spite of these many faults, I am able to sleep in my own home. I am not forced to spend my nights—"

Frey took two steps forward, struck heavily with his right fist. The director had no protection from the blow. He threw up his right arm slightly, but it did no good. His legs gave way under the weight of his body; he fell almost in the center of one of the rugs thrown over the control platform's wooden floor. He was unconscious as he went down.

The mixer was on his feet; he was a young, blond-haired man. He stuttered toward Frey:

"For God's—sake—Mr. Frey—"

Frey looked down at the motionless form of the director. He smiled with his lips pressed together. Then he parted them, said slowly and very calmly:

"I could have killed him—for that."

2

Ben Jardinn sat across the small table from Ernst Reiner. His lean, pale face was expressionless as the director finished speaking. He nodded his head, but he did not speak. Reiner said:

"My contract, thanks to a good lawyer, could not be broken. Maskey had a choice to make—it meant money, a lot of money. He chose to keep me. I might easily have prosecuted Frey. I did not. Since he struck me down, three days ago, several things have occurred. I am not exactly afraid—but at the same time—"

He stopped again, smiling with his eyes. Jardinn said:

"I think you've told me about these things. Frey went to Maya Rand and appealed for help. She turned him down. He then went to your assistant, George Hillard, and offered him twice the amount of money he would make on this picture—to quit. He was turned down again."

Reiner nodded. "I have said nothing about the affair. But these things get around. Perhaps Frey is not so great a writer as he thinks. He will find it difficult to find work. It will enrage him, because he is vain. I am afraid of the result."

Jardinn nodded. He had dark eyes and hair. His body was lean, but it had firmness. He was in his late thirties. His voice was soft; when he spoke he had a habit of turning his head away from the person to whom he talked.

"What fear have you?" he asked.

Reiner frowned. He had small, brown eyes. They were narrowed back of glasses he wore. He replied hesitatingly.

"There is Maya. Frey was a very ardent admirer. I don't think he was in love. Now she has placed herself definitely on my side. There is George Hillard. I understand that Frey got him into pictures several years ago. George is staying with me."

Jardinn smiled. "You are afraid Frey will do something to them?" he asked. "Isn't that taking it a bit big? After all—you got sore at each other and he knocked you down. In the final settlement you won out. That's happened before. Most directors are more important than writers. What do you think Frey will do?"

Reiner shrugged. "It is not so small—this matter," he said. "The money—I do not think of that. Frey has money. But I have won—and he has lost. It will infuriate him. And he will hear about it on all sides. That is Hollywood. It is not a small thing."

Ben Jardinn nodded. "What do you want me to do?" he asked slowly.

Reiner smiled. It was a peculiar smile. Jardinn could not get the meaning.

"Remember what I have told you—merely that," the director replied. "There is nothing else to do. And remember also that Frey said, as he looked down at me: 'I could have killed him for that.' "

Jardinn frowned. "*You* didn't say a very nice thing," he reminded. "You've both been under a big strain. But I'll jot our talk down, when I get home. I don't like to write—it will cost you fifty dollars."

Reiner nodded. "That is very good," he said. "You have done some nice work in Hollywood. Several have spoken of you to me. I have an envelope in my desk, addressed to you. There is a check inside. It is for the amount of five thousand dollars. It is payable to you, dated a month from this time. If it comes to you—you will help?"

Jardinn smiled. "You think Frey will murder you?" he asked, almost cheerfully.

Reiner rose from his chair. "I think he will try to hurt me in some way," he said quietly. "I'm very sure of it."

Jardinn rose and shook hands with the director.

"You've made some fine pictures," he said. "They

show a good deal of imagination. Cities of the future, and that sort of thing. Perhaps your imagination is working now.''

Ernst Reiner continued to smile in his peculiar way. He stood near the small table as Ben Jardinn moved toward the door of the studio office.

"It would be nice to think that," he said steadily.

3

Jardinn and Max Cohn had dinner together at the Brown Derby on Vine Street. Cohn was short, chunky, quiet. He had come into the agency two years ago; Jardinn considered him their best man. Nothing excited him; he had killed two radicals in five seconds, six months ago— and had got in return only a bullet in the left arm. He knew Hollywood. Surface talk meant nothing to him; he got beneath every word.

He said in his nasal voice: "I agree with Reiner. It isn't such a small thing. Frey comes from a bad family. His father served a ten stretch for a shooting down south. He's got a cousin on the Los Angeles police force. A lieutenant. It's a rotten police town, and he could count on help."

Ben Jardinn smiled. "He's made good money for three years—and he's saved most of it. After all, Reiner said something pretty harsh—and Frey had the satisfaction of knocking him down. He might try to do him some harm in pictures, but not personal harm. Reiner has imagination—he's worried. I don't think he's a coward."

Cohn raised a glass of water to his lips, spoke into it.

"Frey's coming this way—easy!"

Jardinn laughed rather heartily. They were eating in a booth at the rear of the Brown Derby; he said in a loud voice:

"—and my horse finished fifth. I'd have had better luck if I'd stayed at the Casino."

Howard Frey reached their table, let his dark eyes meet Jardinn's. He smiled, said slowly:

"You're Jardinn. Tom Bender said you were over here. I'd like to talk with you—not here. At your office, say. But tonight, if possible."

Jardinn smiled up at the writer. "Unless it's pretty important—" he commenced, but Frey cut in.

"It is. I'm perfectly willing to pay for the inconvenience to you. It's damned important."

Jardinn kept on smiling. "All right," he said. "I'll cut the coffee and we'll go right away. Max—you take your time. Come over later."

Cohn nodded. Jardinn rose, got his soft, dark hat, went out with Frey. The writer took short nervous steps; when they got outside and were moving along the Boulevard from Vine Street, he kept moving his head from side to side. He didn't talk.

The agency was located in a frame building two blocks from Grauman's Chinese Theatre. The rooms were not particularly well furnished, but the chairs were comfortable. Jardinn closed the outer door behind him, locked it from the inside. He led the way into his own office, gestured toward a leather chair. From his own seat, with two table lights switched on, he could catch every expression in Frey's face. It was a sensitive face.

"You did a nice job on the Sarrell thing," Frey said immediately. "Getting her off with a year was splendid work."

Jardinn nodded. "*I* think so," he agreed. "If she'd come to me a little sooner I might have been able to get an acquittal."

Frey was sitting tensely in the chair. He said slowly:

"*I've* come to you soon enough. You've probably heard the rumors. I wrote *Death Dance* for Famous. Ernst Reiner was directing. He still is. We had an argument; he insinuated, after I'd called him a few names, that I was forced to have affairs with women who are impor-

tant, in order to hold my job. I knocked him unconscious.
I'm pretty strong. He went to Maskey—and I was let
out. It was one of the two of us. Maskey's a businessman.
He kept Reiner.''

The writer paused. Jardinn said quietly:

"I'd heard this much."

Frey nodded. "I want you to hear it from *me*," he
said. "I was wrong, of course. My nerves were in bad
shape. Reiner's last picture was a million dollar flop.
This'll be another—and it's my story."

Jardinn sat motionlessly and waited. There was something about Frey he liked. The man was direct enough.
He wasn't beating around the bush.

"I'm not afraid of anything that Reiner will do to me
directly." Howard Frey was speaking more slowly now.
"I'm afraid of something else. I'd like you to listen to
it. If a retainer of five hundred would help any—"

He let his words trail off. Jardinn nodded. He spoke
quietly.

"That will do nicely. You think that someone might
take Reiner's life, and that, under the circumstances, you
would be suspected?"

Frey looked faintly surprised. He leaned forward in
the chair.

"Yes, that's it," he said. "Was it that obvious?"

Jardinn shrugged. "Just a guess," he replied. "What
makes you think Reiner's life is in danger?"

Frey said slowly: "He's done some rotten things. Not
so much with women, but with men. Men he's worked
with out here. He's pretty ruthless. He's hurt a lot of
people. Now these people know that finally someone
knocked him down, on the set. I'm not sure of anything,
of course. But I wanted to protect myself. I heard in-
directly, today, that when I looked down at him I said:
'I'll kill you for that.' I didn't say it. But it's got around.
And knowing what I do—"

The writer stopped again. He smiled a little. Jardinn nodded his head.

"Why do you come to me with this explanation?" he asked.

Frey reached for his cigarette case, offered it to Jardinn. They both lighted up.

"You took Reiner's statement," Frey said quietly. "I wanted you to take mine."

Jardinn got up, went over to the window, and looked out. It had been a jolt, and he wanted a few seconds to think. When he faced the writer again Frey was looking thoughtfully at the tip of his cigarette. Jardinn said:

"How do you know Reiner gave me any sort of a statement?"

"It cost me money to find out," the writer replied. "I'm honest with you. Money will buy almost anything—in Hollywood. It didn't buy that dark-haired secretary of yours. But I'd let out the blue-eyed stenographer you took on last week."

Jardinn whistled softly. He grinned at Howard Frey.

"Cohn took her on," he said. "I figured he had a reason but I wasn't sure. I'll fire her tomorrow, and kick Max in the rear end. You got a transcription of Reiner's statement, eh?"

Frey took it out of an inside pocket and handed it to Jardinn.

"I'm through with it," he said. "He quoted me correctly. I did say: 'I could have killed him—for that.' But I'm through. I'm square with Reiner, and I'm sorry I knocked him down. He doesn't have to worry about me."

Jardinn said: "You're going out of your way to play safe. You know something. You've made this same statement somewhere else."

"Naturally." Frey chuckled. "You are working for Reiner. Perhaps for me, too. But I am playing safe. I've

a cousin on the police force. Lieutenant Charles Bracker.
In Los Angeles. He and I—and a notary got together. I
told them what I've told you.''

Jardinn's dark eyes narrowed. He sucked in cigarette
smoke, let it issue from between his lips in a thin stream.

''It isn't worth a damn, your statement,'' he said.
''Neither is Reiner's.''

Howard Frey swore softly. ''Mine's worth as much
as his,'' he reminded. ''That makes mine worth something. While he's alive *he* tells you that if he's murdered
I did the job. That's it, in effect. And while he's alive
I tell you that if he's murdered, I didn't do the job.''

''And you are willing to pay me five hundred dollars
to listen to the statement, after you've already placed it
in a nicer spot,'' Jardinn said.

Frey took a wallet from his inner pocket and counted
out five hundred-dollar bills. He placed them on the table.

''Your agency has always been fair,'' he said. ''I don't
know how much Reiner has paid you. A lot more than
this, I can guess. He's going to be finished, and he knows
it. I'm not going to be the goat. I'm in a tough spot, and
I know it. When it happens—I'll work with you. Will
you work with me?''

Jardinn said: ''Yes—but get this straight. A statement
and a retainer doesn't clear the way for you. Because
you come to a man who has listened to Reiner tell him
that he feels you will try to hurt him—and deny it—that
doesn't mean so much. Because you tell me that if anything happens to him you will be suspected but you won't
be guilty—that doesn't mean you won't be guilty.''

Frey smiled with his lips. ''I wouldn't want your agency
hounding me,'' he said. ''I want you to have to worry
just as much about my statement as Reiner's. I think you
will.''

Ben Jardinn narrowed his eyes on the writer. He nodded.

''Why don't you come through, and let us help Reiner?''
he asked.

Howard Frey rose from his chair. He laughed bitterly.

"I couldn't help him if I wanted to," he said quietly. "And I don't want to help him. Why should I? Hasn't he tried to fix it with you so that I'll be suspected?"

Jardinn sighed. "It all sounds like two picture people getting dramatic over nothing much," he said.

Frey went toward the door, followed by Jardinn. When it was unlocked the writer spoke.

"When I'm dramatic I don't spend five hundred dollars," he said steadily. "You know damned well I'm not going to murder Reiner. Yet he's afraid. You know that. He hates me—and he doesn't know—"

The writer checked himself. He swore softly. Jardinn said with mockery in his voice:

"When does the killing come off?"

Howard Frey smiled. "If I knew that I'd be eating dinner with three people at just that second," he replied grimly. "My idea is—to hell with Ernst Reiner—but give *me* an airtight alibi!"

He went out and down the stairs. Jardinn, frowning with his dark eyes, moved back into his office. He was tapping on the surface of his desk with his right-hand knuckles, and whistling softly, when Max Cohn came noisily in.

"Fire that blue-eyed woman of yours in the morning," he said. "She sold out on us—gave Frey the stuff Reiner dictated."

Cohn grunted, dropped into the chair that Frey had vacated.

"The dirty brat!" he breathed. "Does it hurt us much?"

Jardinn grinned. "Not a damn bit," he said cheerfully. "But when you fire her—it'll hurt *you*."

"She isn't a businesswoman," Cohn replied. "Her place is in the home."

Jardinn nodded. "Ger her a single apartment up along Franklin Avenue," he suggested. "*Keep* her in the home."

Cohn looked hurt. He lighted a narrow, black cigar.

"What about Howard Frey?" he asked.

Jardinn looked out of the window, toward Hollywood Boulevard.

"Reiner's spotted to go out," he replied. "Frey thinks he's been picked for the goat—by Reiner. He came in to retain us. He wants us to play fair. Someone's going to do for Reiner, and they're going to get after Frey. Planted evidence against him. We're to be nice—and get him clear."

Cohn grunted and pulled on his cigar.

"Maybe he knows things, this Frey," he suggested nasally.

Jardinn ran long fingers over the pallid skin of his lean face.

"It's a queer layout," he breathed. "Ernst Reiner comes in and says if anything quick happens to him—look up Howard Frey. Then Frey comes in and says that Reiner can't get away with that. If anything happens to Reiner—don't bother with Frey."

Cohn said, without humor. "Maybe it'll be two other fellows."

"They're both paying money—and neither of them is dumb," Jardinn said. "Reiner isn't asking for protection. He's pretty cool about it. Frey acts half amused. He pays five hundred. Reiner gives me fifty for getting his statement down—and there's five thousand coming if he gets the dose."

Cohn cocked his head to one side. He whistled cheerfully.

"We've got to wait for a murder," Jardinn said slowly.

Cohn grunted. "Wait, hell!" he breathed. "We've got to *pray* for it."

·2·

DEATH IN A BOWL

The next afternoon, at four o'clock, Max Cohn called the agency. Carol put him through to Jardinn, who had just come in.

"Did my little girl get packed up?" Cohn asked. "I've got another one for the office."

Jardinn swore at him. "One woman in here is enough," he said. "Carol can do the stenographic work and we'll give her a raise. Your blue-eyed brat has gone, and it'll take us two days to get the odor of cheap perfume out of the office."

Cohn said: "Ernst Reiner has a brother. Know anything about music?"

Jardinn groaned. "You mean Hans Reiner has a brother," he corrected. "He's conducting tonight at the Bowl. What about it?"

Cohn's voice held a disappointed note. He spoke slowly.

"It's a big doing," he said. "All the picture crowd will be there. Ernst has Box Twenty-two. That's in the second tier of boxes, just about in the center. Maya Rand will be in the party. And that Maskey son-in-law. And

Durling, the guy that's supervising *Death Dance*. Some others, not so important.''

Jardinn said: "Good enough—how about Howard Frey?"

"Box Seven," Cohn replied. "That's in the first tier, off to the right as you face the shell. I checked up at the Bowl. It'll be a big crowd, some twenty thousand or so. It's Hans Reiner's premiere in the west. Getting a lot of publicity—and Ernst shares it, of course."

"Sure," Jardinn replied. "All right, you needn't come back here. If you can get away from that woman of yours for an hour or so, better go out and take in the concert. Maybe you can snare a seat somewhere near Reiner's box. I'd like to know just who sits with him. Might help. Stick through the racket."

Cohn made clicking sounds. "Will I see you out there?" he asked.

Jardinn said: "It's a social event I wouldn't miss. But don't bother with me unless I give you an opening. One has to be careful at these sort of affairs."

Cohn called him a bad name, and Jardinn hung up. He called out loudly: "Carol, you bum!"

His secretary came in. She was good-looking in a substantial sort of way. She had dark eyes and hair, and though her features were rather large they were also well formed. Her mouth was firm, and she had nice, even teeth.

"Thanks for the raise, Bennie," she said, smiling. "How much is it?"

She only called him Bennie when she was pleased, and it always annoyed Jardinn. He said savagely:

"Ten a week—and you won't be worth it. For God's sake learn how to punctuate, anyway."

She chuckled like a man. "I can use a better brand of face cream," she said. "Maybe it'll get me a man."

Jardinn grunted. "Hollywood's a hell of a spot for a

homely woman," he said, "but I wish you luck. Got my ticket?"

She laid the ticket on the desk before him. She had nice fingers. Long and not too pointed. They were strong fingers. He could tell that by the way she crushed things in them. She wasn't afraid to use them.

"Row B, second tier," she said. "About four seats to the right of Box Seven—and two rows behind it, above it. Too far to the side for the best music. You'll get too much brass and not enough of the strings."

Jardinn smiled mockingly. "Hans Reiner does not play the brass," he said. "He likes fugues in string, and some of the Debussy music."

Carol laughed at him. "He's playing 'Afternoon of a Faun,'" she said. "You won't get the French horns right."

Jardinn swore at her. "If you weren't so damned stubborn I'd marry you," he told her. "Where are you sitting?"

She laughed at him again. "I'm not," she replied. "I'm going down to the beach and dance at the Ship, with a wop named Abe Montelli."

Jardinn got up, slipped the ticket in a vest pocket and reached for his hat.

"Carol Torney," he said slowly, rolling the *r*'s, "and Abe Montelli. What in hell you going to call the kids?"

She straightened up some papers on his desk.

"He isn't that kind of a wop," she said quietly. "His brother is Frey's bootlegger."

Jardinn stopped moving toward the door and stared at her. He started to say something, changed his mind. He went over to her and gripped her right arm just above the elbow. He said harshly:

"Don't mix up in this, Carol. It's going to be nasty. A lot of loose ends. Max and I can take care of it. Stay away from this Montelli bird."

She smiled at him. "All right," she replied. "I'll stay

home and catch up on my knitting. With the back door locked and Uncle Laurie to keep an eye on—"

Jardinn swung her around "Max and I can handle this," he repeated. "Stay clear, Carol."

She looked at him with her dark eyes half closed.

"A girl's got to have fun," she said tritely.

He took his fingers away from her arm. He grinned at her.

"Go home tonight," he said. "I'll buy the drinks tomorrow night."

She kept smiling at him through her narrowed dark eyes.

"Maybe," she agreed. "But if you do, it'll be to forget what a job you've got on your hands."

She started for the door of his office, but he got in the way. It wasn't the first time he'd heard her make half stabs at future events.

"Listen, Irish," he said, "did Frey's bootlegger tip someone off that Howard was going a-gunning tonight?"

His mockery didn't bother her. She looked him in the eyes.

"Max doesn't know an oboe note from a first violin A," she stated. "You tell him to pick a good, center spot tonight. You know music—you pick a bum location. How come?"

He stepped aside. "It's just a funny idea of mine," he replied.

She nodded. "Sure," she agreed. "It's funny as hell."

And her voice held a hard, brittle note. He'd never heard her get that sort of feeling into her words before.

2

It was ten after eight when Jardinn turned off Hollywood Boulevard to the right, moved up Highland toward the Bowl. There was a jam of machines; experience had taught him that it was simpler to walk to the symphonies under the stars. He kept on the right side of Highland, walked with his head bent slightly forward.

Jardinn loved music without knowing too much about it. He had a natural ear for massed tones; it pleased him to note the varied effects of visiting conductors, maestros—upon the Los Angeles orchestra. There had been, this season, the Spanish maestro. He had used the baton during two concerts. The men had played raggedly, without feeling. The audience had liked Bandosa, but that had been because he had waved his arms a good deal. Spanish music had lift, even if badly played. The critics had sneered, and that had pleased Jardinn because *he* had sneered. The season lasted six weeks. Luigo Crusant and Browkowski had each conducted, but they were established symphonic leaders. You did not attempt to criticize them, except in their interpretation of individual composers. They were always musicians, where Bandosa had often been a showman.

Hans Reiner was famous, very famous. He was on from Berlin, to conduct at the Bowl for the remaining nights of the season. Jardinn sympathized with him; his brother's position would mean, in Hollywood, much running about. After Berlin, Rome and London, Jardinn felt that the maestro would be puzzled, if not slightly bewildered, with Hollywood. It amused him to think of Hans Reiner at, say, one of Maya Rand's affairs. But then, Maya had absorbed some culture.

"A foot, perhaps—of the five-foot shelf," he muttered.

A voice behind him said: "Hello, Jardinn—going to the circus?"

It was Billy Long; he was flushed and bright eyed. He wore no hat, but his overcoat was a heavy one. Jardinn grinned at him.

"What the hell?" he demanded. "A Tin Pan Alley man going in for better things?"

Long chuckled. He was in a cheerful mood. He wanted
to talk, and as they walked along he did.

"Got thrown out of Tod Lister's house," he said.
"Went over for dinner; there was a gang at the place.
Tod got talking about a lot of things that he'd read about,
only he told them as though they'd really happened. We
hissed him down, and he got sore. Threatened to put
through a call to Georgie Nathan, and have him tell the
crowd over the wire that Tod Lister was a swell actor.
I said that was all very nice—but who in hell was this
Nathan. Tod kicked me out. So I decided to take in the
noise show and grab off a tune for a theme song I've
been trying to drink out of my system for a week."

Jardinn said: "You're getting too damned highbrow,
that's the trouble. How'd you come with the lady from
La Jolla?"

The songwriter swore with feeling. He pointed toward
a highly polished town car that was crawling toward the
Bowl entrance under the expert guidance of a well-rigged
chauffeur.

"There goes Bee," he said. "We used to say that in
New York, only she'd be walking out of Childs headed
for her boardinghouse on West Fifty-fourth then. Give
the little girl a big hand—she did it with her whisky
whisper, and two of my songs. Her voice has the studio
mikes grinning."

Jardinn said: "How'd you come with the lady from
La Jolla?"

Long swore. "Gave her that first lot I bought, up in
the hills," he replied. "She went back to La Jolla a
gladder and nicer gal. Nicer because she'd known my
pure love—"

He chattered on, and every once in a while, as they
walked up the winding dirt path into the hills, Jardinn
picked out something that was funny. He decided that
Long and Hollywood were well mated; both were noisy
and colorful. And clever.

Near the entrance he told the songwriter that he was waiting for a friend. Long looked very serious, and shook hands solemnly.

"I know how it is," he said. "These things will happen. Be good to her, Jardinn—set yourself up as an example. Don't let the world know that—"

A feminine voice squealed "Billy!" in an excited tone. Jardinn turned, saw two girls in blue rushing toward them. They were twins, apparently. Noisy twins.

Billy muttered: "My God—a sister act! Get clear, Jardinn—"

Jardinn walked down the path, bought cigarettes, lighted one and moved toward the entrance again. Long and the twins had disappeared. There was a crowd at the gates; beyond he could see tier after tier of seats. The hills rose darkly beyond the lights that fringed the Bowl. There was no moon as yet.

The orchestra was tuning as he reached his seat. The shell was dimly lighted—there was a babble of voices over the Bowl. Across Cahuenga Boulevard, set atop a hill, was the white cross that marked the spot, below, where the "Passion Play" was given nightly. There was a chill in the air; it would be almost cold before the concert ended.

Jardinn stood beside his seat and looked around the Bowl. It was a nice show; he guessed that twelve thousand or so persons were already on hand. And they were still pouring in through the gate, climbing the steps of concrete to their particular tier, or walking up the wide, sloping path on the right. He looked back toward Box 22. Maya Rand was standing; she was wearing an ermine coat. Many eyes, as usual, were turned toward her. An aisle cut along behind her box; people were strolling back and forth, watching her closely.

It was a four chair box, in the second tier, almost directly in the center of the Bowl. As perfect a spot for the reception of music as there was to be had in the

Bowl. Beside Maya stood Charlie Durling, his browned, handsome face turned toward the dimly lighted shell. Durling, who was supervising *Death Dance,* had a sunburn complex. Maya's skin was white—very white. They attracted much attention, these two. And Jardinn smiled as he thought that attention was something neither of them disliked. Dave Harris was seated, behind Maya. He was a thin, boyish looking chap—the son-in-law of Lew Maskey. Jardinn had met him while working on the Carroll case; he had found him not too artistic for pictures—and decidedly shrewd. He was studio business manager at Famous.

There was no fourth party in the box. Jardinn sat down and looked at Box 7, ahead of him and to the left. It was empty. It was, also, a four chair box. The orchestra was tuning up more earnestly now; in less than five minutes the concert was supposed to begin. But concerts at the Bowl were often minutes late in starting.

Jardinn took a long, thin cigar from a leather case, lighted it. An elderly woman had the seat on his left. The one on his right was as yet unoccupied. He had no program of the concert; he wanted none. Several times he turned, glanced back toward Box 22. Ernst Reiner had not arrived. Jardinn breathed to himself:

"In the shell—with his brother, I suppose. Wonder how he likes—playing second fiddle?"

He smiled at the thought. Somewhere he had heard that Ernst Reiner idolized his brother. But it was difficult, in Hollywood, to distinguish truth from publicity.

A voice reached him from the aisle that cut across the Bowl behind the first tier of boxes. It was Howard Frey, moving toward Box 7.

"Hello, Jardinn! Great evening, eh? Nice crowd."

Jardinn smiled, nodded. Frey was in evening dress; he carried a dark stick in his right-hand. He waved it carelessly toward someone seated back of Jardinn. His

face held a drawn expression, but his eyes were smiling.
He called out again:

"Oh, Eddie—give me a ring tomorrow, will you?"

Then he was entering the box, with three companions,
all men. They were all in evening clothes; Jardinn recognized none of them. He knew many people in Hollywood; it was a part of his business. It struck him as a
strange thing that he should not know any of Frey's
companions. Rising, he looked back at Box 22. The
short, heavyset figure of Ernst Reiner had entered. The
director was bowing before Maya Rand; he raised her
white fingers to his lips as Jardinn watched. The tuning
of the orchestra suddenly stilled.

Conversation died gradually. Jardinn seated himself
again. A man was taking the seat next to him. He was
dressed in dark clothes, wore a dark hat. He had coarse
features and bushy eyebrows. Jardinn's eyes went to the
fingers that held a program; they were long, tapering.
They were almost girlish. Such fingers were strange; they
contrasted the head, the face of the man.

Silence came suddenly as the lights at the side of the
Bowl died. The shell lights flared brightly. A woman in
a trailing, black gown came from the left wing and made
a speech about Hans Reiner. It annoyed Jardinn. He
cursed her under his breath, and kept his eyes on the
fingers of the man beside him.

Humans were still pouring into the bowl. Ushers were
holding them on the wide path at the right. They could
only seek their seats between numbers. The woman in
black finished her speech in something that was supposed
to be a graceful tribute to a famous maestro. She gestured
toward the left wing—Hans Reiner came into the white
light of the shell.

The applause was good; first and second violinists
tapped their instrument wood with bows. There were
cries from some of the foreigners, hoarse calls of *bravo*

and *hoch*. Hans Reiner bowed shortly as he moved toward the platform from which he would conduct. He was tall, slender, rather graceful. There was nothing in his body or head that suggested he was related to Ernst Reiner. Seated more than a hundred feet from the shell, Jardinn could not distinguish the maestro's features. His hair was dark and slightly waved; he had an erect bearing. Reaching the platform, he faced the Bowl audience, bowed. There was a storm of applause.

Jardinn turned, looked back toward Box 22. Ernst Reiner was standing. He held his fat hands above his head; he was applauding vigorously. The others in the box were applauding, but with less enthusiasm. Jardinn turned his head to the front again, glanced toward Box 7. Frey was seated in the front, on the right. He was not applauding, but was talking to the man beside him. In the reflected light from the shell Jardinn could see that he was smiling.

There was a hush as Hans Reiner faced the ninety-odd musicians, raised his baton. A woman sitting behind Jardinn said in a low tone: "They're beginning just three minutes late." The baton was tapped sharply against the music rack. The cello section droned sound into the silence. Jardinn relaxed in the seat, narrowed his eyes. The man beside him was breathing slowly, regularly. His program covered the long tapered fingers. His eyes were closed.

The second violins were coming in. A French horn sang countermelody as the first violins came in, sweeping over the deeper tone of the seconds. The music died; it was a tone poem that Jardinn had not heard played before. There was too much sentiment for him. He thought of Howard Frey, watching the brother of the man he hated, and smiled faintly. He wondered what Frey's feelings must be. He wondered why the writer had come at all.

There was a cymbal crash; the tympani fought with the brass in a sudden, fierce crescendo of sound. All instruments were playing now; Reiner was conducting well, assuredly. The orchestra was playing with vigor. The violins held the motive strongly, sweepingly.

Jardinn kept his eyes on the conductor. Hans Reiner was graceful. His body was motionless; only his rather long arms moved. He stood with feet close together—the right was slightly advanced. He turned his body at the hips, when he worked with one section or another. Jardinn nodded his head slowly.

"If he can play music," he breathed, "they'll like him here."

Cymbals were crashing again—brass was sending strident, staccato notes out over the crowd. As the greater fury died away there was a drone from above. It grew louder; the man beside him swore softly, shifted and tilted his head. Jardinn smiled.

Planes had disturbed more than one concert at the Bowl, this season. The location for the symphony was a scooped-out spot in the hills. Exhaust roar was picked up easily. Valencia, playing a piano concerto, had been drowned out for almost a minute. Protests had been made by the Bowl authorities, but the planes still flew close enough to be annoying.

Jardinn raised his head, looked up at the stars. They were not so bright tonight; there were clouds hanging over the Sierra Madre Range. The drone of the plane was becoming louder. Jardinn decided that it was a tri-motor ship. The man on his right swore again, in a half whisper.

"Damned planes!"

The music was swelling again. Brass and tympani could compete against the ship's engines; the strings reached Jardinn only faintly. All about him people were stirring, muttering. The drone was becoming almost a roar now. Jardinn frowned; he had never heard engine beats so loud. The plane seemed to be coming from behind, and very low.

Hans Reiner was working with the orchestra. His body
was swaying; the baton moved in greater and lesser arcs.
The tone poem was rising to a climax; brass dominated,
with the strings singing a rising melody, and steadily the
beat of the plane's engine increased. It was a roar now.
Only the crash of cymbals—the brassy flare of massed
cornets and French horns sounded above the exhausts.

And then, flying less than five hundred feet above the
Bowl, the ship flashed into sight. She was a big monoplane, but Jardinn could see no markings on her under-
wing surfaces or fuselage. She was a tri-motor plane,
and her roar completely drowned the orchestra now. The
man beside Jardinn cried hoarsely.

"It's a—damned shame!"

The Bowl was suddenly in darkness. Jardinn was tense
in the seat, staring toward the faint outline of the shell.
The musicians were lost in the blackness—not a light
shone. The roar of the plane's engines filled the bowl of
humans, beat down upon it.

The shell lights flared again. Jardinn stared toward the
orchestra, toward Hans Reiner. He caught a glimpse of
first violin bows, moving in unison. He could not hear
the music. Then his eyes were on the maestro. Reiner
was not leading now. He was swaying on the platform,
before the white pages of music on his rack. His baton
slipped from his fingers—he was twisting now. His legs
were giving away—his right-hand fingers were clutching
toward the small of his back!

His slender body was slumping as Jardinn rose in his
seat. The roar of the tri-motor plane was becoming a
drone again; he could hear the first violins; they were
playing raggedly, off tempo. Hans Reiner was pitching
from the platform to the floor of the shell. His body
struck heavily. Somewhere across the Bowl a woman
screamed.

For a second Jardinn stared. Music had died now.
Members of the orchestra were on their feet. Two of

them were moving toward Reiner's body. Jardinn turned, looked toward the box behind and above. In the reflected light of the shell he could see Ernst Reiner. The director was standing, staring toward the maestro's platform. His lips were apart; his heavy lower jaw was sagging.

A confusion of sound was rising. Jardinn swung around; he had almost forgotten Howard Frey. His eyes swept the box to the left, below his seat. He said grimly:

"Frey—not there!"

And then, for the second time, the shell lights were extinguished. Blackness hung over the Bowl. A voice, coming from a spot near the sloping path, reached Jardinn.

"Jardinn—this way. Hurry!"

It was Frey's voice. Jardinn moved past the man on his right. Frey had got into action, left the box as he had seen Hans Reiner pitch forward. He was trying to get down to the shell.

Jardinn reached an aisle and moved along it toward the path. He called out sharply:

"Coming, Frey!"

There were hoarse shouts in several sections of the Bowl. A voice down near the shell reached Jardinn clearly.

"Lights—lights!"

But there were no lights. Figures loomed ahead of Jardinn, indistinctly. He moved around them. He was out on the sloping path at the right side of the Bowl now. He called sharply:

"Frey!"

There was no answer. A woman's voice, from somewhere behind, reached him. It was pitched high, shaken:

"He fell—he went down—"

Jardinn swore softly, moved down the path. Still there were no Bowl lights. Men's voices called hoarsely for them; there was the tiny beam of a flashlight, below Jardinn's position and toward the center of the Bowl. Matches flared here and there—a figure suddenly was beside Jardinn. He was knocked off balance. A voice said thickly:

"Sorry."

It was a half whisper. Jardinn turned his head, muttered.

"That's—all right."

Something flicked downward, scraped his right ear. There was a battering blow on his right shoulder. He groaned, let his body pitch downward. He went to his knees—no one was near him as he turned his head. Bushes of the hill beyond the path crackled. He got to his feet. He called out:

"Hold up—or I'll—"

His words died. That was no good. He wanted to get down to the shell—someone had not wanted him to do that. Pain stabbed through his body. A blackjack or a gun had been used. It hadn't worked so well. But it hurt.

It would have hurt more if the blow had struck his head. He went on down the path. The lights flashed on again as he neared the huge Grecian vase at the right of the shell. Humans were surging toward the grass before the shell; a few uniformed police were trying to keep the crowd back. A group of musicians were bending over the figure that was motionless on the floor, near the platform.

Jardinn went around back, went in through the right wing, out on the platform. He groaned as a white faced musician turned suddenly, struck against his right shoulder. Then he was close to the motionless figure. As he looked down at the face of Hans Reiner he realized that Brendt was straightening up. The doctor said slowly:

"He's dead—shot in the back—four times."

Jardinn knew Brendt. He was one of the best medical men in Hollywood. He said in a steady voice:

"Rifle bullet wounds?"

Brendt shrugged. "Nasty wounds," he said. "Good sized bullets. Two low—two high. One of the high ones almost between the shoulder blades. In at different angles.''

Jardinn said slowly, "We can get that—in the autopsy. That plane went over—the lights were out—"

Brendt said: "Let's pick him up, get him into the conductor's room."

Several musicians lifted the body. Police were keeping the crowd from the platform. Ernst Reiner broke through, calling hoarsely, brokenly:

"Hans—Hans—what have they done—to you—"

Brendt caught the dead maestro's brother by the arm, spoke to him in a low, sharp voice. Jardinn saw that the director's body was trembling; he went slowly to the edge of the Bowl shell. He looked at his wristwatch, frowned. It was eight-fifty-five. Max Cohn came up to him, said nasally:

"Can't spot anyone in the crowd who heard shots or saw the flashes. What got him—rifle fire?"

Jardinn shrugged. "A human on each side path, sweet with a rifle—they could have done it," he said in a low tone. "The plane had the crowd looking up and the exhaust would take out most of the rifle sound. You can use a Maxim silencer on a rifle—there wouldn't be any flash, and the silencer might dull the sound some. But they had to shoot in the dark. The thing is, why did—"

He checked himself, turned his back to the tiers of seats. He lifted his left wrist.

"What time have you got, Max?" he asked.

Cohn got his watch from a vest pocket. They compared faces; Cohn whistled softly.

"You're twelve minutes fast," he said. "We checked to the minute, this morning. That watch of yours has always been accurate. Ben—it's a damned good make."

Jardinn nodded. "Hans Reiner *was* a good conductor, until four bullets dug into him," he said. "Things come along—and change things."

Cohn stared at him. Then he narrowed his eyes on the detective's lean face.

"I don't get you," he said softly.

Jardinn shrugged. "Supposing you want to kill a guy, Max," he said in a low tone. "How do you do it?"

Cohn swore softly. "Get him in a dark alley and give him the whole load from an automatic," he replied simply.

Jardinn nodded, reached for his cigarettes. His voice was steady when he spoke.

"That's the way I'd do it," he said. "*Unless* I had a damned good reason for being spectacular."

·3·

WRISTWATCH

Burkel said, his left eye closed as the right looked through the lens of the watch glass:

"She's running perfectly. She's twelve minutes and some thirty seconds fast. She hasn't gained or lost in the twenty minutes you've been in the store, Ben. I couldn't do much with her to make things better. She's a beautiful watch."

Jardinn leaned against the counter and smiled a little.

"I must have set her carelessly, a few days ago, Burkey," he said. "But I thought you should look her over."

The watch expert snapped the inner case shut, took the glass from his right eye, snapped the outer case. He handed the wristwatch back to Jardinn.

"Want me to set her back?" he asked.

Jardinn shook his head. He saw the mild surprise in the watch expert's eyes; he said smilingly:

"I'll do it, Burkey."

The watch man said: "It's just ten-forty. That was a terrible thing, out at the Bowl, eh?"

Jardinn fumbled with the wristwatch. He nodded, said slowly:

"Ten-forty—thanks, Burkey. Yeah, it was pretty bad."

Burkel narrowed his blue eyes on the dark ones of Jardinn. The detective was strapping the watch on his left wrist.

"Did the police get anyone?" the watch expert asked.

Jardinn grinned. "Sure," he replied. "Anyone that looked like a good bet. They always do."

Burkel chuckled, then frowned. "It's a job for you and Cohn, maybe," he said.

Jardinn let his left arm drop to his side. He said slowly:

"It's a *job*, all right," he agreed. "A job for anybody that sits in."

He thanked Burkel, moved toward the door of the little shop. The watch expert lived in the rear—he had come into the shop because Jardinn was a good customer, and a friend.

Ben Jardinn walked over to Hollywood Boulevard and turned up toward the building in which his office was located. A detective's car, with siren wailing, streaked down Highland and turned down Hollywood toward Los Angeles. Jardinn said softly: .

"So much noise—they must have picked up a drunk."

There was light back of the frosted office door. But the door was locked; Jardinn let himself in with his key. Carol was sitting at her desk, putting lipstick on with the little finger of her right hand. She twisted her head, smiled at him.

"How was the concert?" she asked. "Did you hear anything but the brass?"

Jardinn went around and stood near the wall on her right. He took off his wristwatch, wound it. He said slowly:

"There wasn't any concert, Irish. Just a few tunes. My clock ran down—what's the hour?"

Her eyes widened. She opened a drawer of her desk, took out a man's watch. She said in a steady voice:

"It's just ten minutes of eleven, Bennie. What do you mean, no concert?"

He grinned at her, set the wristwatch back twelve minutes.

"Some guys were busy killing Hans Reiner," he told her. "They shoved him out just after the start. So the concert was called off. Where've you been?"

She stared at him. She spoke slowly, deliberately. There was doubt in her voice.

"You mean—the maestro—was murdered?"

Jardinn swore at her. "Come out of it," he added. "There're enough actresses in this hokum town as it is. Get up off that chair and come into my office. I want to ask you some funny questions."

Her eyes narrowed. She wiped lipstick from her little finger with a tiny handkerchief. Her voice was suddenly amused.

"I didn't do it, Bennie—I swear to God I didn't!"

He turned at the door of his office, smiled at her.

"And you didn't stay at home with Uncle Laurie and your knitting," he said. "Come on in here, and leave the lies you're thinking up outside."

He went into the office. Max Cohn stood near a window, frowning.

"Get anything?" he asked.

Jardinn grunted. "Carol did it," he said. "She shot him from one side of the Bowl, then ran around to the other—and shot two more times. I'm disappointed in her, Max. Ain't you?"

Carol Torney stood in the doorway and swore at Jardinn.

"You'd better quit the game," she advised. "It's got you using bad English."

Jardinn nodded. His face held a peculiar, grim expression.

"I'm giving you that raise, Irish," he said, "only it's a different kind of one. I'm kicking you out of the agency. How much have you got coming?"

Max Cohn sucked in his breath sharply. He stared at Jardinn.

"For God's sake, Ben—" he commenced, but Carol cut in.

"Let him alone, Max—he's been working hard. Why the kick-out, Bennie?"

Jardinn seated himself in the chair back of the center table, near his desk. He said in an easy tone:

"I didn't like the gentleman you seated on my right, at the Bowl tonight. The one with the shaggy eyebrows and the nice, long fingers. And it isn't of you to fool with a fellow's wristwatch."

He heard Cohn mutter something that wasn't distinct. When he looked at Carol she was staring at him with wide, dark eyes.

"You're 'way over my head," she told him.

He relaxed in the chair. Cohn had come away from the window and was standing near him. Carol stood near the opened door that led into the other office. She was pale, and her eyes looked frightened.

"You got hold of my watch when I was washing up this evening," Jardinn said slowly. "You set it twelve minutes fast. I think I know why. You got my seat, and you got another one at the same time. That bird followed me down the aisle, when I was trying to get to the path. He took a swing at me—missed my head and got me on the right shoulder."

Jardinn pressed fingers against the coat cloth over the shoulder, winced. Carol said:

"You're running wild, Bennie—if you're trying to joke—"

Jardinn got up from the chair and started toward the girl. Max Cohn grabbed him by the right arm, and the detective shook him off.

"You went and got yourself bought off, Irish," he said. "I've checked you on the seats—you bought two. My wristwatch doesn't run fast. I could keep you around the office, but it's too much trouble for what I'd get out of it. I can choke the truth out of you. Who bought you off?''

The fear went out of her eyes. She threw back her head and laughed.

"You're walking in your sleep, Bennie," she mocked. "If you think I—"

His fingers closed over the material of her dark dress, just below her throat. He pulled her up close to him.

"If you can rat it with me—you can do it with the other fellow!" he snapped. "Who'd you sell out to, Irish?"

Cohn cut in sharply: "Take it easy, Ben—you may be wrong—"

Jardinn twisted his head and swore at Max. Then he got his eyes on Carol Torney's again.

"There was money in this kill," he said slowly. "You like money. Come on, talk!"

She tried to twist away from him. He shoved her around, up against the wall of the office. Her fingers were trying to twist his loose from the material of her dress. Max Cohn called out.

"She's a woman, Ben—for God's sake—"

Jardinn pulled her toward him, then snapped her head back. Her dark hair broke the force of the wall blow, but it hurt her. He gritted at her:

"I hate a rat—male or female! I'll break your damned, white neck—"

She cried, with terror in her voice:

"Let me go, Ben—let me go!"

He spread his fingers a little. His eyes were narrowed on hers.

"Well?" he demanded. "Give me the name!"

She twisted sideways, threw up her arms and started to sob. Cohn said slowly and with feeling:

"Oh, hell, Ben—that's no way to maul a woman."

Jardinn laughed harshly. He reached out and caught

the material of her dress again. He snapped her head
back against the wall.

"Come through!" he gritted at her. "I'll knock it
out of—"

She twisted loose, putting all her strength in the effort.
There was a swift movement of her right arm—the fingers
of her right hand held the gun muzzled toward him. She
said bitterly:

"Now you—get back! Now you get away from me,
Ben Jardinn. I'll shoot your goddam heart out! You—
get away—"

Ben Jardinn moved back from her. He said without
turning his head toward Cohn:

"You see what a—rat she is!"

Carol Torney stood with her back against the wall,
near the door. She was breathing heavily.

"I didn't—touch your damned watch!" she breathed
fiercely. "I only got one seat—you're framing me. You're
sore because you can't run—my private life. I go out
with the man—I *want* to go out with—and you can't
stop me from—"

The phone bell rang. Jardinn looked at the girl and
shrugged. He reached into a pocket and pulled out some
bills. He tossed her a twenty.

"That's too much for a rat," he said. "Take it—and
get the hell out of here. Better jump the town. When we
grab others we're liable to get hold of you."

He sat down in his chair and lifted the receiver. Cohn
was staring at Carol. Jardinn said:

"She isn't here. I don't know when she'll be in. Who's
calling?"

There was a sharp click from the other end of the wire.
Jardinn swore, hung up, called Central and asked where
the call had come from. He swore again, called the Hollywood Police Station and had Evans tell Central it was
all right. She told him the call came from a pay station
at Ninth and Olive, Los Angeles. Jardinn thanked her

and hung up. Carol stood in the doorway, her gun held low. She was smiling nastily. She said:

"You haven't got a thing on me. I've got plenty on you. I can make it hot—"

Jardinn cut in. "Get rid of that case of Scotch up at your apartment," he advised. "I can use that for a starter. I think you're sitting in with Ronnie White. Better take a trip away—"

Cohn said: "Listen, Ben—what's the use of making it rough for her? If she played rat—we know about it."

Jardinn smiled grimly. "It would be all right if she'd done it in a big way," he said. "But she didn't. Maybe she got a few grand for tinkering with my wristwatch, and buying a seat next to mine. Maybe not that much. Go on, Irish—put the gun up and make a duck."

The voice of a newsboy, shouting "extra," reached the office. Cohn looked at the girl, muttered thickly:

"I can't figure her—ratting it, Ben."

Jardinn grinned. "That's what makes it good," he said grimly.

Carol Torney stood looking at Jardinn, her body swaying slightly, from the hips up. Her voice was tight.

"Maybe you're in on this, you two. Maybe you're framing me out. You're sore because I went to the beach with Frey's bootlegger, Bennie. Max hasn't got guts enough to do anything but stick with you. I've seen it coming. Didn't he let you fire Belle? Didn't you try to—"

Jardinn yawned noisily. There was color in Carol Torney's face now. She jerked her gun hand up a little.

"You better not try—" Her voice, pitched high with rage, died suddenly as Jardinn got to his feet, moved around the table and headed for her. He walked in on the gun.

She cried: "Cut it out, Bennie—cut it out!"

She didn't squeeze the trigger. He knocked the gun out of her fingers with a swift, hard blow. He grabbed her by the shoulders, used his knees to boost her into the outer office. She was sobbing incoherent words at him.

He went back into his office, closed the door, locked it on the inside. Picking up the baby automatic, he slipped it in a pocket of his coat. Then he went over and sat down, lighted a cigarette. Cohn said:

"God, Ben—you may be wrong. I figured you were strong for her. She's been with us a long time. Maybe she didn't rat. Maybe she—"

Jardinn inhaled, swore out white smoke into a two syllable word.

"Maybe she didn't, Max. But she's running with the wrong crowd. I figured for a while she was just being big hearted, doing it for anything she might pick up. But—"

He stopped. A door slammed. He pointed toward the outer office.

"Go out and see if she's gone," he ordered. "Lock the outside door."

Cohn went out. He came back in a few seconds.

"She's gone," he said. "Why in hell would she set your watch ahead?"

Jardinn smiled. "Someone has brains," he said. "They might be able to take care of the police. It's been done. But a private dick is something else again. That plane was mighty important. I might be able to trace it. Supposing she wings along the Valley somewhere and sets down. Then I catch up with her. Twelve minutes is a lot of time in the air. About twenty miles—for a tri-motor ship. That murder occurred at about eight-fifty-two, by my wristwatch. But I'm twelve minutes fast. Maybe that tri-motor ship has been checked down—and checked down honestly—at eight-forty-five. I'd figure that ship out of the deal, wouldn't I? She was on the ground when Hans Reiner was murdered. I was supposed to count the plane out."

Cohn swore softly. "What made you check up with my watch?" he asked.

Jardinn said: "It was eight-fifty-five when I looked at my watch, on the platform. It didn't take me more than three minutes to get down there, from my seat. It wouldn't have taken me that long if Irish hadn't planted that bird next to me. A woman seated behind said that the concert was starting just three minutes late. I didn't look at my watch then—Reiner had his baton raised when she said it. He was shot down at eight-fifty-two, or within a minute either way of that time. That was by my watch. And I knew the orchestra hadn't played any nineteen minutes. When I checked with you it made me twelve minutes fast. That set the kill time back to eight-forty. And that's just about right. The concert had been on for about seven minutes."

Cohn said grimly: "But the police—they'd get a check on the time. You wouldn't be the only one in the place—"

"I might be the only one there who knew that Ernst Reiner was worried about Frey—and that Frey was worried about Ernst Reiner," Jardinn replied.

Cohn narrowed his little eyes. His thick lips parted. But Jardinn spoke first.

"I'd be more apt to be on the job. And it was just a helper, fixing that watch. It was a cinch for Carol to do. It was a cinch for her to put a guy close to me, so that he could try to slam me down. He nearly succeeded."

Cohn said: "He took a big chance. What was he stopping you from doing?"

Jardinn grinned. "Ernst Reiner will be here pretty soon," he said. "He'll figure that Howard Frey had his brother done in—motive revenge. If that bird in the Bowl had hit me hard enough I wouldn't be here to take five grand from Reiner, along with the job of finding his brother's killer. That's *one* thing he would have stopped me from doing."

Max Cohn went over and looked down on Hollywood Boulevard. He said with feeling:

"Carol Torney, crossing us up! It don't seem right."

Jardinn tapped ashes from his half smoked cigarette. He said grimly:

"It don't, Max—that's why I gave her the bum's rush out of here. She's gone Hollywood, maybe."

Max Cohn groaned. "I liked her, even if she was Irish," he muttered. "She had brains."

Jardinn tilted his chair back and closed his dark eyes. He said in a tired voice:

"She got careless in the way she used them, Max. I always did like her figure better."

Cohn grunted. "I like 'em heavier," he returned. "Who's going to tag her—and see what she does next?"

Jardinn whistled something from Dvořák's "New World Symphony" badly. He tapped his fingers against the side of his chair.

"I'll call someone she can't buy off," he said slowly. "Maybe a woman would be the right idea. That Gunsted woman. I've seen her a lot and I can't remember what she looks like. She's negative enough for a tailing job."

Max Cohn frowned at Jardinn. "Torney's got brains," he repeated.

Jardinn nodded. He smiled a little.

"I get more money for using mine," he said cheerfully. "Maybe that means something."

2

It was almost two in the morning. Jardinn got up and shoved the window wide. There was nothing on Hollywood Boulevard but streetcar tracks and the sidewalks. The air had a snap to it. Back of him he heard Ernst Reiner's voice. He'd been hearing it for several hours, and it always got back to the same words.

". . . used to talk to Howard Frey about Hans. He

knew I loved Hans. He knew this was the way he could hurt me most. I was instrumental in having Hans conduct in the Bowl. He didn't want to come. It isn't exactly a cultural center, out here. I tell you, Jardinn—''

Jardinn turned away from the window. He raised a hand, said briefly: "Don't."

Reiner shrugged wearily. His eyes looked bad—they were shot with red streaks. His shoulders had a droop. He was a pasty-faced bulk collapsed in the chair. He was emotional, and it annoyed Jardinn to see a man cry. He had wished, more than once in the past few hours, that the director would get up and smash things.

He looked at the oblong slip of paper lying on his table. He went over, picked it up, folded it, slipped it in a vest pocket. Reiner said:

"I don't want publicity. Hans is dead—publicity won't bring him back."

Jardinn swore softly. "It'll bring back newspaper circulation that hasn't had a story like this since a certain star sprayed lead all over a director named Naylor," he said. "You can't keep this off the front pages. It's red meat. A famous conductor shot down while he's leading an orchestra in the Bowl. His brother looking on—''

Ernst Reiner groaned, raised a protesting hand. Jardinn said quietly:

"If you want to get your brother's killer you can't be sensitive. I know how you feel. But death is just as complete one way as another. Hans Reiner's dead. We can't go around whispering about it."

The director got up from his chair. He got up slowly, with an effort. He said:

"I am convinced that Frey did this terrible thing. It will ruin me—I can't go on with the picture. Do you not suppose he thought of that? He is clever—a devil to do this to poor Hans. And to me. I could kill him—''

Jardinn said again: "Don't." He looked at his wristwatch. "It's getting late—or early. You need sleep."

The director stared at him. "You think I can sleep—
after this? I shall never be able to sleep again. I can see
him, swaying there—"

Jardinn said brutally: "In six months you'll hardly
remember how things happened. In two years it'll be an
incident you can regard as something rather remote. The
sooner you start forgetting—the better."

Reiner narrowed his eyes. His face was slightly flushed.

"*Gott*—you are like ice!" he breathed. "He was—
my brother."

Jardinn nodded. "I've got your check for five thousand," he said. "I think it will carry me all the way
through. I don't think it will be easy. Things went rather
smoothly. Don't talk too much. You're worth consid-
erable money, and if Howard Frey is as clever as you
think he might start a suit for defamation of character.
I'll do everything I can."

Reiner started to cry again. Jardinn lighted a cigarette.
He spoke quietly.

"I'll remember what you've told me, and I'll keep in
touch with you. I don't think your life is in danger. If
you want to avoid being hurt, don't read the papers. I'll
want to get inside the studio—there'll be people to see.
You can arrange that. Don't bother too much about what
the police dig up. They'll get a half dozen humans they
think killed your brother—and most of them will have
perfect alibis. They work that way, out here."

Reiner said thickly: "So many things—and I can't
think clearly."

Jardinn smiled. "If you don't get sleep—take something," he suggested.

The director stuffed his handkerchief back in a pocket.
"What?" he asked.

Jardinn shrugged. "Scotch," he suggested. "Get drunk
and sleep it off. Get sick and that'll give you something
else to think about."

"*Gott!*" Reiner muttered. "You *are* hard."

Jardinn went toward the outer office door with the director. Reiner was in bad shape—he leaned heavily against the detective.

"My car is down below—a block away," he said. "Can I take you to your home?" he asked.

Jardinn smiled his thanks. "I'm going to stay in the office a while," he explained. "I've got some notes to go over—and some more to get down."

Reiner said: "I must have the one who was responsible. I must!"

Jardinn nodded. "A killer is a rotten thing," he replied. "You may have to rip open your inside affairs—in order to get this one. It isn't pleasant. But it'll be something done, if we succeed."

The director straightened a little. His small brown eyes held momentary hatred.

"I will do anything—to succeed!" he said harshly.

Jardinn said: "You may have to do a lot. Start in by getting sleep—one way or another."

The director went out of the room and along the corridor. Jardinn listened to his heavy footfalls, went back into the outer office. He closed the door, locked it, went into his own office. He called a number, told Central to keep at it. After about thirty seconds he heard Carol Torney's voice.

"Yes?" It had a sleepy note.

He said: "Listen, Irish—you get too damned much sleep. It'll make you soggy. Slip a fur coat over your pajamas and come up here right away. Don't make a parade of it. I want to ask you things."

The sleepiness went out of her voice. She said:

"Okay—I'll be over. 'Bye."

She hung up. Jardinn scribbled words on a pad for fifteen minutes or so. They filled five sheets of paper. He burned four of them—and let the ashes drift over

Hollywood Boulevard. The fifth he tore into little pieces,
let a match singe a few of the pieces, and slid them from
an ashtray into a wastepaper basket near his desk.

When Carol came in he was leaning back in his pet
chair and smiling. He said:

"I'll send Max over to your place tomorrow for the
keys to the office. We can't have you running in and
out. You can get sore with him, if you want, but give
him the keys. When he comes back and points out that
you could easily have had some more made, I'll tell him
we'll change the locks around."

Carol Torney nodded. She sat down in a chair and
unbuttoned her squirrel coat.

"Like the pajamas, Bennie?" she asked.

He swore at her. "I don't like green," he told her.

She made a clicking noise. "Cut it out, Bennie," she
said. "You know I love red."

The pajamas were a pale blue. They were very nice.
Jardinn tossed her a cigarette. They lighted up. She said:

"Did he fall for it?"

Jardinn shrugged. "I can't figure Max," he replied.
"Maybe he did. We'll play he did, anyway. You put on
a good show."

She smiled. "What a sweet one they put on at the
Bowl!" she said.

Jardinn narrowed his dark eyes. "What a sweet one
who put on?" he asked.

She swore at him. "I can think of fifty easier ways of
shoving out a guy—than that way," she said slowly.
"How come?"

Jardinn frowned. "What gets me," he said softly, "is
why Max Cohn fooled around with my wristwatch. It
was right on the dot, before I went in for a wash."

The girl's long fingers played with the cigarette. They
rolled it from side to side as she held it on a level with
her lips.

"He knew you'd try to trace that plane," she said.

"He wanted the ship down at the time of the kill. So he set the watch ahead. That's my guess."

Jardinn nodded. "Maybe it's all right," he said. "But I like Max. I sort of hated to put on that act for him."

"Yes you did!" she replied.

"I'd like to know who got to him," Jardinn said quietly. "It's the first time an outsider has worked into the agency."

Carol eased her body down in the chair. She stretched well shaped legs aslant with the faded carpet.

"There's the blonde you kicked out of here," she suggested. "It costs Max money to keep her. I can name a lot of people in Hollywood that have the gold, Bennie."

He nodded. "That's what's going to make this hard," he said. "There's plenty of money around for the cover-up."

She said: "You were pretty rough, Bennie. You didn't have to rush me out like that."

He grinned. "That was just thrown in for good measure. What do the papers read like?"

She shrugged. "The usual bunk. They name all the pictures that Ernst directed—and list all the symphonies that Hans conducted. The reporters are all writing their heads off, naturally. The damn thing was spectacular, Bennie."

He swore softly. "It was a nice, colorful job," he agreed. "Thirty-thirty rifles—one on each side of the Bowl. Not too far back, but far enough to make it touch. Two boys at the triggers, just to make sure. And neither of them missed. Plane engine drowned the cracks from their guns—silencers killed the flame red. Got a hunch the gun boys were pretty well hemmed in by their own pals. The guy that throws the switch was outside smoking a pill when he was slugged. That tone poem runs twenty odd minutes. They had their own man at the lights—and he worked them right. It was smooth—and sort of simple."

"They shot in the dark," Carol reminded, frowning. "That was something."

He nodded. "That was hours of practice at just the same angle—somewhere in the hills," he said. "Probably they used a dummy—and they figured the slope of the Bowl. The conductor's platform is always in the same place. Reiner didn't move around much. My guess is that they had their guns raised when the lights went out."

The girl smiled grimly. "How'd they know just when they were going out?" she asked.

Jardinn frowned at her. "You *were* sleeping heavily," he said. "They had the plane coming right over the spot. When she hit the spot—the lights went out. And so did Hans Reiner."

Carol Torney shook her head. "Why the big show?" she demanded. "Why not a knife in the back?"

Jardinn laughed at her. "That answer would help a lot," he agreed. "It won't be easy to get."

She said: "Max was trying to cross you—maybe *he's* got it. Making him think that you figured *I* played with your wristwatch was not a bad idea, Bennie."

Jardinn said slowly: "It's a jolt for me. I always figured Max was just about right for the agency. It's hard to take. He figures you about the same way. He couldn't seem to believe that you'd cross us."

She smiled with her lips pressed together.

"He's keen," she said. "Doing that watch job himself, and then trying to make you believe that he didn't think I'd do it. Not agreeing with you—that wasn't so dumb." Ben Jardinn looked at his wristwatch. It was two-thirty. He smiled at Carol Torney.

"Reiner was in," he said. "He thinks Howard Frey directed the kill. Getting even. Knows how Ernst loved his brother. He's taking it pretty hard. I told him to get drunk and sleep it off."

Carol chuckled. "He's not the type," she said. "Frey been in?"

Jardinn shook his head. "Expect him in the morning," he replied. "I'm getting hungry. Max should be sleeping, but we'll play safe. I'll order up some beer and sandwiches. Then you can run along home and sleep. Have any of the papers got the studio fight stuff?"

She nodded. "The *Press* has got something about a rumored knockdown of Hans Reiner's brother by a well known picture writer," she replied. "It's carefully worded, though."

Jardinn frowned. He said suddenly: "By God! I forgot to take that lighter out of my blue suit when I sent it to the laundry this morning!"

Carol Torney snuffed her cigarette in the ashtray.

"You don't take this murder seriously enough," she mocked.

He grinned at her. "Business is business," he said slowly, and reached for the phone. He ordered four bottles of beer and two Limburger on rye. He hung up, went over and kissed her roughly on the lips. Then he went back and sat down again.

"And pleasure is pleasure," he said.

She kept her eyes on his. "Bennie—" she said after a while—"you're kind of nice."

He didn't seem to hear her. There was a half puzzled expression on his pale face; his eyes were looking beyond her.

"I'd like to know who got to Max," he said softly.

·4·

POINT-COUNTERPOINT

Ben Jardinn got to bed, in his Laurel Canyon bungalow, at four o'clock. He didn't sleep well. The beer hadn't been too good, and the Limburger sandwiches *had* been too good. At nine o'clock he got up, washed, dressed and cooked some eggs and coffee for his breakfast. There was an accumulation of papers on the patio grass—he picked out the right one and read seven columns of bunk on the maestro murder. Los Angeles and Hollywood police were working hard—they had accomplished little, so far as the newsprint showed. Hans Reiner had been cheerful before the concert. Ernst Reiner had stated that his brother had apparently had no worries. They had not seen each other, except for a few hours, in the past two years. Ernst was not familiar with the murdered conductor's personal affairs.

Hans Reiner had led a rather solitary life. Music was everything to him. He was unmarried, had no secretary. He traveled alone. Ernst Reiner had appeared "stunned," according to one reporter, "dazed," according to another—and "was a broken thing," according to the sheet's

sob sister. The one fact of which the police were sure
was that two expert rifle shots had loosed thirty-thirty
bullets from positions in the Bowl. No humans had been
found who had seen the riflemen or had heard the sound
of the guns. No one had seen the flame. The plane had
been traced—it was a tri-motor Fokker whose appearance
at the precise time of the murder had been a ''colossal
coincidence,'' according to a writer named Lunden, who
got a by-line for his stuff. The plane had come over from
Mines Field—it had been piloted by one Johnny Carren.
Six people had been aboard. They had paid five dollars
for the privilege of having a look at the Bowl from the
sky. Carren had gone the limit and had dropped down
low. It was alleged that one passenger had offered him
a hundred dollars to wing over at a hundred feet. Carren
had denied this and the police had been unable to find
the passenger who had made such an offer. Carren's
license was to be suspended for six months. The police
believed that the arrival of the plane, just before the lights
had been extinguished, had been chance. They were convinced of the fact—and were not holding Pilot Carren.

Jardinn sipped his coffee and read that the shooting
of *Death Dance* would be called off until after the funeral
of Hans Reiner. Studio officials sympathized deeply with
their star director. They were ''shocked,'' as were many
famous musicians in Berlin, London and Paris. Hans
Reiner had been a ''genius whose spark of divinity often
flared into flame.'' There was a column of such stuff. It
annoyed Jardinn; he tossed the paper aside and lighted
a cigarette. He didn't like words without reason, and it
was his opinion that Hans Reiner had been a pretty good
fellow who had been shot out of life for a pretty good
reason. The thing was that Reiner was dead, murdered.
And that the police were running around in circles. That
necessitated reporters using words in place of facts.

The phone bell rang—a reporter from the Los Angeles

Times was calling. There was a rumor that Jardinn had been called into the case by Ernst Reiner. The reporter wanted a verification. Jardinn asked:

"What case?"

The reporter, not without sarcasm, stated that Hans Reiner had been shot to death in the Hollywood Bowl, last evening. Hans Reiner had been conducting—he was a famous maestro. He had been murdered.

Jardinn whistled softly, as though in surprise. He said:

"That's too bad—who did it?"

The reporter muttered something that Jardinn didn't understand, hung up. Almost immediately the phone bell rang again. Max Cohn spoke.

"Ben? You coming down here today?"

Jardinn grinned. "Anything doing?" he asked.

Cohn swore at him. "I've got a line on Irish for you," he said. "And Howard Frey has been in. He'll be back in an hour. And the Gunsted woman is here now."

"Keep her there," Jardinn ordered. "I'll be down in thirty minutes or less. Got anything important on Irish?"

Cohn was silent for a few seconds. He seemed to be thinking something over. Jardinn said impatiently:

"Well—say something or hang up."

Cohn said: "Maybe it's important. She's running around early in the morning. I spotted her."

Jardinn set his cigarette on an ashtray and spoke steadily into the mouthpiece.

"Tell me the rest when I get down there. Call up Famous Studios and tell someone that Jardinn wants to get in touch with Maya Rand. Ask how. How's the blonde?"

Cohn swore at him again. "She's raising hell," he said. "A fiddler's got the apartment above her—and all she hears is off-key 'Cradle Song.' "

Jardinn chuckled. "It's the mother yearning that's got her," he told Cohn. "How does Frey look?"

Cohn hesitated again. "Worried," he said finally. "He told me that this put him in a bad spot."

Jardinn nodded. "It's liable to put a lot of people in a bad spot," he said. "You and I included."

Cohn said: "You better get right down here, Ben. There's no girl in the office, you know."

"That's tough," Jardinn admitted. "But you can look out on the Boulevard."

He hung up during Cohn's reply, got his soft hat from the floor near the decanter of Scotch, and went outside. There was a flivver down the canyon about fifty feet, in the paved roadway. It looked familiar. He walked around the tiny patio of the small, Spanish bungalow and stopped as he looked toward his roadster.

"Hello, Bennie!" Carol greeted. "I thought you were in the garage. I was going in."

He frowned at her. It was a warm day and the house windows were opened. He'd been talking over the telephone, and there was nothing the matter with Carol's ears. He said:

"You shouldn't come up here. You know Max thinks I've kicked you loose. If he gets wise to our little play—"

"He won't," she cut in. "He's at the office. I saw him go up. The Gunsted woman's there—she went up a few minutes after. I drove right out here."

He kept on frowning. "Why?" he asked.

She came up to him, spoke quietly. "I've got something on Max. He was prowling around last night. I left the office at three. He was in back of the house. I sent Uncle Laurie around back—and when he headed for the front I worked the porch light. He didn't see me, but I caught him."

Jardinn smiled. "Maybe he was figuring you'd give him a lead," he suggested. "But be careful. Better not call the office."

She nodded. "I wanted you to know that he's giving me a play," she said. "He figures I really did fool with that wristwatch of yours, and I'm a suspicious character."

Jardinn nodded. He said slowly: "The police figure the plane was just around by accident. Carren, the pilot's, got a nice story. Maybe the wristwatch stuff wasn't worth much, Irish."

There was a peculiar expression in her eyes. She nodded, moved out toward the roadway.

"Mind if I stroll around the Bowl?" she asked.

He grinned at her. "There'll be a mob out there—sightseers," he said. "But go ahead. The dicks don't know you. Max won't be out that way—I'll send him downtown."

She narrowed her eyes. "Downtown?" she said. "I'll keep my eyes open for him, Bennie, if you're sending him somewhere else."

She moved off, climbed into her flivver, and clattered down the canyon road. Jardinn got into his car and drove slowly out of the driveway. He backed around, killed some time in front of the bungalow—rolled at low speed down the grade. When he turned into Hollywood Boulevard there was no sign of Carol Torney's flivver.

Max Cohn was in the outer office, talking to Marie Gunsted. She was a middle-aged woman with a passive, rather flat face. Her eyes were almost colorless. She was dressed in dark clothes and wore a dark, ugly hat. Jardinn smiled at her.

"Just a few minutes, Miss Gunsted," he said. "Come on inside, will you, Max?"

Jardinn went in and sat down. He glanced toward the wastepaper basket. It had been cleaned out. The charred bits of the sheet he had written on last night were gone. He was looking at the calendar hanging over his desk when Cohn came in. He shut the door back of him, came over to Jardinn.

"Let's have it," Jardinn said. "You ran into Carol Torney running around town, early this morning?"

Cohn nodded. His little eyes were half closed; his short, chunky figure stood near the chair in which Jardinn sat.

"About three-thirty last night," he said. "She was walking, wearing a fur coat. She was going toward her house."

Jardinn said: "What in hell were you doing out at that time?"

Cohn grinned broadly. "I figured I might be able to pick something up—something on the Bowl murder. I didn't feel sleepy, so I went out. Just walked around."

Jardinn nodded. "All right," he said. "She was walking toward her house, at three-thirty. What of it?"

Cohn stopped grinning. "She was walking in that direction, but she didn't go there," he said. "She went somewhere else."

Jardinn said quietly. "I don't want the three guesses. You're being paid to tell me things. Don't let's play games."

"She went to Ernst Reiner's place," Cohn said. "Went around to the back."

"Did she get in?" Jardinn asked.

Max Cohn nodded. "Right away," he said. "She didn't make any fuss about it. Either she had a key, or she didn't need one. She got in—and at four-ten she came out. She went home. She went right in and undressed in the dark. Or maybe she didn't undress. I went home and got some sleep."

Jardinn reached for his cigarettes, tapped one on the desk surface, slipped it between his thin lips. He said quietly:

"All right, Max—that wasn't a bad stroll. Don't talk about it—I'll handle that end. Go down to the *Times* and ask Connors for a look around the morgue. Get everything you can on both Ernst and Hans Reiner. See if they've ever printed anything about Frey. You might look up Maya Rand, too. The clippings are all indexed. There'll be A.P. stuff from abroad. If you can get anything on Hans Reiner from the other side, it might help. I'll be here at four this afternoon.''

Cohn nodded. ''You putting the Gunsted woman on Carol?'' he asked.

Jardinn nodded. ''Better drop over and get the office keys from her,'' he said. ''Don't get in an argument— just get the keys.''

Cohn said: ''She's had time to have more made.''

Jardinn smiled a little. ''We'll have some different locks put on the doors,'' he said. ''But get the keys, anyway. On your way out tell the Gunsted woman to come in. See you at four.''

Cohn moved toward the door of Jardinn's office. He turned with his left hand on the knob. His little eyes were very small as he looked at the detective.

''It gets me—Carol working against us, Ben. It don't seem right.''

Jardinn smiled grimly. ''It don't, Max,'' he said for the second time. ''She's afraid of something. Afraid of the agency, maybe. Afraid of what we might do. We've had some luck lately. Someone else knows that, other than Carol.''

Cohn said: ''They've offered her money to cross us up, big money. And she's grabbed it.''

He shook his head, swore and went outside. Jardinn heard his voice, very faintly through the thick door, as he spoke to Marie Gunsted. He rose from the chair, faced the window and looked down on Hollywood Boulevard. Jane Winston came out of the Pig 'n' Whistle, across the street, and walked slowly along the paving. An Isotta-Fraschini, with a New York license, rolled shinily along. There was the sound of the door opening. It was Marie Gunsted, but Jardinn was still thinking of Max Cohn.

Ernst Reiner working against Howard Frey and Frey

working against Reiner. Max Cohn fighting Carol Torney—and Carol watching Max. A score for one—a score
for the other. Point-counterpoint. For the first time the
agency gears were grinding. Money could do that. Money
was doing it. But who was lying—Carol or Max? Reiner
or Frey? The human who had planned the murder of
Hans Reiner was a mystery. Little mysteries were trying
to keep him so.

Jardinn turned slowly from the window. Marie Gunsted
said in a flat tone:

"Is there anything I can do, Mr. Jardinn?"

Ben Jardinn shook his head. "I'm sorry," he said,
"but there was a mistake. There was a person I wanted
you to sort of watch, but she knows you. I wasn't aware
that she did."

He saw the questioning glance in her eyes. He said
quietly:

"It was Carol Torney. She left us, and I had an idea
you might keep track of her."

Marie Gunsted showed him something that was meant
for a smile. She said:

"Carol Torney wanted me to keep track of Mr. Cohn.
She changed her mind. Odd, wasn't it?"

She went quietly from the office. Jardinn sat down
and stared at the faded carpet. The only conclusion he
could reach was that it was about as odd as hell.

2

The girl had a baby face and figure and a husky voice.
She was dressed in a blue sport outfit that fitted nicely.
She had brown hair and eyes and she looked right at
Jardinn when she talked. She didn't seem too bright; he
liked her. After she'd got through explaining he said:

"All right—what do you know about this agency, or
me?"

She didn't smile. "You're the Ben Jardinn who went

after the bunch that framed Clara Sarrell," she said.
"You got her out of jail. I don't think much of detectives—but that was a nice job. I don't know much about
the office. I'm a fair stenographer, and I can keep quiet."

Jardinn nodded. "We'll take you on," he said. "The
last girl we had in the outer office couldn't keep quiet.
It's hard sometimes—when you want a fur coat or something."

The girl said: "I've got a fur coat and a Chevy that
gets me around. All I want is a job. If I change my idea
about men I may marry one next year."

Jardinn grinned: "Don't change your idea," he advised. "Thirty a week. Your name is Edith Brown. We'll
call you Ede around here. Familiarity is said to breed
contempt—and that's one of the funny things we like.
Howard Frey, the writer, will be here soon. Show him
a chair—and come in and tell me he's outside. Call the
agency that sent you and tell them you'll do. I'll go out
and show you how the buttons work."

He went out into the other office with her. When he
got back at his desk he took a slip of paper from a drawer
and started to scribble. His head felt better than his stomach. He wrote: "Ask Frey about his brother serving ten
year stretch. Ask him if he's got in touch with that cop
cousin, Bracker. Talk about his yelping for me at concert.
Are the bulls working on him? Call off any appointment
that Max may have made with Maya Rand. Get out to
Mines Field and see this bird Carren. Important. Check
on those in the box with Frey. Find out why in hell Carol
went into Reiner's place, *if* she went in. Carol and Max—
watch. Find out who gets Hans Reiner's money. Ask
Frey why he tried to buy Hillard off. Also about his play
with Maya. Get dope on Abe Montelli, Frey's bootlegger. Frey's bootlegger's brother—correct. Check on where
Carol was night of concert. Look up Ronnie White. See
if—"

He stopped scribbling as the new stenographer came in and told him that Howard Frey was outside. He nodded, folded the slip of paper, got it carefully in a small, inside pocket of his vest. He tilted his chair back, got his shoe leather on the small table and hunched down a little.

"Start him this way," he said. "Can you do short-hand?"

She frowned. "Not so good, but a little," she replied.

He smiled more broadly. "It isn't important, but try it," he said. "Snap that green button the right of your desk and use the headset that's hanging near it. Take down as much as you can—it'll come through to you clearly. But don't let it bother you any."

She nodded, went out. Howard Frey came in. He looked as though he'd missed some sleep. There were circles under his eyes. His lips were pressed tightly together. He was dressed very carefully, perfectly. He took a chair across the table on which Jardinn had his feet. He said:

"This is pretty bad, Jardinn."

Jardinn offered the writer a cigarette; he refused it. After he had lighted up the detective said:

"Anyone working on you?"

Frey nodded. "Some plainclothesmen from the D.A.'s office have been around to the apartment. They joke a lot and drink my liquor, but they're damned persistent. It's got around that I knocked Ernst Reiner down, on the control platform. That's the thing."

Jardinn grinned. "Knocking down the brother of a murdered man can't put you in San Quentin," he said slowly.

Frey shrugged. "They're after me, just the same," he muttered. "They always have to find a goat—when a name gets smeared out, around here. I hear Ernst Reiner has offered ten thousand reward. That counts, too."

Jardinn took his shoes from the table, got to his feet.

"You're a name, yourself," he reminded. "They can't railroad you so easily."

Frey made an impatient gesture. "Oh, they're decent enough about it. But they're working on me. One of these dicks said he'd heard that I got drunk at one of Maya's parties, and said I was fed up on hearing Ernst talk about his love for his brother. Said I wished he'd do a flop overboard, on the way across. This was weeks ago."

Jardinn said: "Did you talk like that?"

Frey groaned. "Why not?" he asked. "We were trying to get the story in some sort of shape. That was tough enough. And every half hour or so Ernst Reiner would yap about how much he loved his brother. It got on my nerves."

Jardinn nodded. "Don't let it get on them now," he said. "Got any ideas?"

Howard Frey's sensitive face was twisted. His dark eyes stared at Jardinn, then narrowed. His face was passive again. He shrugged.

"You're working for Reiner," he said. "I know that."

Jardinn smiled. "I don't think you killed Hans Reiner," he said quietly. "Does that help any?"

Frey swore fiercely. "You don't *think* I did!" he said bitterly. "You know goddam well I didn't! I called to you, up there in the Bowl—

Jardinn interrupted. "Take it easy, Frey. You can help us both, maybe. You got out of that box in a hurry—what was the idea?"

The writer said bitterly: "*You're* suspicious, too. Figure I was trying to alibi myself by calling to you, showing you where I was. You're taking Ernst Reiner's money and—

"I've taken some of yours, too," Jardinn reminded. "We have a wonderful organization here, Frey." He smiled ironically. "We can handle two angles at one and the same time. By God, but we're efficient!"

Howard Frey was staring at Jardinn; his eyes were puzzled. The detective leaned back in his chair.

"I know you didn't use a thirty-thirty, if that's what you're getting at," he said. "I just wondered why you happened to be trying to get down toward the musicians' shell in such a hurry. Most of the crowd weren't sure what it was all about."

Frey got up and walked around near the wall. He stood still, frowned down at the carpet.

"You hadn't met Hans Reiner, had you?" he asked abruptly.

Jardinn said. "I didn't have that honor."

Frey laughed bitterly. "I had it," he said grimly. "It was a hell of an honor. I met him at Maya's place. Maybe it was her idea of a joke. She's funny that way. Anyway, he bowed and said: 'The pugilist, I believe?' I could have taken him by the throat—he used that nasty, Continental superiority that gets me. But I didn't take him by the throat. He took Maya by the arm, and they went into the music room. I went downstairs and got tight. Not too tight—just nice. About an hour later I went up to say good-night to Maya. She was out on the patio, walking around alone and talking to herself. She was sore as the devil."

Jardinn asked: "What night was this, Frey?"

The writer said: "Two nights before the concert. Ernst Reiner wasn't there. They were shooting some night stuff without Maya."

Jardinn nodded. "What was she sore about?" he asked quietly.

Howard Frey sat down again. He leaned toward Jardinn, said in a steady voice:

"I'm in a tough spot—and I'm going to be in a tougher one, Jardinn. I can see it coming. Are you going to be square with me?"

Ben Jardinn smiled with his lips. "It depends on what you mean by square, Frey," he said.

Frey said: "I'm slated to be the goat. I'm almost broke, Jardinn. I've made money, but I've never saved it. I made a play for Maya—and you know what that means. If they frame me I won't be able to get Cummings, or Jallett. I need help—and I need it now. Those big lawyers will be too expensive for me."

Jardinn tapped ashes from his cigarette to the tray. He said quietly:

"My job is to get the man who brought the guns in for the sharpshooting deal. If I get the man—we'll get the boys who worked the rifles. I know you didn't work a rifle, Frey."

Frey said: "And you know Ernst Reiner didn't work a rifle."

Jardinn whistled softly. "Come out in the open," he said. "You think Ernst Reiner did a murder job on his brother?"

Frey smiled coldly. "Talk straight," he replied. "You think I didn't work a rifle—but maybe I put the boys there?"

Jardinn said: "I *know* you didn't work a rifle. And I just told you I thought you didn't murder Hans Reiner."

Frey relaxed. He was silent for several seconds. His voice was very calm, when he spoke.

"Ernst Reiner insults me on the set. He then comes to you and makes a statement with a basis that he fears harm from me, after I've knocked him down. Does that make sense?"

Jardinn said quietly: "Not the way you tell it, Frey. He insulted you. You knocked him down. He got you fired. *Then* he came to me and said he was afraid of trouble. That makes better sense."

Howard Frey smiled. "I came to you and told you that if anything happened to Ernst Reiner, I wouldn't be guilty. That gave you a laugh, didn't it?"

Jardinn shook his head. "Just a smile," he corrected. "What you're trying to tell me is that Ernst Reiner is going to frame you for the murder of his brother. All right—what about it?"

Frey said: "You're cold as hell—but I think you're honest."

Jardinn bowed. "You were saying that you found Maya Rand, two nights before the concert during which Hans Reiner was killed, out in her patio, sore as the devil."

Frey nodded. "She didn't hear me come up—I was behind her. She was talking to herself, as I said. Gritting words out. She can use them, when she's being herself. She played burlesque in Philly for two years before she got money enough to come out here and take the pies for Sennett, as a start. Well, she was using words. I caught a few."

Jardinn said: "For God's sake be right with me, Frey. Don't make any mistakes. They'll count like hell. I don't mastermind to get a killer. I go out and fight for a break. I'll fight Maya Rand just as quick as anybody else. But be right with me."

Frey's face was white—almost as pale as the natural color of the detective's skin. He said slowly:

"I could go to some other agency, Jardinn. I've come to you. From the very beginning, I've got to have a chance—and you can give it to me. Even if you are taking Reiner's dirty money."

Jardinn said: "What was Maya Rand saying?"

The writer spoke very quietly. His voice was almost toneless.

"She said: 'I got up here alone—I'll stay here. He's rotten, but he can't pull me down. I can get to him—before he gets to me—use his brother—' That was all, Jardinn."

Jardinn said: "You're not making any mistake?"

Frey swore bitterly. "It's a rotten time for me to make

mistakes,'' he replied. ''That's what she said, Jardinn.
Only she gritted out some nasty words in between. Just
the regular words one human uses on another—when
there's hate.''

Jardinn nodded. He relaxed in his chair. Frey had been
leaning forward; he got up, rubbed the palm of his right
hand across his face. He said:

''Maya's mixed up in this—I'm a dirty rat for telling
it! But I'm not going to be framed! I'm not—''

His voice was pitched high. Jardinn said sharply:

''Steady! It's all right, Frey. Want to tell me something
else?''

Frey faced him. He shook his head. His eyes had a
strained expression.

''That's the biggest thing I know,'' he replied. ''Doesn't
it mean a damn thing to you?''

Jardinn smiled faintly. ''It's a nice thing to know,''
he replied. ''Someone was trying to kick the star rating
from under Maya Rand, for some reason. That someone
had a brother. Maya figured she could keep on shining
if she could 'use' someone's brother. It might mean
something.''

Frey said: ''If you don't go after her I'm going to the
D.A. with—''

Jardinn got up and swore at the writer. He said grimly:

''You keep away from the D.A.'s office. A lot of
people use words and don't mean them. You did that,
with Ernst Reiner unconscious at your feet. You should
know. When you've got anything to say—come and say
it. I'm after a killer—man or woman. It's my business.
I'll take your money and Ernst Reiner's money. I'll take
anyone's money, if I can give something for it. This isn't
a hobby with me. I don't work in a library, or go into
trances. I don't dope out involved codes. And I don't
bother too much with the D.A.'s office or the harness
bulls. Your brother did ten years in stir, down South.
What for?''

Howard Frey clenched his fists at his sides.

"Manslaughter was what they convicted him on," he said harshly. "He wasn't guilty."

Jardinn said: "What city was he tried in?"

"Atlanta," Frey replied. "Want me to pay for the wire you're going to send for a transcript of the court testimony on the case?"

Jardinn went over to a window, turned his head away from Frey and grinned.

"How about this cousin of yours—this cop Bracker?" he asked. "Been talking to him?"

Frey said slowly, steadily: "I've come to you. You're as hard as the thing Maya Rand calls her soul—but I think you're white."

Jardinn turned, faced the writer. He said:

"Get some sleep—I've got a lot to do. Don't talk too much."

The writer moved toward the door. He said grimly:

"I suppose you give Ernst Reiner the same advice."

Jardinn nodded. "It's damn good advice," he stated. "But it's harder to follow when a couple of dicks have got you in a soundproof room with a length of rubber hose."

Howard Frey's eyes were little, dark slits. But there was no fear in them. He said very quietly:

"I didn't even plan to knock Ernst Reiner down. It was instinct."

He went out. Jardinn stared at the half closed door, nodded his head, sat down. The outer door slammed. Edith Brown came in with a notebook in her hand. She said:

"I missed some of it. The receivers don't fit just right over my head. But I got the best part."

Jardinn regarded her narrowly. "What part was that?" he asked.

She smiled with her brown eyes. She set the notebook on his desk.

"What Maya Rand said, talking to herself," she answered.

Jardinn got up and stood beside her. He said in a tone that was so hard it was unpleasant:

"I don't know you well enough to break your neck, Ede. But I'll break it—if you don't do just one thing for me. I swear to Christ I will. Do you know what that one thing is?"

She nodded. "To forget what Maya Rand said, talking to herself," she replied.

"Just that," he said softly, and got his hat from the dust on top of the cabinet. "Just exactly that!"

·5·

LOVELY LADY

Maya Rand sat in the chair that was something of a throne at Famous, sipped tea, and nibbled at small crackers with her perfect teeth. She had a face that was slightly oval in shape—her eyes were very beautiful. Her hair was dark; she had a small but exquisite figure. There was a great deal of confusion on Set Two; the din had no effect on Maya. Her colored maid hovered in the background; she was called Nina, and she had one of the most perfect primitive faces that Jardinn had ever seen.

Maya said in tones that were very precise and clear:

"Things go badly today. The lighting is not good. George does well enough, but he is not Ernst Reiner."

Jardinn nodded. He was seated on an uncomfortable chair, very close to the star of *Death Dance*. He said:

"I read somewhere that work on the picture was to be called off until after the funeral."

Maya Rand lifted her shoulders a little, made a helpless gesture with her white hands. She had slender, tapering fingers.

"We are behind schedule, as it is. There will be re-takes. The set is wanted. Or the space for another, rather.

There was the fire, you know. The studio is in rather
fearful shape. It isn't that the officials don't sympathize
with Ernst. They do.''

Jardinn leaned back a little in his chair and watched
the electricians working with the lights. The set showed
a corner of a richly done living room. Maya was in
evening dress; her scarlet wrap set off the pallor of her
makeup startlingly.

Jardinn said: "You were acquainted with Hans Reiner,
Miss Rand?''

She said. ''Yes, acquainted.''

She had a peculiar way of clipping off her sentences.
He decided that she would be difficult. She had assur-
ance. She wasn't a wide-eyed child—there was her background. She had come up from a low theater. He wondered
how far she had come, and how much fight she had lost
on the way up. Or gained.

"You were in the box with Ernst Reiner," he said.
"Do you mind telling me your reactions. I mean, at the
time of the murder? It will help.''

She narrowed her eyes on his. She said:

"I wasn't thinking much about the concert. I dislike
music. It was an affair, of course. I go often to the Bowl
and think about other things. My work, mostly. It's relaxation, you know.''

She smiled at Jardinn; he smiled back.

"Of course," he agreed. "And publicity.''

She nodded. "And publicity," she agreed. "But that
isn't as important as the relaxation.''

He laughed at her. "After all, Miss Rand," he suggested, "you've worked under greater strain, with less
chance for relaxation.''

She set her teacup on the tray near her and kept her
dark eyes on his. She said:

"You're getting at something. You are not direct.''

He shrugged. "Neither are you," he replied. "After
all, it's nice to hear you talk. You have a lovely voice.

I like Hollywood—because it's pleasant to look at beautiful women. I'd like to know, though, some truths. Why did you go to the Bowl for Hans Reiner's concert?''

She smiled. "Publicity," she said.

He made a little bow. "Now, that's nice," he told her. "The seats out there are pretty hard for relaxation. There was almost a snap in the air. You don't like music. The orchestra was playing—what next?''

She said mockingly: "If I do *The Affair at Vendome* you must play Lernier. I think you'd screen well, and you could just live the part.''

He nodded. "It's something for me to look forward to," he said. "That would be because I'd be working with you. Actually, I don't like pictures.''

She said, as though the subject had not been changed:

"I was wondering what Ernst must be thinking—with his brother rather the whole show. Then I heard a plane engine. It grew louder. Everyone seemed to be looking up. I couldn't see the plane. Mr. Durling—he was with us, you know—was disturbed. . . . I think he swore. The plane engine noise was growing very loud. Then the shell lights went out. When they came on again Hans Reiner was swaying—his hands were groping toward his back—''

She stopped. There had been no emotion in her voice. She said, with a faint tremor:

"It was—terrible.''

Jardinn said: "What next?''

She shrugged. "There was a great deal of excitement. I didn't rise—the others did. I remember Ernst; his body was very tense. He was staring toward the shell. He cried out something—I think it was 'Hans.' I'm not sure. The lights went out again. Mr. Durling said something about Hans Reiner fainting—overwork, perhaps. He stayed with me. Mr. Harris stayed, too. Ernst went down toward the shell. I think we were all standing by this time.''

Jardinn nodded. "Did you look around the Bowl, after the lights came on again?" he asked.

She nodded. "I was quite excited," she said. "I had an idea there might be a panic, a stampede. Even though we all were outside, right in the hills."

Jardinn smiled. "When you looked around, did you see Howard Frey?" he asked.

Her eyes widened. She shook her head.

"No," she said. "Should I have seen him?"

He said slowly: "It would have been just chance. He was present, you know."

She said, carefully: "I've heard that he was. I believe there was a party—several men with him. I didn't see him—not at all. Not before, or after. Does it matter?"

Jardinn shrugged. "It might," he told her. "So many things seem unimportant now—later they assume importance."

She leaned toward him. "What you mean is that you want to learn whether I'm lying to you or not," she said quietly. "I'm not."

Jardinn said: "Without trying to frighten you, it wouldn't be wise to lie. It never is. But I don't think you are. I was trying to determine how observant you are. Or perhaps testing your memory."

George Hillard came over. The assistant director was a slow moving, handsome man of about thirty-five. He had a nicely waxed mustache and a pleasant voice. He said:

"Pardon—it'll be about ten minutes, Maya. Hank is doing things with the spots. Are you all right for that time?"

She nodded. "I'll look like hell in a close-up," she stated calmly. "Better not, George."

He said: "You look like a million. The front office is yelling for it. Ernst may be busted up for a few days. Got to, Maya."

He moved off, calling for the boss electrician. Some bit players in evening clothes moved across the set languidly. A tall, good-looking boy said in a rather high-pitched tone:

"I think she's a lovely lady."

Jardinn tapped fingers against the wood of the chair. Maya Rand smiled and said:

"My memory is just fair. I haven't a too bad past, but sometimes I forget portions of it. I was merely acquainted with Hans Reiner—just the usual entertaining one would do for one's director's brother, a stranger in town. I doubt if we were ever alone in a room together."

Jardinn nodded. "You haven't any idea regarding the murder?" he asked.

She shook her head. "It seems an incredible thing to me," she replied. "Such a sort of stupendous way to do—such a thing. I don't think anyone knew Hans Reiner out here, with the exception of his brother. That is, really knew him. And Ernst loved him deeply."

Jardinn rose from the chair. He said very quietly:

"Perhaps you knew Howard Frey better?"

She rose also. But there was no change of her expression. She smiled at him.

"I know Howard quite well. He tells me the police are bothering him. That is all very silly. He couldn't control his feelings—and Ernst has been working very hard. That affair had nothing to do with the Bowl—knocking down Ernst—"

She checked herself. Jardinn said in a low tone:

"You don't want to be dragged into this. You aren't big enough to beat it. I'll want to talk to you—not here."

She stood quite stiffly. There was a faint contempt in her eyes.

"I *can't* be dragged into it," she said emphatically. "I'm not afraid, and I don't care to talk with you."

He smiled. "I'm easier to get along with than the

police," he said. "On the surface I may not pretend to be so impressed with your importance as they will. But I'll be fair."

She said coldly: "I don't know what you're getting at. What more would we have to talk about?"

Jardinn looked toward the group of bit players near the edge of the set. He said in an easy tone:

"We might talk about the night Frey was introduced to Hans Reiner, at your home. We might talk about Reiner insulting him. And just to be out in the California air while we talk, we might wander out to your palmy patio—"

Her eyes showed fear—but only a flash of it. Then she was shaking her head.

"I've a rather difficult scene to do," she said steadily. "I must have a little quiet."

He nodded. "I'm sorry to have bothered you," he told her. "When shall I come to your house?"

She glanced toward her white slippers. She said very quietly:

"Tonight—if you wish. But you don't think—"

Fear caught at her words, gave them an uncertainty of tone. He touched her right wrist with his fingers.

"I think you're a very lovely lady," he said quietly, and went slowly toward the thick door of the soundproof stage.

In the studio street he lighted a cigarette and gazed toward the stars' bungalows. He said softly:

"A *very* lovely lady—but a liar, just the same."

2

Brenniger came in the Hotel Christie as Jardinn was buying two-for-a-quarters at the cigar counter. Brenniger was a short, heavyset man. He had a cherub-like face. He looked not unlike a Y.M.C.A. secretary with sufficient income to eat well. He slapped Jardinn on the back.

"Didn't know you used cigars, Ben," he greeted.

Jardinn grinned at him, and passed one over. He bought two more.

"Don't," he said simply. "How's business?"

Brenniger coughed heavily. "It's way over my head," he replied. "The rotten part is I've got to work just as hard as you—only no one slips me five grand for it."

Jardinn said. "You've been reading the papers. My client did a wise thing when he slipped me the five grand—but he wasn't so wise when he talked about it, afterward."

The police detective grunted. "It's a tough one, eh, Bennie? How's Max and that swell kid, Miss Torney?"

Jardinn struck a match and held it near the tip of Brenniger's cigar. He lighted a cigarette.

"They're both fine," he replied. "Carol isn't with me anymore. Max is working hard, though."

He watched the police detective closely. Brenniger was intelligent, even though he didn't look that way. He inhaled with satisfaction.

"What happened to the kid?" he asked. "I thought she liked her work."

Jardinn grinned. "Her uncle's been sick," he said. "She's sticking close to him."

Brenniger grunted. "He didn't look sick, when I saw him down in Los Angeles this morning," he observed. "Say, this is a good smoke."

Jardinn nodded. "Just a nice one," he replied. "It isn't anything fatal—the uncle has spells."

Brenniger said: "Sure, we all have spells. Know anything I can use without hurting your graft too much?"

Jardinn rolled his cigarette around and appeared to think the answer over. Brenniger swore and said:

"Anything that isn't too funny, Bennie."

Jardinn nodded. "Lay off Frey a little," he suggested. "He's all right. His nerves were just a little shaky, that's all."

"That's what I told the chief," Brenniger said slowly. He had a peculiar smile playing around his thick lips. "But he said a guy that hates another guy is kind of likely to hate another guy's brother."

Jardinn groaned. "With that kind of reasoning my spot isn't so tough," he said. "I won't have too much competition."

The city detective smiled good-humoredly. He inspected the ash on his cigar with narrowed eyes.

"I hear this Rand gal is calling Madame Wakun in from Pasadena," he said. "She's going to put on a show and look in the glass. She's naming the gent that put the guns in the Bowl—and then the Rand gal is going to put us wise. All we have to do is to go out and grab off the gent she names."

Jardinn nodded. "Bonsall's a good publicity man, but if he spreads that stuff around he's a damn fool. He'll pull her into the case—and it may not be so funny."

Brenniger grunted. "I'm going out to the Bowl and wander around," he said. "I'm a sociable chap—come along?"

Jardinn shook his head. "You won't find ejected shells, footprints that are worth anything much, or bloodstains," he said. "I was out there when they let things loose. It was smooth, Brenny."

The city detective nodded. "It's all nice, so far," he agreed. "Still, there are a few guys sitting on the edges of cots up in San Quentin that got along all right for a week or so after they shoved other guys out."

Jardinn grinned. "*You* didn't send them there," he said.

They moved toward the street. Jardinn said:

"I'm going down to the beach and take a swim. It stimulates me."

Brenniger let his eyes show what he thought about that. He pulled on his cigar.

"Sure you are," he agreed. "And I'll give you a tip—

Carren's hard to get along with. We've been talking things over. He's got guts, but he's nervous as hell.''

Jardinn said: "You think he just happened to wing that plane over there, Brenny?"

The city detective shrugged. "He's had ships flying over Bowl concerts before: He was warned twice by the Department of Commerce. They got complaints from the Bowl committee. He admits he never flew so low. Says he must have misjudged the distance."

Jardinn swore softly. "Maybe he did," he said.

Brenniger nodded. He gestured with his chin toward Jardinn's roadster.

"When you get through with this job you can go buy yourself a nice shiny one," he said.

"Or sell this one," Jardinn replied. "If you did a human in, Brenny, and had a hundred thousand in cash, you'd use it to keep out of stir—yes?"

Brenniger said: "I'm ahead of you—I wouldn't have any trouble in finding a lot of humans ready to take it and *help* me keep out."

Jardinn went toward the roadster. The city detective called after him:

"If you see Miss Torney tell her I hope her uncle gets rid of the spells."

Jardinn grinned back at him. "She'll like the thought," he said.

But he wasn't smiling as he climbed back of the wheel. He drove out Vine to Wilshire Boulevard, turned westward toward the ocean. He decided that Jerry Bonsall was too good a publicity man to send out Maya Rand's name tied up with a fake crystal gazing stunt. He decided that Howard Frey had told him the truth about finding Maya in the patio alone—using words that she didn't want to be repeated now. Her eyes had showed him fear.

He decided that Brenniger, who was one of the best men the city had on the force, wasn't convinced that Carren was telling the truth. And Brenniger was suspi-

cious about Carol having left the agency. The thoughts
came to him separately—they didn't exactly tie up. The
thing was—he had to go slowly. There was the matter
of Max Cohn telling him he had seen Carol go into Ernst
Reiner's house. He had to go at that carefully, very
carefully. There was the matter of the wristwatch. He
couldn't be sure there—he could only play the girl against
Max—and wait for a break.

The agency had been lucky. They had got inside of a
few things. That had meant a reputation. Someone was
afraid. It was the money that would stop him from getting
anywhere. Certainly there had been leaks—where none
had existed before. It wasn't a pleasant situation.

It took him forty-five minutes to reach the field. He
parked the car near the line of hangars, went into the
Administration Building. A red-haired clerk scribbled
him a pass, when he asked for Pilot Carren. He said in
a tired voice:

"He'll be around the tri-motor ship hangar. It's up to
the right when you get on the deadline. Someone can
point him out. You're a reporter or a cop, I suppose?"

"Whichever annoys you the least," Jardinn replied,
and went out to the deadline.

He walked along past the propellers of little cabin and
open cockpit ships, reached the big hangar where the tri-
motor planes rested. Two were inside—one was on the
deadline, two of the propellers whirling at idling speed.
The third propeller was not turning. A mechanic in over-
alls came near him; Jardinn said:

"I'm looking for Carren. He around here someplace?"

The mechanic pointed toward the far side of the big
ship. Jardinn went around. Two men were talking to a
third. The two had slips of paper in their hands and were
using pencils. One of them walked away as Jardinn came
up—the other smiled at the man who stood with his back
against a wing tip of the big monoplane.

"Just a tough bit of luck, Carren," he said, and went away slowly, writing stuff on the slip of paper.

The pilot regarded Jardinn with narrowed, weary eyes. He was dressed in a gray suit and wore no hat. He had a rather long face and a stubble of beard. His arms hung loosely at his sides, but fingers clenched and unclenched nervously. Except for his fingers there was no movement of the pilot's body.

Jardinn said loudly, against the rumble of the two engines:

"My name's Jardinn. Ernst Reiner has asked me to do some looking around for him. I haven't rushed out here because I figured you just blundered into the killing."

He paused. Carren said, in a voice that was flat:

"Too bad the rest don't figure that way. It's tough— for me."

Jardinn nodded. Carren had brown eyes, and they held a lifeless expression. They didn't seem to meet Jardinn's—they appeared to focus on some spot beyond him.

"I was in the Bowl, the night Hans Reiner was murdered," Jardinn said steadily. "You were flying pretty low."

The pilot wet his lips with the tip of his tongue. He said:

"I thought I'd do it right. There was a girl aboard who wanted to get down low—maybe I sort of fell pretty hard for her."

Jardinn stepped up close and said sharply:

"You're a goddam liar! You're too good a pilot to do a stunt like that for a girl."

Carren's face was white. He said in a hoarse voice:

"You can't talk like that to me! I know who you are! You haven't got anything on me. You won't get anything on me—"

Jardinn laughed at him. It was a nasty, mocking laugh.

"I'm *getting* enough on you!" he snapped. "Every time you pull one like that last—I get something on you. Better be right with me."

Carren stood with his body hunched forward a little. He was breathing heavily—both hands were clenched at his sides. Jardinn let his eyes drop, slipped his right hand into a side pocket of his coat. He said:

"I know you're nervous as hell. But don't get too nervous. I'm holding something that quiets any kind of nerves. Don't try to pull one of Frey's tricks on me."

Carren sucked in his breath sharply. His body was tense, his eyes wide. Then his facial muscles relaxed. He ran the fingers of his right hand over his face. He said hoarsely:

"There was a party made up—they wanted to see the Bowl. I took them over. There were two girls aboard. I don't know where any of the people live. I take lots of them up. They've all been asking me where the passengers are—I don't know. Why should I?"

Jardinn said: "I'll tell you why—most of them sign a release slip. Most fields get addresses. There might be an accident."

The pilot shook his head. "There wasn't enough time— they got here late."

Jardinn smiled narrowly. "You got over the Bowl just after the concert started—you had plenty of time," he said.

Carren walked a few feet away from the wing tip of the big plane. Jardinn said:

"You're lying, Carren—and you'll catch plenty of punishment for it. If they get you downtown—"

The pilot swung around, faced him. He said hoarsely:

"The ship just happened—to be there! Do I look like a killer?"

"I never saw a man who looked like one," Jardinn said more quietly. "You look like a liar to me—I've seen them before."

A mechanic came up. He grinned at the pilot.

"Phone call from Detective Headquarters, Hen," he said. "A guy named Bonner wants you to wait out here until he gets here. He says it's nothing important—he just wants to talk with you."

Carren nodded. Jardinn smiled grimly. He said nothing. The pilot asked the question.

"Who's Bonner?"

Jardinn shrugged. "You'll like him," he said with irony. "He has technique—with a hunk of rubber hose."

"They haven't got anything on me," the pilot muttered. The rumble of the two throttled-down engines almost drowned his words. "It was just a passenger joyride. I didn't think I was so low."

Jardinn said: "You didn't circle the Bowl. You didn't come back. You didn't give your passengers much of a show. You just got there—winged over very low—and kept on going. And while you were over the Bowl— Hans Reiner was murdered."

Carren kept his clenched hands at his side. His face was white, twisted. His eyes stared at Jardinn's.

"It was just—luck!" he cried. "Just damn, rotten luck!"

Jardinn stepped in close to him. He said sharply:

"You know Frey pretty well—you'd better talk first. It'll be easier—"

Carren struck with his left hand. The blow caught Jardinn over the right temple—it battered him backward, rocked him on his heels. The second blow caught him under the left ear—he went down heavily. He didn't lose consciousness. His body was numb, almost helpless. He pulled himself to his knees, fumbled for the weapon in his pocket. It had slipped from his relaxed grip as he had gone down.

He got it from the pocket—his head was clearing. He swayed to his feet. There was a roaring in his ears; it seemed to be increasing in tone. The great tri-motor shape was moving, rolling forward. Jardinn saw it as a blur as he swayed on the turf. Wind whipped at his body; he bent forward against the force of it. Raising the gun, he fired once. His hand wasn't steady enough, his grip strong enough, to prevent even the recoil. He didn't fire again.

His vision was better now—in the distance he saw the big plane getting into the air. Men were running toward him from the deadline. A voice said:

"Carren's grounded—he shouldn't have done that!"

A middle-aged man, with a gray mustache, was staring at the gun Jardinn held loosely at his right side. He said:

"What's the matter—you got a gun there—"

Jardinn slipped the gun in a pocket. He said thickly:

"He knocked—me down. He's got—that ship for a—"

A voice, hoarse and strained, broke in on Jardinn's weak tone.

"She's—slipping off—it's a crash!"

Jardinn stared desperately in the direction he'd seen the tri-motor ship take off. Two hundred feet above the earth, he saw her. She was in a bank—headed back toward them. But she was slipping—the scream of wind through her rigging reached him as she came down.

Someone cried out: "She's only got—two engines—"

Jardinn stood motionless. The nose of the big plane seemed to whip downward in the last fifty feet. She was plunging almost straight toward the field surface when she struck. There was the terrible, vibrating roar of a big plane crashed to earth. Then only a distant hissing, drowned by the wail of the field siren and the shouts of running men.

Jardinn raised his right-hand fingers to a cut beneath his left ear. The pilot had worn a ring. He walked unsteadily toward the wreckage of the big plane. He muttered to himself:

"I didn't think—he'd do—that."

When he reached the wreckage they had carried Carren from the ship. It had taken time for Jardinn to get to the spot. Every foot of the distance hurt. The man with the gray mustache walked toward him, shaking his head. There was no color in his face.

Jardinn said: "Dead?"

The man nodded. "Everything came back on him," he muttered. "She slipped off on a wing."

Jardinn moved around the wreckage. He didn't go near the body of the pilot. A tall man with rounded shoulders and thick lensed glasses came over and stood beside him. He said in a stunned voice:

"Something must have happened—to Carren. I designed that big girl. She was a—tested plane. Something went wrong—"

He broke off, moved away shaking his head from side to side.

Jardinn turned away from the wreckage. He went over and sat down on the grass, lighted a cigarette with shaking fingers. He smiled a little, with his dark eyes narrowed. He said unsteadily:

"Brenniger was right—Carren knew things. He couldn't be pushed—too far. Maybe the ship was fixed—maybe he slipped her off—he might have been too shaky—"

Fifteen minutes later, as Jardinn was getting into his roadster, a Headquarters car drove up beside it. Ed Bonner climbed out of the rear seat and frowned at him.

"What in hell happened out here?" he demanded.

Jardinn smiled with his lips. "There was an accident," he replied.

Bonner grunted. "Your face looks as though it happened to you," he returned.

Jardinn said: "Part of it did," and got the roadster moving. "But most of it happened to a pilot named Carren."

Bonner called after the moving car: "I came out—to see that fellow."

Jardinn twisted his head, grinned. "Go ahead," he called back. "He won't mind—not now."

·6·

"IF YOU HURT ME—"

Edith Brown was frowning over a clipping from a newspaper, when Ben Jardinn shoved open the door of the agency office. She looked up at him, started to work her baby smile, stared. He smiled down at her.

"I know," he said. "But I'll survive. What are you clipping—ads for other jobs?"

She shook her head. "Stories about the murder in the Bowl," she replied. "Gun experts are disagreeing—I thought you'd want to see the items."

He nodded. "It's safer to stay in the office and read," he agreed. "Anything happen?"

She chuckled at something, looked a little startled, set the shears on the surface of the desk and nodded.

"A nifty boy came in and said you might want to give him a job as an operative. I said that you might. He tried to make a date with me, but I told him I was broke. A man named Squire called up from Pasadena and said that he could handle that matter himself—that he'd learned who the man was. He said to tell you he was getting sick of his wife, anyway. A woman called and said she'd

read you'd been retained by Ernst Reiner—and she had
something of interest to tell you. Her name's Degonné,
and she lives in Glendale—the address is on your desk.
She sounded Frenchy like. I guess that is about all."

Jardinn nodded. "You're earning your money," he
said. "If you're broke—"

He tossed her two tens. She said: "Thanks," and
narrowed her brown eyes on his. He said:

"I wasn't hit hard—that is, not very hard. I was a
delicate child and I still bruise easily. I'm going down
to a barbershop and take a nap under some cold towels.
If a little, Jewish looking man comes up here tell him
I'll be a half hour late. He's Max Cohn, and he's my
assistant. Don't let him kid you too much."

Edith Brown chuckled. She scooped up some of the
clippings, offered them to him.

"How about reading them in the barbershop?" she
asked.

He shook his head. "I can't see through towels," he
reminded. "Put 'em on my desk. How do you like the
job?"

She shrugged. "Just so long as I don't get hurt it'll
be all right," she replied.

Ben Jardinn had got over near the door; he paused,
frowned at her.

"Who's going to hurt you?" he asked.

She shrugged again. "I didn't say anyone was," she
said. "I said so long as—"

"All right," he cut in. "I remember the speech. But
don't kid yourself—you won't get hurt. You may get
killed, but it'll be so sudden there won't be pain."

He went out and down the stairs. In the chair of a
barbershop across the street, he decided that Edith Brown
would be all right around the office, even if he hadn't
got her by the usual method of running a trick ad in the
paper. She seemed smart enough about a lot of things,

but she'd been dumb in suggesting that he bring the clippings along. She was better than the blonde Max had brought in, anyway.

The barber, who thought Jardinn ran an agency for motion picture people, seemed to believe his story of a wild party at the Cotton Club, and agreed that the towels would help his face. While Jardinn tried to think of other matters, the barber advanced his own theories about the murder in the Bowl. It all came down to the point that he figured Hans Reiner had been shot from the plane, by a super-sharpshooter. Jardinn mumbled that he agreed and tried to get the man's idea of a motive. The barber didn't have any, but he consumed ten minutes in an effort to make his customer believe otherwise.

When Jardinn got back to the office Max Cohn was sitting on the edge of Edith Brown's desk and talking about Tampa, Florida. He grinned at Ben.

"Miss Brown's been living in Tampa," he said. "We got something in common."

Jardinn went on toward his office. "I doubt it," he replied. "Come on in and tell me some things."

Cohn followed him in. He looked pretty cheerful. His dark eyes worked on Ben's face; he spoke in his nasal voice.

"Where'd you get this Brown kid, Ben?"

Jardinn frowned and slid into the chair back of his desk.

"You lay off her," he warned. "We've got a job on—and it might be tough. She's a nice girl. Did you get the keys?"

Cohn tossed them on the desk. He kept on grinning.

"Irish raved a lot, but she gave them to me," he said. "It's her idea that I wanted her out of the office. God— women are funny. She thinks I wanted her out because I couldn't make her."

Jardinn put the keys in a pocket. He said slowly:

"What happened at the paper?"

Cohn shrugged. "I spent two hours working around the files," he replied. "There's damned little on Hans Reiner. Just the usual stuff. He's conducted all over the Continent. No one ever took a shot at him over there. Or if they did it didn't get sent over the cable. Maya Rand gets a lot of the usual publicity. Nothing that counts in this thing. Just the regular bunk."

Jardinn nodded. Cohn asked: "What's the matter with your face—it looks hurt?"

Edith Brown came in with some clippings. She handed them to Jardinn.

"Busy girl," Max said. "You'll get yourself a nervous breakdown around here."

She went out without speaking, but she smiled a little. Ben Jardinn said:

"I want you to cut using a line with this kid. I'm not joking. Lay off."

Lines in Cohn's face wrinkled with surprise. He looked hurt.

"Relative of yours, Ben?" he asked in a sarcastic tone.

Jardinn tapped on the desk surface with fingers of his right hand. He looked at the clippings.

"You didn't spend all your time on the paper morgue," he said finally. "Did you see Glenning?"

Cohn nodded. "My old pal Glenning," he mused. "He's got himself a bad throat—doesn't feel like talking. It got better when I reminded him that I helped get him that experting job down at bull headquarters. He talked a little."

Jardinn waited. Cohn lighted a cigarette and sat down.

"One bullet mushroomed after it got inside Reiner— the other didn't. Both thirty-thirty in caliber. The one that mushroomed finished him. The other one slapped into some bone, and didn't do too much damage. It's Glenning's idea that the bullets were fired from different guns. He likes the idea of one sharpshooter being on each side of the Bowl, on the paths.''

Jardinn smiled a little. "What made the bullet mushroom?" he asked. "A cross, cut at the point?"

Cohn shrugged. "That's one way of doing it," he agreed. "Though Glenning didn't say that. Only one was a soft-nosed bullet. It struck under the left shoulder blade, dug into the right. The other struck his back a little low, and traveled to the left. Glenning's guess is that they were fired from a distance of about two hundred yards—not much less. Impact force showed that."

Jardinn nodded. "That's nice shooting," he murmured. "Nice distance—and in the dark. Just the two bullets—none banged around the orchestra after a miss."

Cohn nodded. "We poked around there pretty carefully, at the time," he agreed. "Jeeze—what we need is a motive lead. It would be a sweet stunt to get this fellow Carren talking."

Jardinn grinned. "It would be a miracle," he said grimly. "He's dead."

Max Cohn took the cigarette from between his rather thick lips, muttered a surprised "huh," and stared at Jardinn.

"There was an accident," Ben stated. "I was getting him all worked up calling him a liar and a few other things. He cracked me down, got aboard a tri-motor ship and took off. She crashed over the field. He got killed. Bonner was on the way out—he wanted to talk with him."

Cohn kept on staring. He said slowly:

"Maybe you played him the wrong way. Maybe you should have agreed with him, Ben."

Jardinn nodded. "Maybe," he agreed. "But you're never around to give me advice when I need it."

Cohn got a foolish expression on his heavy face. He said slowly:

"Carren's dead—Jeeze, that's tough. I think he knew something."

Jardinn picked up a small slip of paper, read aloud the name "Degonné," handed the slip to Cohn. He looked toward the window.

"Trot out that way tonight and see this woman," he said. "She called here and said she had something of interest to tell me about Ernst Reiner."

Cohn grinned. "The name's French," he announced. "She probably had some relation killed in the war, and thinks she can tell you something that'll hurt Ernst."

Ben Jardinn picked up a clipping and read it. While he was reading he said:

"Just as sure as hell this is a cover-up job. We can't afford to miss anything. Don't be smart with her. Listen to everything she says."

Cohn swore. "It seems to me you took a chance— getting this Brown kid in from an agency."

Jardinn went on reading the clipping. He nodded.

"No doubt about it," he agreed. "But we were pretty careful when we got the others we've had outside—and they went bad. Even Carol."

Cohn frowned. "I can't figure her going inside of Ernst Reiner's place," he said slowly. "She should be worked on."

Jardinn set down the clipping and smiled nastily. He said slowly:

"There's just the two of us, Max—and we've got enough to do. The police don't know what it's all about. We won't learn much from them. Never mind Irish. If we want her I'll take care of that."

Cohn shrugged. "She fixed your wristwatch," he reminded. "Even if that didn't count, she knows something."

Jardinn nodded. "Carol Torney's stubborn as hell," he said. "I think she put a bad boy next to me—the one

who tried to slug me down. I think she did tricks with
the wristwatch. But I don't think she knew what it was
about. Someone just came along at the right time—with
plenty of money."

Cohn got up and put the slip of paper in his pocket.

"How about the passengers in that tri-motor plane?"
he asked. "Maybe they knew something."

Jardinn nodded. "Maybe," he agreed. "I'll get back
to the field later. The police are working that end. They
can't find any passengers. Things seem to have been
worked sloppily out there. Carren said he didn't even
remember what his passengers looked like. He made up
some story about a girl wanting him to fly low—one of
those aboard. He was lying. The officials at the field
don't seem to have paid much attention to the night
flights. Carren's dead—and that end is going to be plenty
tough."

Cohn grunted. "It's ten to one the passengers didn't
know what it was all about, anyway," he said. "Carren
made a deal—and carried it through. He was getting in
a jam, lost his nerve—and finished things. That's the
way I see it."

Jardinn leaned back in his chair and smiled. He said
quietly:

"I've got a hunch you're right, Max. And look here,
this murder fits in with a theory of mine. It looks like a
big, spectacular job. But it's smooth, Max. After you
get through with the woman out in Glendale, say tomorrow, I want you to get after the light end—out in the
Bowl. Those lights were turned off—then flashed on,
and then turned off again. See what you can get on that.
The fellow that was slugged is Murphy. You might talk
with him, though the police have been doing most of the
obvious things, and the reporters have been sticking close
and printing most of the stuff they learn. I'll look up
Carren's family."

Cohn nodded. He kept his dark eyes lazily on Jardinn's. He said:

"Sure. You were saying the kill fit in with a theory of yours—but you didn't mention the theory."

Jardinn yawned. "Didn't I?" he said. "Well, maybe I was just using words. But what I was trying to get at was that it might not have been such a fool stunt to do in a human with twenty thousand other humans around, at that. Not with things right. None of them saw anything—and they were all in the way, after the kill."

Max Cohn grunted. "That's a hell of a theory, Ben," he muttered. "It doesn't mean anything."

Jardinn grinned. "Maybe I'm getting old," he suggested. "I've always tried not to have theories. The first thing I know I'll be chasing fingerprints."

Cohn chuckled. He moved toward the door. Jardinn said:

"You might go up to the Bowl headquarters tomorrow and talk to Mrs. Winfred-Neeley. She likes to talk. There's a lot of politics in the Bowl stuff, so they say. Find out if they canceled any other maestro, to let Hans Reiner conduct."

Cohn groaned. "Oh, God!" he breathed. "Not that?"

Jardinn stood up and called for Edith Brown. He said to Cohn:

"These foreigners are hot blooded. You never can tell. Remember, the simple things—

Cohn swore at him and went out. Edith came in, smiling. The outside door slammed. Jardinn walked past the girl, went into the outer office. He heard Cohn going down the steps. He locked the door, went back into his office. He shut the door behind him, went over and sat down.

Edith Brown stood before his desk, her brown eyes smiling at him. He motioned for her to take the chair that Cohn had vacated. She sat down gracefully. She slumped a little. He liked her eyes, and the imperfection of her mouth lines. She had one of the most cheerful voices he had ever heard. The huskiness was nice—but not too nice. It didn't fit in with her baby face and figure; Jardinn liked contrast. He said quietly:

"I've checked you, at the agency. That isn't sufficient, under ordinary circumstances. These aren't ordinary. I'm in a tough spot. The office work around here doesn't amount to a damn. There's such a thing as a sporting proposition. You said something, a little while ago, about liking this job if you weren't going to get hurt. That was silly—it gave me the idea that you didn't know what this was all about. Play fair with me—are you in here for a reason? Or did you just want a job?"

Her eyes met his squarely. "Just for a job," she said. "I came here three months ago, from Tampa. I tried to get picture work—my voice doesn't go with my face. I can't get it. If I could whine maybe I'd do. I needed the job—any job."

He nodded. "Max put one of his girls in here—she sold out on us," he said. "I had one named Carol Torney. It isn't generally known—but I kicked her out. I was suspicious. I'd like to use you—maybe outside the office. I don't want Max Cohn to know that. You won't get hurt. You won't have to think. You'll just have to do what I tell you. Nothing else. No imagination—no police work. I'll pay you sixty a week—while the job lasts."

She said slowly: "You're sure I won't get hurt?"

He grinned. "Unless you walk in front of a truck, or get hit by some falling brick—you won't get hurt," he replied.

She nodded. "I'll do as you say," she said simply.

He leaned back in his chair. "A conductor named Hans Reiner has been murdered, at the Hollywood Bowl," he said. "He was—"

"I've been reading about—"

He interrupted her interruption. "Wait—I know you have. I want you to hear it this way. I'm not just anxious to talk. He was shot. We don't know why. A pilot flew a plane over the Bowl just as Reiner was being shot. His name was Carren. We think maybe he flew the plane over to drown the sound of shots with the engines. He flew very low. He's dead. He was killed about an hour and a half ago, after he knocked me down while I was questioning him. He got into a plane, got the plane in the air—and then crashed. We don't know why he crashed. We're looking for the murderer of Hans Reiner. His murder, and the crashing to death of this pilot, Carren— these are major events. We know they happened. We don't know anything else of importance. We don't suspect anyone, and we have no motive for Reiner's murder."

Jardinn smiled pleasantly. He repeated slowly, emphatically:

"We don't suspect any person."

He waited. The girl's brown eyes closed. She said very slowly, as she opened them:

"We don't suspect any person, even though we know that Howard Frey knocked Hans Reiner's brother unconscious on a movie control platform—and even though we have been told that Maya Rand has used certain damaging words, in the patio of her home."

Jardinn got up, smiling. He looked down at the baby-faced girl. He said:

"You're bright as hell, Ede. I don't know where I stand, with the office crowd wise enough to know the gold is flowing all over the place. I've never been sure of Carol—she was too hard inside. I'm sure of you. I'm positive."

She said, smiling: "Why?"

He smiled, too. He opened a drawer at the bottom of his desk, on the right side, and took out a gun. He held it toward her, still smiling.

"It's loaded," he said. "It's got ten bullets. It's got a Maxim silencer that'll work well killing the racket of one shot. You walked in here and took a job. You've got a baby face and brains. I can use both—and I'm going to use both. You won't get hurt, Ede—not unless you get clever."

She looked frightened. She shivered a little. He laughed nastily.

"I've got to have help. It's all right being crossed—just so long as I know who are crossing me. But I won't be able to know about you. I won't have time. If it happens—I'll just get the idea suddenly."

She started to shake her head, stopped. She said:

"I don't have to stay on here."

He nodded. "You have to stay on here," he contradicted. "You came in—and you looked around. You heard a few things. You're going to stick—and you're going to do what I tell you. Either that or—"

He slipped the weapon back in the drawer, closed it. He sat down and lighted a cigarette. There were tears in the girl's eyes.

"You said I wouldn't get hurt," she said shakily. "You said—"

"You won't," he cut in. "You won't even come close to getting hurt. It'll be the easiest job you've ever had. But I've got to get things right, here in the office."

She said shakily: "Then why'd you show me the—gun?"

He smiled. "Figure it out for yourself," he replied. "I can't shoot worth a damn—but at two feet it's hard to miss."

She dabbed at her eyes with a handkerchief. She tried to smile. Her baby face was pale.

"I'm not tricking you," she said in an uncertain tone. "And you said—I wouldn't get—"

"Christ!" he cut in harshly. "A lot of people don't get hurt. But they get dead."

She got up from her chair suddenly. There was courage in her eyes. Her baby figure was tense.

"You think I came into this agency for a reason!" she flared. "It isn't true. I came just for a job! That was all!"

Ben Jardinn leaned back in his chair, grinned at her cheerfully.

"All right—all right," he said in a soothing voice. "You've *got* it, haven't you?"

2

Jardinn finished scrawling on the fourth sheet of paper, struck a match under the white stuff, let the flames eat upward. He took the ashes over and dropped them into the wastepaper basket. One sheet wasn't completely destroyed; he could distinguish the words "Carren" and "Bonner" and a few broken sentences of unimportance. There wasn't much else in the wastepaper basket. He smiled.

"Twice," he said softly. "Make sure, this time. Think someone's trying to read this stuff."

Edith Brown came in. Her face was still pale, and her eyes were red. But she smiled.

"The woman who cleans the office is outside," she said.

He nodded. "Let her come in, Ede," he told her. "Feel better?"

She nodded, went out. A heavy-bosomed German woman came in. She turned weary eyes toward Jardinn.

"Don't do anything in here tonight," he said. "Just stay outside. Don't come in at all."

She nodded. Jardinn folded a dollar bill, gave it to her. She went out. He followed her into the outer office, watched Edith Brown putting powder on her nose. He said:

"Getting late. Run along, Ede. Give me a number

that I can call. I won't call it tonight. Better go over to the Egyptian and hear Garbo talk. Come down around nine tomorrow.''

She scrawled a phone number on a slip of paper, handed it to him. He held her fingers in a grip that was almost gentle.

"Not sore at me, Ede?" he asked. "*You've* got to be right.''

She said in her husky tone: "There was no reason to think I wouldn't be. You didn't have to be brutal.''

He frowned. "I was just honest with you, Ede,'' he said.

She got ready for the street slowly, carefully. At the outer door she stopped, looked at him. She spoke in a hesitating voice.

"You look—very tired. It would be better if you got some sleep.''

"Better than—what?" he asked her, his eyes amused.

She shrugged. "Better than going out to Maya—''

"Careful!" he cut in sharply. "You know—''

She laughed at him. It was a hard, husky laugh. It wasn't pretty. Her little, perfect figure was erect. Jardinn kept his eyes on hers; his right-hand fingers were twisting near the material of his suiting. He watched fear come into her eyes. But her voice was steady enough.

"If you hurt me, Jardinn—''

Her voice broke. She went out quickly, slamming the door behind her. Jardinn swore bitterly; he went over and sat at the stenographer's desk. He fingered a cigarette, but did not light it. He looked at his wristwatch, spoke as though he were not alone.

"Concert at the Bowl tonight—think I'll go out there. Can make Maya Rand's place by nine-thirty. Early enough.''

There were powder marks on the stenographer's desk. He looked down at them, lighted the cigarette, and frowned.

"Damned little fool," he said placidly. "She walked right into it."

3

It was ten minutes after eight when Jardinn walked up the winding path that led toward the gates of the Hollywood Bowl. Early arrivals were strolling along; the program girls, in their gay colored uniforms, were listlessly calling attention to their printed sheets. Jardinn turned to the right, did not go through the gates. He moved around by the hill-cut parking places, approached the shell near the musicians' entrance.

On his left he could see the lighted, semi-natural theater. Tier after tier rose from the level of the grass that stretched between the shell and the first rows of seats. Only a small portion of the Bowl was filled; he could see the early comers moving up the aisles, the side paths. The brakes of cars squealed on the dirt road that wound from Highland Avenue to the parking spaces. Jardinn said softly:

"Get through with this—get up above for the first number. Move around; see how things look, even if the police have done all that."

He moved among the musicians, into the anteroom at the left of the shell. The brass sections were tuning; he saw the tall, gray-haired concert master standing near the door that led to the shell platform, moved toward him. Brusset smiled as he approached; there was a sadness in the man's eyes. He had a lean, cadaverous face; he spoke with an accent.

"You have—learned something, Mr. Jardinn?"

Ben Jardinn shook hands with the concert master, said quietly:

"Very little. I have come to you to learn something, perhaps."

Brusset spread his hands in a gesture of hopelessness.

"It seems difficult," he said. "But if I may help, in any way—"

They moved from the anteroom, went out along a narrow path that circled around toward the grass that fronted the shell platform. Among palms they found a secluded spot. Jardinn said in a low voice:

"You were in the shell—when the lights went out?"

Brusset nodded. "I was with Madame Volten, the soloist who was to sing during the second half. We were talking. When the airplane came over we both complained rather bitterly—there has been so much of it this season. The other maestros had complained, and I was worried about Herr Reiner. Then the lights went out. It startled me—I looked toward the shell platform. We were in the anteroom across the platform from the one in which you met me. The switch that operates the lights was across the platform from us. As I looked—the lights came on. Herr Reiner was falling. I think he had one hand at his back. The lights went out again—and I started toward the platform. There was much confusion. Finally one of the tympani men reached the switch and turned the shell lights on. The Bowl lights came on very soon—perhaps ten seconds after that—"

Emil Brusset's voice died; he stood looking toward the outline of the shell, the great curve of it, frowning. Jardinn said:

"When this tympani player found the switch there was no one near it?"

The concert master shook his head. "Not a soul," he stated. "The electrician had been outside smoking—he knew the time the piece would take. He had been struck down, and as he has said—he did not recognize the one who assaulted him. But I do not understand why the lights flashed on—then off again."

Jardinn said: "The police theory seems to be that Hans Reiner was shot from the two paths of the Bowl. The shots were fired in the darkness. But the lights were needed—it was necessary to see if there had been hits. When Reiner fell—they were not needed. Darkness was better. So the switch was thrown again.''

The concert master frowned. "That was remarkable shooting," he said softly.

Jardinn smiled a little. "That is the police theory," he repeated. "For the present I am accepting it. As a matter of fact, the shooting was not so remarkable. Two hundred yards or so, with perfect sights and perhaps much practice at a similar angle. If the men with the rifles were well screened by friends, they could easily have raised their weapons and sighted—just before the lights went out. It is only a matter of ten feet across the paths—these men could have fired from the growth beyond. The bushes are tall enough to hide a human.''

The concert master said quietly: "It was a horrible thing, Mr. Jardinn.''

Jardinn nodded. "This is confidential, of course," he stated. "I would like you to take me to one or two musicians in each of the sections. First violins, second violins, brass, cellos, tympani. I would like to have you show me on the score of the tone poem Hans Reiner was conducting—the approximate note sounding when the lights went out.''

Emil Brusset whistled softly. "You mean, of course, on the maestro's scoring," he said. "The sections would be all in variance. There was a crescendo, I think—''

Jardinn said: "Yes, on Reiner's score. I want to get his exact position—which section he was facing as the lights were extinguished. There are one hundred and ten musicians—surely some of them must have seen his exact position.''

Brusset said, smiling sadly: "They would have sensed it, of course. He was working with them. He was a brilliant conductor, Mr. Jardinn, and was getting everything from them. Yes, I think we can learn these things.''

Jardinn said: "Good, but it is to be done in a casual

manner. You do not feel there was hatred between Hans Reiner and any of the musicians. You, as a musician—"

Emil Brusset said emphatically: "I am very certain Herr Reiner was only loved. He was admired very much. He was gentle with the men. In the rehearsals he was much liked."

Jardinn nodded, smiled at the concert master. He said slowly:

"We haven't much time—I'd like to question the musicians."

Brusset nodded. "The first piece is scored for a limited number of strings," he said. "Many of the musicians will not be on the platform."

Jardinn said: "Well, let's get at it, anyway. None of them spoke of seeing anything, out in the audience, that looked like a flash—a streak of red?"

Brusset shook his head. "It was a crescendo," he explained. "Almost all were working hard. The men seldom are aware of the audience, in any case."

Jardinn nodded. They moved along the path toward the shell. Brusset spoke in a low, puzzled voice:

"It was such a spectacular, daring way to shoot down—" He broke off, then said grimly: "It was almost like a gesture. The supreme indifference of the method—"

Jardinn said: "Sure—it looked like all that at first. But it begins to look like something else now. It wasn't so daring and it wasn't worked indifferently. Certainly it was no gesture."

Brusset made a clicking sound. "It was a very terrible thing," he reiterated.

Jardinn said grimly: "It was a damn, smooth job."

Thirty minutes later, as he moved slowly along the right path of the Bowl slope, he was repeating the words. The orchestra was playing the second number; Bern, the local conductor, was wielding the baton. There was only a fair crowd in attendance. Near the spot where he had been knocked down, Jardinn paused, stood looking down at the musicians. The music reached him; it was a jest in tone. There was a quality of mockery in the string sounds; the brass section superimposed gay notes against the motif of the violins.

Jardinn stood motionlessly for several minutes. His eyes, half narrowed, searched the whole slope of the Bowl, rested on the conductor's platform, on the squat, ungraceful form of the maestro. The strings died, brass was subdued to the thin tones of a reed.

Above him, in the upper rows that rimmed the crest of the hill, there was muffled laughter. Lovers occupied the upper rows—it was an ideal spot. He looked in that direction, said softly:

"Too far—even for rifles, back there."

A feminine voice reached him faintly. It was protesting, half jokingly.

"Charlie—stop! If you hurt me—"

It died suddenly. Jardinn glanced back toward the shell again, smiling grimly. He muttered to himself:

"Yeah, but that Brown kid isn't afraid of being hurt *that* way. It isn't hugging that worries her. And there was Ernst Reiner, pretty worried about something—and Frey—"

He stopped muttering as the music ceased, the Bowl lights flared. He said slowly, in a half whisper:

"Damn—D'Este might be the man—"

He moved suddenly down the sloping path and toward the Bowl entrance.

·7·

PATIO SCENE

Leon D'Este twisted the ends of his waxed mustache, smiled at Jardinn with his dark eyes, and spoke with the voice of a roughneck.

"Hell—I been with the Central Casting Bureau for two years, Ben. She sounds like an extra type to me. Hundreds of these would-be Gish brats think crossing a street in a mob scene is a bit. How's this one?"

Jardin shook his head. He was looking at photographs; the table beside which he and D'Este stood held hundreds of them. They had been at the job for thirty minutes, with no luck.

"I don't think she's worked in studios out here on the Coast," Jardinn said. "More likely in New York or Jersey. Or out at Long Island."

D'Este grunted. He continued passing photographs to Jardinn, and Ben kept on dropping them on the table's surface. D'Este said:

"We'd get a still of some scène or some damn fake scene, or a shot of the kid's face, even if she hadn't worked out here. That's part of the lousy game. But you know I'd go out of my way to help you, Ben—you've done your stuff for me. Why don't you let me look at this brat? I'll get you the dope, all right."

Jardinn said: "I'd like to know right away. A quick job'll help. If it don't go, then I'll fix it so you can see her. If I get what I want—I can use it tonight."

D'Este chuckled. "First time I've seen you togged to kill," he said. "Know who I think did the Reiner job?"

Jardinn grinned: "That nance O'Reilly?" he replied. "Maybe thinking he was losing Hans to Ernst."

The casting bureau man winked at Jardinn. He handed him a half dozen photographs.

"All baby-faced kids," he said. "Maybe she's in there. No, not O'Reilly. Just some guy who wanted to try something. No motive, see. Just a clever guy trying to get away with the old, perfect crime stuff. That's what's making it rotten for you, Ben."

Jardinn smiled down at the pictures. He shook his head.

"Money is what's making it rotten for me, Leon," he replied. "It always counts—the spend stuff. Nothing here."

He dropped the last picture. D'Este swore. He said slowly:

"That about finishes the sweet kid type. Sure you grabbed off the right idea? Maybe she does heavy stuff."

Jardinn lighted a cigarette, shook his head.

"Not with that face and figure," he replied. "But maybe I've got the wrong hunch. Maybe she never worked in pictures."

D'Este turned around and stared at Ben; he groaned heavily.

"For God's sake!" he muttered. "After all this hunting around, you tell me she may never have worked on the lots!"

Jardin grinned. "Like my old friend, S. Holmes," he returned, "I'm a very careful worker. You know Ernst Reiner, Leon?"

D'Este was twisting the ends of his waxed mustache again. He was small in size, very dapper in appearance. He had always been small in size, but he hadn't always been so dapper. It was a Hollywood affectation.

"Sweet director," he said. "But, Jeez, he's fussy. When he's casting—he's casting. He does a smooth job."

Jardin nodded. He got on his light coat, buttoned it over his dinner clothes. He said cheerfully:

"Come up to the office tomorrow, about twelve, will you. We'll have a bit of lunch. On your way in look at the stenographer. Then forget her until we get outside. She'll take your name."

D'Este widened his dark eyes. He nodded. Jardinn walked around to the far side of the table and looked down at the writing on the back of a photograph. He lifted the picture, turned it over. D'Este said:

"You saw all that stuff, Ben."

Jardin shook his head. "I didn't see this one—must have slipped by. Not that it makes any difference."

The casting bureau man came around and looked at the photograph. He said in an irritated tone:

"Just another baby face—God, I see 'em in my dreams."

Jardinn grinned. "That's better than falling off a cliff," he said. "I get that dose every week or so."

D'Este grunted. "Ever hit bottom?" he asked.

Jardinn shook his head. "If I'd do that little thing once I think that would end it," he replied. "That would be swell. Any suggestions?"

The casting bureau man toyed with his waxed end mustache and chuckled.

"Out of my line, Ben," he said. "See you at twelve."

Jardinn nodded, went toward the door of the office. He stopped, swore softly, faced D'Este again.

"Damn near forgot about Max Cohn," he said. "Can't make it tomorrow, Leon. I'll give you a ring in the afternoon. Not so much of a rush, anyway."

D'Este nodded. "Not sneaking out of buying me a lunch, are you?" he asked. "Say, want to take that photo along?"

Jardinn narrowed his eyes a little and said absently:

"Which one?"

D'Este held up the last one he had looked at; there was a peculiar expression in his dark eyes. He said:

"This one."

Jardinn got a puzzled expression in his eyes. He said nastily:

"What in hell would I want to take that one along for, Leon?"

The casting bureau man dropped it back on the table with the others. He parted his lips, yawned as he tapped them carefully with the tips of his fingers. When he got through yawning he said in a pleasant voice:

"If I can help you any, Ben—"

Jardinn grinned at him and went outside the office. There was a frown on his face as he walked along the paving toward the spot where the roadster was parked.

"Hell!" he muttered as he slipped back of the car's wheel. "Every one seems to know more about this kill— than I do."

2

Maya Rand sat across from him, gracefully indolent in the huge, fan-backed chair. She wore a jet-black evening gown—white pearls in a long string contrasted the color. Her skin was beautiful; with no harsh, studio lights to strike her she was a gorgeous thing. She sipped her cocktail with narrowed eyes upon the liquid in the long stemmed glass. She said:

"I feel more and more as though it had nothing to do with pictures or picture people, Hans' death. I think that Ernst is standing the shock wonderfully. Of course, anything that I can do to help, you know I'll do."

Jardinn leaned back in his wicker chair, got his hands from the pockets of his dinner coat and smiled at her.

"It's nice to know that," he said, and turned his head away from her, keeping his dark eyes on the patio palms. "Even if you did start in by lying to me."

She was very quick. On her feet, she took a step toward him, her eyes blazing. He turned his head toward her, kept on smiling.

"You did, you know," he said quietly.

She brought her right hand downward; the cocktail glass shattered on the patio tile. She said in a twisted, distorted voice:

"You can't be a beast—with me!"

Jardinn said: "I can do a lot of things with you, Maya. To hell with your temperament. Hans Reiner went under dirt today. That's more important. Sit down and stop acting."

She turned her back on him, moved away from the fan-backed chair. He called after her, softly:

"You knew Hans Reiner—before he came to Hollywood."

She stopped, swung around. Her eyes held denial. She shook her head. She said in a strained tone:

"I didn't—I didn't know him! You can't do this to me. You can't! If you try—"

"Take it easy," Jardinn cut it, and slumped down in his chair. "Howard Frey was at your place, here. Hans Reiner was here. Ernst was working at the studio. Hans had heard about Frey knocking his brother down. You introduced them, and Hans referred to Frey as the 'pugilist.' Then he went out in the patio, out here, with you—"

"That's a lie!" Her voice was sharp, steady. She sat in the fan-backed chair, but she didn't relax. Her eyes were on the dark ones of Jardinn.

"Hans Reiner went into the music room with me. Howard Frey started to drink. He felt he'd been insulted.

Hans played some of his own compositions—he left in about a half hour. I came out here and strolled around, going over some of my scenes for the next day. There were lines to be spoken.''

Jardinn smiled with his thin lips. He said:

"What next?"

She was calmer now. She spoke in a low voice, making graceful gestures with her hands. She knew how to use them; it was a nice show. Jardinn kept his eyes away from her face, watched her hands. They were very perfect.

"After a half hour or so I was chilly. It was two nights before the concert at which Hans was—"

Her voice wavered. She relaxed in the chair, smiled wanly. Jardinn nodded:

"Yeah, go on," he said. "You got cold."

She spoke very perfectly now, using words and her picture voice. It amused him and he fought away a grin.

"I had finished doing the scene—talking it. I went inside, looked around for Howard Frey. He'd gone, my Jap told me. There were some other guests—there almost always are.''

She spread her hands in a gesture of completeness.

"That was all," she said.

Jardinn leaned forward, got a cigarette from his case, remembered Maya. He apologized, offered her the case. She shook her head.

"My voice," she explained.

He lighted up, said very casually:

"Rather a nasty spot for Frey—meeting Ernst Reiner's brother."

She drew her wrap about her shoulders, touched her dark hair with pale fingers.

"It was unavoidable. Frey came without calling. He does that, often. Hans chanced to be here."

Jardinn nodded. "Want to hear Frey's idea of what happened?" he asked.

She frowned. "Is it important?" she asked.

"Might be," Jardinn said. "Frey's in a mess—and getting in deeper. He's right about the police wanting a goat."

"He has friends," she said.

Jardinn smiled. "Sure," he agreed. "But wait until things start to move—the friends will forget a lot of things. They'll know him, but not very well. Or maybe they'll take trips for a few weeks. Anyway, friends may not help too much. Want to hear his story?"

She nodded. Jardin said: "After you left the room with Hans Reiner, Frey went downstairs somewhere and had some drinks. In about an hour he came up, went out to the patio. You were excited, pacing back and forth. You were talking to yourself. You said: 'I got up here alone—I'll stay here. He's no good, but he can't pull me down. I can get to him—before he gets to me. I'll use his brother.' Or words to that effect; I may have slipped up somewhere. You didn't know Frey was listening."

She widened her eyes, looked surprised. Then she relaxed, laughed. It was a low, throaty laugh. Her slender body moved with the laughter. Jardinn smiled:

"I'm glad you've got a sense of humor," he said. "It's nice."

She stopped laughing. She leaned toward him, speaking mockingly.

"You believe that sort of thing?" she asked. "Frey comes up and crouches in the shadows of the patio—while I parade back and forth dramatically, involving myself in a nasty mess by telling terribly important things to the goldfish in the pool."

Jardinn smiled pleasantly. "Frey had reason to hate Ernst Reiner," he said. "He took a nasty insult, and when he physically resented it he was fired. His contract was broken. He was shelved. It isn't much fun to be shelved, in Hollywood. Frey may be sensitive. He was working under a nervous strain. He hasn't much money—he'd spent a good deal in attempting to show his admiration of you.''

''Oh, God!'' She got up, started to laugh again. She walked a few feet from the chair, came back and stood beside it. ''Howard Frey spent money on me? *He* spent it—on me!''

Jardinn said: ''All right, you spent it on him, then. The point is, he hasn't much money just now. And Maskey had shoved him out, started him on a slide. It happens that Ernst Reiner had come to me; he felt his life was in danger. Right after that Frey comes to me and tells me he's learned that Reiner suspects he will try to injure the director. Frey says it's the bunk. But he thinks he may be framed for some injury that will occur.''

Maya Rand looked down at him with narrowed eyes. ''Well?'' she said.

Jardinn shrugged. ''Frey couldn't revenge himself on Ernst Reiner, even though he had told me he might be framed. Reiner had made it too tough for him. But he knew that Ernst idolized his brother. He knew that Hans Reiner was to have his little moments of triumph. If he could smash Hans Reiner down, murder him—with the man he hated looking on—''

''No—no!'' Her words were half cries. She turned away from him. Her arms were raised; he guessed that her fingers were pressed to her lips.

''It's a theory the police seem to like,'' he said. ''What Ernst Reiner can do with this picture, after the shock of his brother's murder—that's problematical. Perhaps Frey thought it would finish him—the Bowl kill. Or perhaps he thought that such a crime, done in such a big way, would turn suspicion away from him. Or perhaps he thought he had a perfect alibi.''

She said quickly: ''He did!''

Jardinn shook his head. "You mean you've heard that
he called to me, just after the lights went out—and that
I tried to follow him. No, that's far from perfect."

She faced him again. She said in a calmer tone.

"You suspect Howard Frey?"

Jardinn shrugged. "You've just hurt him a little," he
said. "You've caused me to doubt that he told me the
truth when he said he'd spent money on you. You laugh
at what he told me he heard you saying—"

She shook her head. She said in a hard tone:

"I shouldn't have laughed, perhaps. That was wrong.
But it seemed funny. I'm an actress, of course, and I
couldn't believe you'd believe that a plotter in crime
would walk about muttering things that would be dangerous."

Jardinn stood up, propped his cigarette stub in the
ashtray near the fan-backed chair, smiled coldly at the
actress.

"I'd rather believe that than the explanation you are
about to offer me," he said simply.

She showed her surprise in an involuntary gesture of
her hands. She spoke in a controlled tone.

"What explanation am I about to offer you?"

Jardinn let the skin at the outside corners of his eyes
crinkle in a smile.

"You might tell me that you were just rehearsing your
lines for a scene the next day," he said.

She nodded. She sat in the fan-backed chair again, her
wrap drawn tightly about her shoulders.

"Yes, exactly," she said in clipped sentences. "Yes—
that's it. That's what I was doing. Rehearsing lines."

Jardinn sat on the arm of the wicker chair. He frowned
at her.

"Don't be a fool, Maya," he warned. "The lights
are bright enough just now. That throne chair over at
Maskey's is comfortable enough. When you snap your
fingers things happen. But I saw Jean Carewe a week

ago, down at Tia Juana. She sat in a chair like the one they move around for you. And the studio lights burned just as brightly for her. She didn't have to snap her fingers—they anticipated that. Know what she's doing now? Taking anything that's easy around Caliente—and nothing's easy.''

Maya Rand said stolidly: "I haven't done anything. Publicity can't hurt me. Jean Carewe was mixed up in a killing.''

"So are you.'' Jardinn nodded his head. "By God, you are, Maya. The reporters will be down on you like a pack of dogs. They helped make you—and they'll pull you down so damn quick—''

He got up, walked over close to her. She said quietly: "Want to see the script of *Death Dance*?''

Her eyes were half smiling. Half amused. She was sure of herself, he knew that. She was sure of herself on this point. He felt beaten, and he didn't like to feel that way. He tried to keep the flatness out of his voice.

"How many scripts are there?'' he asked.

She shrugged. "God knows. Twenty—thirty—forty. You can even choose your favorite color—they type them on pink, yellow, white paper. The lines are in all of them, you know.''

He said slowly: "Howard Frey did the story—he knew the lines were there. He must have recognized them. Even if he hadn't written them in, he knew the script.''

She said in a flat voice: "He's been terribly nervous— perhaps he didn't recognize them.''

Jardinn said grimly: "Even knowing that he came to me, telling me something that would drag you into this mess, you try to excuse him.''

She drew a deep breath. Her voice was expressionless.

"He didn't—murder Hans Reiner,'' she said.

Jardinn got off the arm of the wicker chair. He laughed bitterly.

"It's a close job," he said steadily. "How long have the lines been in the script, Maya?"

She smiled. "Months," she replied. "The story was ready for me three months ago. We hadn't finished the last picture. It's a stock market story—and I play one brother against the other. In the end, I lose. *Death Dance*."

Jardinn nodded. "Sure," he said. "The old hokum. I believe you, Maya—the lines were in the script. They've been there for months. Howard Frey just didn't recognize them. He thought you were acting a *real* part."

Her eyes met his squarely. "Yes," she said. "He didn't have anything to do with Hans Reiner's death. He wouldn't come to you and deliberately lie about me. He'd know I could show you the script. He simply was upset, terribly upset. He didn't remember."

Jardinn said in a very calm voice, "But what made him think that those words of yours might mean something? Why didn't he just laugh, step out and speak to you?"

Her eyes showed momentary fear. The tapering fingers of her right hand played with the soft material of her wrap. She said unsteadily:

"What are you—getting at?"

Jardinn leaned over her dark head. He spoke clearly, in a very low voice.

"Frey knew something—he didn't think of the script lines because something *else* was more important. What you said fitted in. To save his neck he squealed on you—"

She was on her feet; she pushed him away from her. She said excitedly:

"Oh, why don't you go away? Why don't you hunt for the murderer the way—others do? The police haven't bothered me! They are at the Bowl. They don't come here. They don't try to make things out of nothing!"

Jardinn smiled at her. "I do things my way," he said steadily. "Just like Carren did things his way."

Maya Rand walked a few feet and placed her left hand against the fan-backed chair arm. Her face was turned toward his. She said thickly:

"Carren—the plane pilot?"

Jardinn nodded. "Know him?" he asked.

She was breathing heavily. She shook her head. It was as though the movement had been an effort, a great effort.

"See tonight's papers?" Jardinn asked.

She didn't speak. She shook her head again.

"What—" she commenced, and stopped.

Jardinn said carelessly. "He had an accident. His plane crashed."

Her eyes closed. She opened them. He waited while her lips framed the words. Her voice was very weak.

"He's—hurt?"

Jardinn nodded. "A little," he said. "He's dead."

Her body swayed, but he wasn't prepared for the utterness of her collapse. His rough grip prevented her head from striking the tiles of the patio. She was light; he carried her easily toward the door that led to the living room. The Jap butler met him just inside; his eyes became saucers.

"Madam—she sick?"

Jardinn nodded. "Sure," he replied. "We can't all be strong—like you. Where does she sleep?"

The Jap moved quickly toward the stairs. Jardinn followed him. The Jap said, in a frightened tone:

"Madam—she very sick?"

Jardinn grunted. "Sick as hell," he replied. "She had a shock."

·8·

NOT JEALOUS

It was eleven-fifteen before Carol Torney reached the beach speakeasy designated by Ben Jardinn; he had been in the place a half hour, sipping two old-fashioned cocktails, smoking a half pack of cigarettes and watching the door that led to the narrow street. In the distance an amusement park concession shrilled stupid music; at intervals there was the rush of a scenic railway car. Carol came in quickly; her eyes caught the lift of his hand. She moved over the wooden floor, reached the booth. A weary-eyed waiter followed her.

"Beer," Carol said. "Hello, Bennie. Got a start?"

He shook his head. He rose, strolled past the booth next in line, turned and came back. The booth was empty. There was none on the other side—he'd picked the last one in the line. A radio suddenly got into action, but no couples were using the small dance floor. There was only the faint murmur of voices, at the far end of the room.

Jardinn slid along the bench across from Carol. He smiled at her.

"No start—not drinking much," he said. "Sure you weren't tagged?"

She leaned back a little and narrowed her eyes.

"Killed ten minutes, making sure," she replied. "But I spotted Max standing on a curb, as I drove through Hollywood. Came around the block—passed the place again. He wasn't there. Drove all over the place getting here. Maybe he followed—maybe not. Sure thing he didn't follow all the way."

Jardinn said: "Where'd you spot him, Irish?"

She was looking in a mirror and fooling with her lipstick.

"He's in this," she said. "You better watch him, Bennie."

Jardinn sipped his drink. "Where'd you spot him, Irish?" he repeated.

"Down near the Montmartre," she said. "Between the entrance and the corner of Highland. On Hollywood. Just lolling around, but he wasn't there when I turned the block."

She finished with her lips, lifted the glass of beer. She made a face that wasn't pretty, set the glass down.

"Rotten," she said.

Jardinn nodded. "Get something else," he suggested. "Listen, Irish—you keep away from the office, see?"

He signaled the waiter. Carol looked at him, then at the beer.

"Take it away," she told the waiter. "Whisky sour, and don't make it too sweet."

The waiter wanted to know what was the matter with the beer. Carol said:

"It's rotten."

He took the glass away, muttering to himself. She kept her eyes on Jardinn.

"You don't look so good, Bennie," she said. "Maybe we're going to get licked."

Jardinn said grimly: "Maybe we are. Did you hear what I said about keeping away from the office?"

Carol Torney looked around the place curiously.

"It's a dead spot, eh?" she breathed and shivered.

Jardinn lifted his right hand, clenched his fist and pounded it on the surface of the wooden table. His glass danced—things vibrated. Carol's black eyes got wide. He said angrily:

"Goddam it—you stop doing that, Irish! When I ask you questions—you answer them. Remember, I can fight women just the way I fight men. I'll do it—"

"Easy, Bennie," she interrupted. "You've been losing sleep. What makes you think I've been around the office?"

He sat back and smiled nastily at her.

"You're curious as hell," he replied. "You'd like to know who's doing the stenographic work."

She smiled. The waiter brought the whisky sour. He said in a hoarse voice:

"If it's too sweet I'll get you a lemon."

Carol nodded. The waiter moved away. Carol sipped the drink, smiled.

"It's all right, Bennie," she said. "It's pretty all right. Who *is* doing the office work?"

Jardinn looked at her strong fingers. He said slowly:

"A baby-faced kid named Brown. She's dumb, and I want her to stay that way. After she got the job she started getting scared. Afraid she'll be hurt. I want her to stay that way, too. I got her from an employment agency."

Carol chuckled. "Max Cohn's the only one that'll hurt her," she said. "Any special reason for throwing this party, Bennie?"

He said: "Just a chat. What happened while you were out at the Bowl?"

She shrugged. "Walked around and tried to figure distances, things like that. Had a talk with Mrs. Winfred-Neeley. Asked her about how she'd happened to sign up Hans Reiner. She said she'd been trying to get him to conduct in the Bowl, for three years."

Jardinn said: "You want to be a little careful. Max thinks you've been kicked out. If he picked up the idea that you've been out asking questions—"

"Newspaper woman," she interrupted. "I told her my name was Briggs. No one out there from the police. It was all right, Bennie."

"All right." His voice was very low. "The night of the murder you were down here—that is, at the beach somewhere. You wanted to be. What happened?"

She shook her head. "Abe didn't show," she replied. "You know I'd tell you anything that had happened, if it were worthwhile. I met this Montelli somewhere. Think it was at the Cocoanut Grove. Someone said that his brother was a big guy. Some picture boy, I think. Anyway, I heard his brother was Frey's bootlegger. Thought maybe I'd get a line on why Frey had rushed to you. But Abe didn't show. I came down to my aunt's—you know, the red headed one."

Jardinn nodded. Carol Torney kept her eyes on his face. She said:

"Carren hit you—before he killed himself, eh? I'm sorry, Benny."

Jardinn smiled, touched the hurt spots and finished his drinks.

"What makes you think he killed himself?" he asked.

She shrugged. "They were closing in. You went at him too roughly."

Jardinn frowned at her. "How do you know how I went at him?" he asked.

She said: "For God's sake, what is this? A thirder? I've been reading the papers, and I know how you work."

He passed the cigarettes, lighted the two. They were silent for a while. Then Jardinn leaned across the table's surface and spoke in a low voice.

"They're afraid of us, Carol—afraid as the devil. I've got an idea that the D.A.'s office will slow things up, just as soon as it can be done. And the police are slowing up already. Max Cohn's been bought. They came right inside the office—right into us, Irish. It makes me sore."

Carol frowned. "Got anything?" she asked.

He smiled at her. "I've got a job for you," he said. "But we've got to be careful. Max figures he's sitting nice. He's doing the routine stuff I give him—and watching me. I'm not sure he knows who did the job on Hans Reiner, but he knows that it's his job to worry me, keep me away from the real stuff. They bought him out, Irish."

She nodded. "Why don't you get him in a cellar and make him talk?" she asked.

Jardinn shook his head. "That would mess it up. But I've got a job for you. It's a woman job. I'll keep Max away from you. Carren knew what a lot of this was about. Find out where he lived and who he knew. Work it that way. It'll give me some leads. I'm wasting too much time around the office."

Carol nodded. "I can try that," she said. "But it may be slow."

Jardinn smiled. "It may be," he agreed. "Don't make a mess of it. What did you want to put that Gunsted woman on Cohn for?"

Her eyes widened, but she chuckled. She said:

"I thought it would be a nice stunt. Then I remembered that he knew her pretty well. So I called it off."

Jardinn nodded slowly. "I'm running the agency," he reminded grimly. "Don't start things without talking to me."

She shrugged. "I was trying to help you, Bennie," she said. "I can do more than that baby-faced—"

"Don't get that way," he cut in. "There are too many women in this deal, right now. When things clear up I'm going to kick all the women out—put a man in the office."

She swore at him. "Sure—Max is so damn faithful, Bennie."

They sat in silence. Carol broke it by staring out at

the dance floor and speaking against the beat of the Biltmore orchestra, and the voices of the trio.

"Frey could have done it, Bennie. Or Ernst Reiner. Or that picture actress—"

She checked her words. Jardinn beckoned for the waiter, asked for the bill. He said to Carol Torney:

"What picture actress?"

His eyes held a hard expression, and the tone of his voice had changed. Carol looked hurt.

"We're not going—so soon?" she asked. "Listen, Bennie, I don't get to see you—"

"What picture actress?" he cut in again. "Come on, Irish—open up."

She laughed at him. "The English actress—the one he had the affair with, in London. She's been in Hollywood for three months."

Jardinn leaned back and smiled. "If you got something why in hell didn't you get to me with it?" he said. "Now listen, Irish—you come through with this."

She kept her eyes on his; her face was flushed. She said:

"You've got to be good with me, Bennie. Never mind the bill. If you want to be nice—"

He stood up. "You just made a mistake, Irish," he said. "Hans Reiner didn't have any affair in London— not that you know about. There wasn't any English actress. You just made a mistake. You're thinking about some actress like—"

He stopped, grinned at her. She said savagely:

"You're playing around with Maya Rand. I know that. You didn't just *pretend* to kick me out of the office, Ben. You *did* kick me out. You were getting tired—"

"Shut up," he said wearily. The waiter came with the slip of paper; Jardinn paid him. But he didn't sit down. "You're holding back on me, Irish. You'd better come through. A jealous woman can't muss around in this deal."

She got up. "She won't look so pretty with a rope around her neck," she said bitterly.

Jardinn stared at her. He shook his head slowly.

"It beats me," he said. "You're getting too curious, Irish. I don't want you sitting too close on this job. You're supposed to be out of it, and if Max—"

"To hell with Cohn!" she snapped. "You never worked a job like this, Ben. You never played around the way you are. Maya Rand saved her money. She's got plenty. You don't care about Howard Frey. Or Ernst Reiner. If Maya Rand wants to buy you—why not. She's got looks—"

"My God," Jardinn muttered, and sat down on the bench.

Carol Torney laughed wildly. Then, suddenly, she was very calm. She stepped to the side of the table.

"I'm not putting up a yell, Ben," she said quietly. "I'm not jealous."

He motioned toward the bench opposite him. He said very quietly:

"Sit down, Carol. For just a few minutes. I've got to tell you something."

She kept her eyes on his, shrugged. She went over and sat down. Jardinn said:

"Hans Reiner has been murdered. Howard Frey is under suspicion, and unless the D.A.'s office can kill the case he'll stand trial. I can see it coming. He's a good goat. We've had pretty good luck in the agency, Carol—and maybe it'll keep up. But it won't if you get selfish. Or jealous. You know things you shouldn't know. You chased me out to the Rand house tonight, I think. Or maybe you had some friend tail me. Cut it out, Irish. It's no good."

She started to cry. Jardinn swore softly.

"Either you're working for me, or you're not," he said. "Keep me a fair break. If you don't—you can hurt

me. Work the Carren angle and never mind what I do—
or quit. Tell me now.''

Carol Torney twisted her handkerchief in her strong
fingers. She kept her face turned away from his. She
said thickly:

"Bennie—I'm not jealous. I swear I'm not. I was
trying to make you think so, but I couldn't go through
with it. Bennie—I'm scared.''

Jardinn narrowed his eyes on Carol's, said in a low
tone:

"Scared of—what?''

A glass crashed to the dance floor, near the front of
the speakeasy. Carol sucked in her breath sharply; her
body was tense. Jardinn said:

"Good God, Irish! You've never had a case of nerves.
What you scared of—what's happened to make you
scared?''

She shook her head. "It's different," she said shakily.
"All the other jobs we've had—they've been different.
It wasn't so close, Bennie. But this one—it's all around
us. I'm afraid—for you.''

Jardinn grunted. "Never mind about me. If you feel
up to it, work the Carren end. And try to get a line on
any love interest. See if he played around with—well,
maybe a picture kid. Extra or bit player.''

He was watching her narrowly, but when she looked
at him his eyes went across the room. A couple were
dancing—the radio music had a nice beat. Jardinn kept
time with his right foot.

"Just because Max goes back on us—that don't mean
you've got to stampede, Irish," he said. "Reiner's the
only one who got killed from a gun. Maybe that Carren
crash was an accident.''

Carol smiled at him. There were tears in her eyes, but
she blinked them away. She said slowly:

"You've worked blackmail cases, Bennie. You're not

too well liked. This might be another one of them—Ernst
Reiner may be holding back. And the others—they'd get
you if there was a chance to do it right. You know they
would.''

"Sure," he said, smiling. "You'd better get started,
Irish. You're all right, only you don't feel good. You
work the Carren end. Keep under cover and away from
the office. Don't phone in. I'll keep in touch with you.''

She leaned across the table; her fingertips touched his.
She said flatly:

"You're not sure, Bennie. You're not sure of me. Or
anything much. Max or Frey—or Ernst Reiner. There
isn't a trace—''

She stopped. Her fingertips felt cold against his. He
said quietly:

"Hell—you can't expect everything. Go home and get
some sleep. Of course I'm sure of you. Frey and Ernst
Reiner are all right, but I've got to prove it, maybe.''

She got up slowly. "Maybe Carren did the kill, from
the plane—some way. Maybe one of the passengers—''

Jardinn said as he rose: "Yeah, maybe that was it.
Going to work that end for me?''

She nodded. "I'll try. But you're shoving me out of
the way, Bennie. I know that. You're playing safe.''

He started to deny it; her arms went around him; her
lips were pressed against his half parted ones. She turned,
went out. Jardinn stood looking down at the dance floor.
His lips hurt. He wiped the rouge from them, sat down,
called the waiter and ordered Scotch.

He thought: She's wise to something. She's scared,
wishes to God we were out of this thing.

When the drink came he downed it, paid up and went
toward the door. A man's voice sounded from one of
the almost enclosed booths on his left. It had a high-
pitched, expressionless quality—it was the voice of a
pervert.

"Sure she got it—sure she did. Right in the stomach.

Six chunks of lead. And do you know what she did? She kept right on goin'—kept right on her feet. Picked up a meat cleaver and knocked that hunky's brains all over the place. Sure she did. Then she went over and put a record on the phonograph. They found her in front of it, sort of leanin' against it. She was holdin' her stomach and grinnin'. An' she says: 'He was a louse—an' he got what was comin'.' Then she walked over and got on a bed—and died. Sure she did. She should've been a man—that big baby!"

Jardinn opened the door and went outside. He was smiling.

"So many humans like to tell lies," he said almost gently. "It's hell finding out what really happens."

He thought about Irish and frowned. She was either jealous, scared—or lying. He shrugged, stared up and down the narrow, alley-like street that ran north and south the length of the beach towns of Venice and Santa Monica, a square from the sand and boardwalk.

"Not jealous," he said, as though answering a question, and looked for Carol's machine.

It was not in sight; he walked to the northward, but failed to see it. Then he went back to his own car. He drove back toward Beverly Hills, using Wilshire Boulevard. The fog was steadily growing thicker. It was cold.

He parked a half block from Henry's, went inside and had coffee and a sandwich. Al Burr was talking to Chaplin and Kennedy, at a table across from the food counters. He came over to Jardinn's table, grinning.

"What you got for me?" he asked. "The sheet's lousy with everything but news. Anything new on the Reiner kill?"

Jardinn shook his head. "I've been out of town," he said. "Police got anything?"

Burr grinned and swore. "They think maybe the guys with the rifles got the wrong man," he said. "Bonner is out with a statement that they've dug up a cello player.

whose life has been threatened. He was placed in a line with the conductor. Bonner thinks the killers were trying to get him.''

Jardinn grinned. "Well, isn't that news?" he asked.

The newspaper man swore. "Sure," he said. "But it's too funny to be *good* news."

Jardinn kept on grinning. "Bonner's a good man," he said. "He might have an idea."

The newspaper man chuckled. "He has, about you," he said. "He's also out with a statement that a certain private detective handicapped the police by going after Carren too hard."

Jardinn finished his coffee. "I still think he's a good man," he said. "Maybe that's an idea, too."

Burr groaned. "You're too damned good natured, Jardinn," he said. "Say, what did Carren really tell you before he slammed you down?"

Jardinn got up, dropped fifteen cents for a tip, and moved toward the cashier's desk.

"He said never to talk to newspaper men just before the final edition goes to press," he told Burr. "Maybe that was an idea, too."

Burr grinned. "That was just a lie," he said. "Call me up if you get anything, will you?"

Jardinn nodded. "I'll come down to the paper personally," he replied. "It'll add a human touch."

He went outside and bought the Los Angeles *Times*. He read the headline in a low voice.

" 'Police Have Reiner Clue.' "

"Sure," he breathed, folding the paper without reading more. "They've been having clues on the Stannard murder—for three years."

·9·

TELEPHONE CALL

When Jardinn reached the agency office it was after one. There was light showing beyond the frosted glass of the door; Max Cohn and Ernst Reiner were seated in the outer office. The picture director rose nervously as Jardinn entered; Max tilted the chair he was sitting in, grinned.

"Where you been, Ben?" he asked. "Down at Caliente?"

Jardinn went over and shook hands with Reiner. The director's face was pale, flabby. His eyes looked bad. He said in his precise voice:

"I have come for a report."

Jardinn grinned. "Sure," he replied. "Let's go into my office. Come along, Max—maybe we've got something to tell Mr. Reiner."

They went into the office. Max and Reiner seated themselves in chairs near Jardinn's desk. Jardinn pulled his chair over near a window. He got a pack of fresh cigarettes from his pocket, opened it and tossed it on the small table not far from him. As he dropped some bits of the package paper in the wastebasket he saw that the object had been emptied. The charred paper he had dropped there was gone.

Reiner said in a thick voice:

"Well?"

Jardinn got comfortable in his chair. He spoke to Max Cohn.

"Anything new?"

Max grunted. "Not much—but you know what I went out to Glendale about."

Cohn's eyes shifted to the profile of Ernst Reiner, who was watching Jardinn closely. Jardinn nodded.

"Yes—a woman called up and said she could tell us something about Ernst Reiner," he said quietly. "Did she?"

Reiner sat up stiffly, turned toward Cohn. Cohn blinked at Jardinn.

"No," he said. "That was some sort of deal—I couldn't locate the woman."

Reiner smiled. Jardinn smiled, too, but he shook his head.

"Never mind that, Max," he said. "What did she say?"

Cohn frowned at Jardinn. Reiner said in a dignified tone:

"Your assistant has just stated that there was no woman—he could not find her."

Jardinn grinned. "Sure," he agreed. "But we're not playing that way, Mr. Reiner. Come on, Max—talk out."

Cohn shrugged. "I think she's a little off," he said. "Her name's Degonné—she's got a French accent. She lives up in the hills on the outskirts of the town. The house is pretty bad, and she says she stays there alone. There isn't much furniture in the place. She just thought we should know that Ernst Reiner threatened his brother, some months ago."

Reiner got from his chair and swore sharply. He looked at Jardinn.

"That is a lie!" he said. "That is an attempt to frighten me, to procure money. That is blackmail. I will have her arrested—"

Jardinn said sharply: "Sit down, please, Mr. Reiner. All right, Max—what else?"

Cohn hunched himself forward in the chair and rolled his cigarette between thick lips.

"I couldn't get much else out of her," he said. "She says she isn't well, and what she has to say might be dangerous for her. She wants to get away. She said she'd stay in the state. Five hundred dollars is what she wants. She was present, backstage of a theater in Paris, when Ernst Reiner threatened Hans Reiner. She knew the two men because they had been pointed out to her by the stage manager. One was a famous maestro, the other a great motion picture director. She was in charge of costumes—the play was a musical comedy. The two men were backstage to meet one of the female stars. That's the substance of what I got, Ben."

Reiner muttered in German. He clenched a fist, brought it down heavily on his fat right leg, just above the knee.

"She lies!" he state emphatically. "It is absurd. We will have her arrested."

Jardinn frowned at the faded carpet of the office.

"What a story for the yellow press," he breathed. "No, I don't think we'd better have Madame Degonné arrested, Mr. Reiner."

Reiner's blood-streaked eyes widened. He said sharply:

"What, then, shall we do?"

Max Cohn was watching Jardinn with a puzzled expression in his eyes. He said slowly:

"As I told you, I think the woman's off her head. She says she's very nervous, hasn't slept since she read about the murder. Neurotic, probably. Gets all worked up over every murder she reads too much about."

Jardinn grinned. "Is that a professional opinion, Max?" he asked. "Or are you just using words?"

Ernst Reiner said in his accented tone, reaching for a slip of paper from the small table:

"It is preposterous! I shall not put up with this—"

He got the stub of a pencil from his pocket, scribbled something on the bit of paper. Jardinn said quietly:

"Go easy, Mr. Reiner. Better let me handle this. It doesn't make much difference whether she's crazy or mentally fine—not to the press. A story is a story."

The director rose to his feet, glared down at Jardinn. He said in an angered voice:

"You wish to protect a woman who is attempting to blackmail me? She is after the money—the five hundred dollars. I will not agree."

Jardinn said: "How long ago did you make a trip to Paris, Mr. Reiner?"

The director raised a trembling hand to his face, rubbed the palm and fingers over his flabby skin. He said thickly:

"It was perhaps four months ago—I made a hurried trip."

Cohn whistled softly. Jardinn said:

"You went backstage at any theaters?"

Reiner walked around behind the chair in which he had been seated.

"Of course," he said sharply. "Of course. It was a matter of business. It was a matter for the pictures."

Jardinn said very quietly: "Was your brother in Paris at the time?"

There was a little silence. Reiner stood with his stubby fingered hands at his side. He kept his eyes narrowed on Jardinn's.

"I saw him only for an hour, one evening," he said. "He was off to London. I tell you, Jardinn, that this woman is a criminal."

"Sure," Jardinn agreed. "Where'd you see your brother?"

Reiner's face was white. His mouth twisted; he drew himself erect.

"Backstage—at a theater," he said in a shaken voice. "But I tell you, Jardinn, there was a reason."

Jardinn nodded. "All right," he agreed. "I don't want to hear it. Better get me five hundred in cash, as early tomorrow as you can."

The picture director raised his voice. He cried out fiercely:

"No—no! I will not!"

Cohn said. "Jeez, you better, Mr. Reiner. It's a bad spot until we clear it up."

Jardinn said: "You scribbled this woman's name on that piece of paper. You'd better keep away from there, Mr. Reiner. The police aren't killing themselves on this job, but the newspaper boys are working hard. If they get to this woman, by tagging you—"

He broke off, shrugged. Cohn said:

"*They'll* pay her the five hundred quick enough."

"Just like that," Jardinn said, and snapped his fingers.

Reiner walked around and dropped heavily into the chair from which he had risen. He said in a thick voice:

"It is all—no good. It does not bring Hans back."

Jardinn nodded. "It may keep the right person alive," he said grimly. "You bring in the five hundred—we'll get this woman away and watch her. When we need her we'll dig her up."

Reiner let his weary eyes meet Jardinn's.

"Why do you not break her story down now?" he asked. "Suppose you are caught getting her away? The police know that I have retained you."

"We won't be caught," Jardinn replied. "As for breaking her story down—suppose we fail to do it? Suppose she stands up under the strain, insists she heard you threaten your brother. It puts you in a bad spot. It messes the whole thing up. We want to get your brother's killer or killers. We don't want to have to spend our time fighting to clear you. She knows that—she's not so crazy."

Cohn said thickly: "Crazy like a fox."

Ernst Reiner stared at Jardinn and spoke in a low voice.

"I will—get you the money."

Jardinn nodded. "Good," he said. "When you reached the shell, after the lights had come on again, you said: 'Hans—what have they done to you?' Why did you use those words?"

Reiner relaxed in the chair. He held his right hand below the level of his eyes, looked at it, steadied the shaking fingers.

"There was no reason," he said slowly. "I felt that he was hurt, dead. I sensed it. I hardly knew what I was saying. It was instinct—saying that."

Jardinn said suddenly, changing the subject:

"Did Maya Rand know the pilot, Carren, very well?"

Reiner's eye held a stupid expression. He shook his head.

"I do not know this Carren," he replied. "I do not know that Maya was acquainted with him. I have read about him. Why do you ask?"

Jardinn said: "Do you still think Frey is responsible for Hans Reiner's murder?"

The director shivered as he used the last word. He said grimly:

"I think Howard Frey is a dangerous man. You know that. I came to you, even before Hans—"

He stopped. Jardinn looked at Max Cohn. Cohn said:

"It seems to me I saw a picture once—something about a girl who couldn't make up her mind about three guys who were hot after her. There was a lot of singing and—"

"Never mind," Jardinn cut in. He looked at Reiner and smiled.

"You don't like the way I'm handling this job, Mr. Reiner," he said. "It's the best way I know. Because the police are yelling that I caused an important human to get himself quieted, don't think I'm all wrong. That was a tough break. There may be some more of them."

The director said slowly: "I do not know about these things. I have come to you. You do not seem to care about Howard Frey. The police are working on the bullets. They are at the Bowl much, I am told. They are seeking motives. You do not seem interested in such things. It is more as though you suspected me."

Jardinn made a gesture of amusement. He chuckled.

"If the police are working one way—there is no use in repeating that work," he said. "I hear what they are doing. It is undoubtedly good work. I am more interested in the events that occurred before the crime was committed—and in those acquainted with your brother."

Reiner rose with an obvious effort. He said:

"I am in your hands. You have done good work in other instances. I'm tired—it is difficult for me to sleep. If I appear upset, you see there is sufficient reason. The money will arrive tomorrow."

Jardinn rose. "It'll be worth it," he said simply. "I'll get in touch with you if anything happens."

Reiner said: "It is a terrible thing. A terrible thing."

He went slowly from the inner office. Max Cohn went out with him. Jardinn heard him turning the key in the lock of the outer office door, after the director had departed. When Cohn came back there was a puzzled expression on his face. He sat down and waited for Jardinn to speak. A car engine hummed, on Hollywood Boulevard. When the sound of the engine had died away Jardinn said:

"That's just a clever woman, out in Glendale. But we've got to keep her quiet. We don't want her to get talking for a while." He winked at Cohn.

Cohn said: "I didn't figure he'd come through with the five hundred in such a hurry. You're pretty slick, Bennie."

Jardinn smiled. "I'll handle it—when the five hundred gets here. Seen Irish around?"

Cohn shook his head. "She's dropped out of sight," he replied. "Maybe she left town."

He slumped in the chair and started to whistle off key. He stopped and said half to himself.

"Frey—Ernst Reiner—how about this Rand gal, Ben?"

Jardinn lighted a cigarette and shrugged. He squashed the match, dropped it in the wastebasket.

"It's hell to get anywhere—without a motive," he muttered. "A lot of better men than myself have found that out before."

Cohn said with his eyes half closed:

"I don't think we're working Frey hard enough. Reiner may be right."

Jardinn nodded. "Max," he said slowly, "I can't get over Irish trying to cross us up. It's hard to take. And I don't think she got so much. Just a little to try and make it hard. I feel kind of sorry for her."

Cohn swore. "You're too damn sympathetic, Ben," he replied. "She was dirty with us. She deserved what she got—maybe some more."

Jardinn frowned. "Sure," he agreed. "She was rating it. Hell—I hope she finds a hole for a crawl. She may need it."

Cohn said musingly: "If you could get her in a cellar— with something that would scare her—make her tongue get loose—"

Jardinn closed his eyes. "That would only mess things up, Max," he said softly. "Just mess things up, that's all."

2

He hadn't been sleeping long. The phone bell pulled him out of it, insistently. He sat up, found the button of the small reading lamp on the table beside his bed. The wristwatch was beside the lamp—the hands showed it was a few minutes after four. He'd been in bed almost two hours. Rain was tapping the windows of the Laurel Canyon house as he reached for the receiver. He said sleepily:

"Yes?"

Carol Torney's voice came clearly; her words were hesitating, filled with fear.

"Bennie—I've been called up twice in the—last hour. You'd better—come over."

He sat up, swung his legs over the side of the bed. Weariness was leaving him. He spoke stupidly.

"Called up—about what?"

She said: "I can't talk—over the phone. You don't want me—to do that. Uncle Laurie's away—I'm alone in the house. You better come right over, Bennie!"

Jardinn swore softly. "Listen," he told her, "I've only been sleeping a couple of hours. I've got to get more than that. What in hell's the matter with you, Irish? Been drinking?"

Her voice was high pitched, almost shrill as she spoke. It was strange; Carol had always been cool enough, steady about things.

"Bennie—you come over here. For God's sake, Bennie. I tell you I've been called twice—in the last hour."

Jardinn said: "All right, Irish. You sit tight. I'll rush things. Be over there in twenty minutes. If it's something bad, get over to a neighbor's—"

"Like hell I will," she cut in. "I'm not going out. That's what—they want. They called twice, I tell you. You come over—"

"All right," he repeated. "Want to tell me anything—before I start?"

There was silence. Then, her voice low and hoarse, she said:

"God, Bennie—it isn't *you* that's—"

Her words died. He said impatiently:

"Listen, Irish—you're acting up. I don't get you. Who called you—and what did they say? Never mind talking over the wire—we'll take the chance."

She said: "I didn't mean that, Bennie. I was just getting scared. You kicked me out—and I thought—"

Her voice died. She cried out, panic in her tone:

"You there, Bennie—you're coming over, aren't you? Listen, you've *got* to come over! Hear me—you've got to come! If they get me, Bennie—"

He said grimly: "Cut out using that name. I'll be over as soon as I can get there. If you haven't been drinking— take one. If you have been—take another. It's raining like—"

She was talking incoherently. There was a sharp clicking of the receiver—he thought she had hung up.

"Irish—" he said sharply—"I'll be right—"

Her voice was a long drawn whisper. It was one word expelled with all the horror he had ever heard in a human voice. He got the one word faintly:

"Frey!"

He said sharply: "Carol—Carol!"

There was no answer. He heard clicking sounds. Then faintly, he heard a man's voice. It sounded like the voice of Howard Frey. It was hard, very distant. The words reached him slowly. They were spaced. It was almost a beat.

"You—dirty—little—"

There was a crashing sound. The line was dead. He called again and again, then shoved the hook of the receiver up and down. There was no immediate answer. The voice of an operator reached him after a few seconds. It was routine in tone.

"Number, please."

Jardinn said: "I was cut off—"

He checked himself. That was foolishness. Central's voice said methodically:

"What was the number you were calling?"

He stood up. "Never mind," he said.

It took time. He couldn't find the things he needed. When he got outside there was difficulty in getting the garage door opened. The car was inside—it seldom happened that way. The engine was cold. He was shivering as he drove down grade, sped the car along Hollywood Boulevard.

It took him fifteen minutes to reach the section of town in which she lived. There were only three houses on the street, two on one side. The one the uncle rented was on the other. Jardinn braked the car down a hundred yards from the house. His Colt was in the right pocket of the light overcoat he had flung over his suit. He moved rapidly toward the house; there were no lights showing. The place looked like so many other homes at night—it drove suspicion inside of him. He thought grimly, as he reached the curb:

If she tried to—pull me over here—lied—

He went up the steps, walked across the porch, rang the bell. While he listened to it ring, hearing it faintly, he moved back from the door. He was thinking:

That was Irish, all right. It sounded like Frey. Wire distorts voices. I can't be sure.

There was no sound from within the house. No lights flashed on. He rang again—twice. If Carol Torney had been afraid, she wouldn't have waited in the darkness. The house would have been bright with light. She would have been waiting for him. Something had happened—inside.

He got off the porch, went around to the side. Several blocks away a car was speeding toward the center of Hollywood. Laughter and shrill voices drifted back to him as the roar of the engine died. He tried to look through one of the side windows—but there was no light to give him background. He moved on to the rear door.

It was closed, locked. He said to himself, grimly:

"Got to—get inside."

It wasn't difficult. It wasn't the first lock he had picked.
The screen door gave him more trouble than the lock of
the other door; he was forced to cut the screening, shove
up the hook. He had no flashlight.

Inside the kitchen he stood motionless, listening. The
dark had always bothered him; he was afraid. Conflicting
thoughts filled his head; he had to fight down the desire
to turn, go out. In the bungalow living room he could
hear a clock ticking. It helped. It was a symbol of the
commonplace.

He wanted to go into the living room, through the tiny
dinette, in the darkness. Light would make him a mark.
But he wanted light. Carol's fear-gripped voice was still
sounding in his ears. It combined with the dark to make
him uncertain. He fumbled for the light switch, snapped
it. The kitchen was white with the glare.

He called sharply: "Carol!"

He waited long seconds. Then he got his Colt in his
right hand, moved toward the living room. He knew the
house, but he didn't use the knowledge to any advantage.
He walked with his body bent slightly forward, not on
tiptoe. The kitchen light got into the dinette—some of
it reached the living room. The bungalow was very small.

When he switched on the living room light he said
softly:

"All right—all right."

The room was in perfect order. The telephone was on
the little table beside the tinsel doll. The receiver was
hanging in the hook. There were magazines on the divan—a compact and other woman objects were on the
center table. He stood without moving, near the light
switch, and searched the room with his eyes. He needed
the sound of his voice, so he said: "All right—everything's pretty—I've been a target—nobody here."

The rest he did swiftly, carefully. There was nothing
wrong in the bedrooms. Carol's clothes were in her closet—

the brown dress she had worn when he had met her at the beach speakeasy was missing. Things were in fair order. The living room door had no inside bolt. He used a handkerchief, lifted the receiver of the phone. A voice said:

"Number, please."

He hung up immediately, without speaking. There were few things that he touched—nothing with his fingers. When he was finished he switched off the lights, went out as he had come in. A concrete walk ran around the side of the house. He followed it, taking care not to step on the soft earth. It was raining hard.

His shoes were not wet on the under portions; he went up on the porch, tried the front door. He had not done that before. It was locked. He moved from the bungalow, went to his car. There were no lights in the other two houses on the street. The rain made dripping sounds in the palms.

He said in an unemotional tone:

"She could have been—taken out."

He got in the car, drove around the block, turned to the left on Hollywood Boulevard. Frey lived in an apartment not far from Famous Studios; he turned to the left again before he reached Vine Street. He glanced at his wristwatch—it was loose against his skin. It was four-thirty-two, and he had received the call from Carol a few minutes after the hour. About thirty minutes had passed.

The apartment building was a rather pretentious one; Jardinn parked the car before the entrance, went inside. A sleepy-eyed elevator man regarded him dully. Jardinn said:

"Howard Frey in?"

The man grinned. "You with him?" he said. "I just took him up."

Jardinn nodded. "Not with him—just a little behind him," he said. "Is he sober?"

They got inside the elevator. The man chuckled.

"Sober and sore," he replied. "He must have had a hard fall."

Jardinn nodded. He got a little smile on his face.

"I tried to hold him up, but it didn't work," he said. "Hurt much?"

The operator stopped the car, opened the door.

"Cut over the right eye," he said. "It's 5D."

Jardinn nodded. He stood opposite the door of 5D as the elevator descended. He kept his right hand in the right pocket of his coat, buttoned the coat tightly, turned up the collar. He kept the smile on his face, rang the apartment bell.

·10·

DEATH AGAIN

Frey was in dinner clothes; he held a handkerchief over his right eye. At intervals he took it away—there was a nasty cut running above the eyebrow. The skin was bruised, badly swollen. He sat on the gray divan of the apartment living room; Jardinn stood near the radio and grinned at him.

"Better let me pour you a stiff one," he suggested. "It'll help."

Frey shook his head. "I haven't got a thing in the place," he said. "I wanted to cut the drinking until this business was over. Tonight I was getting crazy over the whole thing. Bonner was up again, shooting fool questions at me. And the damn reporters are here all the time. They've caught up to the fact that my brother served a prison term—it's getting rotten. I had to get out. My friends were too damn sympathetic. And then some fool I didn't know got funny. I hit him—he hit me—"

He broke off. Jardinn said: "That isn't a fist cut, is it?"

The writer swore. "He knocked me down," he said. "There was a table edge that got in the way. I nearly went out. But I'll be all right—all set for the dicks again tomorrow.''

He spoke bitterly; his eyes avoided Jardinn's. There was a little silence, then the writer said:

"What are you doing for me, Jardinn? Have you got any trace of the real criminal?"

Jardinn shook his head. He moved away from the radio, sat in a chair opposite the divan. He turned his head slightly away from Frey.

"Suppose you read that the pilot of the plane flew over the Bowl at about the time of the murder—" he started, but Frey nervously interrupted him.

"At *about* the time! At exactly the time, Jardinn. You know that.''

Jardinn smiled. "All right," he agreed. "Anyway, he's dead. Good friend of Maya Rand's, you know."

Frey's breath made a hissing sound as he sucked it in sharply. He got up from the divan abruptly.

"Was he? I didn't know it," he said. "Did know he was killed in that crash, of course. That was a rotten break. He probably knew enough to clear me."

Jardinn said: "You haven't been accused of anything yet—why get all nervous before anything tough breaks?"

The writer stopped near the chair and frowned down at Jardinn:

"I've told you why—it's the reason I came to you," he said. "If they get me in a cell I'll never have a chance to make a case."

He moved around behind Jardinn. With his right-hand fingers Jardinn caught the material of the writer's coat. He said sharply:

"You won't gain anything by lying," and released his grip.

Frey came around and stood in front of him. His face was white; there was a droop to his shoulders. He took the handkerchief away from the injured spot, stared down at Jardinn.

."What do you mean by that?" he asked.

Jardinn said quietly. "You haven't told me all the truth, Frey," he said. "Some of it's been all right. Some of it hasn't. You seem to be pretty sure that you're going to be in a bad place—you have been, from the first time you came to me. The evidence I've got now doesn't warrant an arrest—and I doubt if the police have stronger evidence against you. What is it you're *not* telling me?"

Frey said steadily: "I'm not holding back anything, Jardinn. What would I do that for—don't I need help? They may not have me yet—but it won't be long. I'm nearly going crazy, Jardinn."

Jardinn rose from the chair. "Maybe you've already gone crazy," he said in a hard tone.

Frey was staring at him, his eyes wide. He wet his lips with the tip of his tongue, dabbed his injury with the handkerchief. He said:

"I don't know what you're getting at, Jardinn. I don't know why you came here at this hour. If you don't believe me—"

Jardinn said in a mild tone: "Ever read the script of *Death Dance*, Frey?"

The writer braced himself by leaning against the center table. He swore shakily.

"Read it? I wrote most of it, Jardinn. Hell—you know that."

Jardinn nodded. "Then why did you come to me and try to drag Maya Rand into this murder, because you heard her repeating words that were in your script?"

Frey narrowed his eyes; lines creased his forehead. He said suddenly:

"Good God! And I never thought of that—"

He broke off, turned and walked toward the radio. Jardinn said grimly:

"I hope you don't mind my saying that you're a damned liar, Frey."

The writer swung around. He came rapidly to Jardinn's

side. His face was splotched with red. He said in a voice that shook with rage:

"I don't take that, Jardinn. I don't have to take that. After all, I'm hiring you—"

Jardinn said in a nasty, low voice:

"Sure—but you're not *buying* me, Frey. It takes more than five hundred to do that."

The writer's eyes met the dark ones of Ben Jardinn in a narrowed stare. He said in a steady enough tone:

"I never thought of Maya using the words in the script. I'm not sure yet—"

He broke off, muttered something that Jardinn didn't get, as he turned away. Across the room he turned, faced Jardinn again.

"You went to her, told her what I'd said *she* had said, on the patio—"

"I'm running things the way I see fit," Jardinn cut in. "Yes, I went to her. We're not getting anywhere on this thing. The police are not getting anywhere. A motive is important. If I get that—things will move. You repeated words that involved Maya Rand. But you must have known those very words were in the script of the picture she's making. It's a sweet out for her."

Frey made an impatient gesture. "It might have been just a piece of luck—that there was a connection," he said. "Or she might have been thinking the way she did—and expressed it in terms of the story. You do it— quote something to get it out of your system."

Jardinn smiled coldly. "You don't even come close to believing such tripe as that," he said.

Frey moved toward a door that led into another room. He said wearily:

"I'm all in—I can't think straight. I want to get some iodine on this cut. I'll be out in a minute."

Jardinn nodded. After Frey left the room he moved silently to the chair on which the writer's coat had been flung. It was mud covered—a sleeve was torn. His hat

lay on the carpet near the chair. A side of it was crushed.
It was wet, mud stained. Jardinn went across the room
and faced the doorway through which Frey had made his
exit. When the writer came back—red streaked across
his forehead—he said quietly:

"I don't think you went broke spending money on
Maya Rand—the check stubs don't read that way. What
did you do with the money?"

Frey's eyes showed fear—it was gone instantly. The
writer laughed shakily:

"You can't hand me that—the bank wouldn't let you
see my stubs. I did spend money on Maya—she lies
when she says I didn't."

Jardinn got his cigarette pack from a pocket.

"I asked you to be right with me, Frey," he said in
a cold voice. "By God, you'd better be. I said the bank
check stubs didn't read that way—and I mean it."

Frey raised his voice. "What you trying to do—send
me up for a kill I don't know anything about? Reiner
bought you out—he had the most money. You're not
trying to help me—you're trying to get me!"

Jardinn said: "I'm going to get the killer of Hans
Reiner, Frey. I told you I didn't think you did the job.
That still goes. But you've lied to me."

Frey went over close to the divan, dropped down on
it. He sat stiffly for a few seconds, then his head went
down into his hands. He rocked from side to side, cursing
steadily in a monotone. He put feeling into the words.

Jardinn went over and stood several feet from him.
He said:

"What happened tonight, Frey? Where've you been?
What did you do?"

The writer paid no attention to him. He stopped swear-
ing, but he kept his long-fingered hands covering his
face. His head was bent forward.

Jardinn said: "How about Carol Torney?"

Frey took his hands away from his face. He stared

stupidly at Jardinn. The muscles of his mouth moved, but no words came. He leaned back on the divan, smiled. It was an almost child-like smile.

"Carol Torney—I don't know her, Jardinn. How does—she come in?"

Jardinn shook his head. He didn't smile. He said softly:

"I don't know yet. But I thought maybe you'd met her. I thought maybe you were at her place this morning—say around four."

Frey kept the child-like smile playing around his lips. He said very quietly:

"I don't know her. I wasn't at her house at four this morning. What happened—did someone cut her throat? Am I supposed to have done it? What in hell's it all about?"

Jardinn said: "All right, we'll forget Torney. I just thought you might have known her, might have been with her. Around four, say. You weren't. You got in a scrap somewhere and got your head hurt. I'm sorry, Frey."

Frey's smile lost some of its child-like quality. His voice got hard.

"Sorry I haven't got more coin for you," he said. "Sorry you've got to turn me loose—and maybe string with the police. Reiner got there first—and he had more money—"

Jardinn interrupted: "Never mind the heroics," he said. "Don't get all self-sympathetic before anything happens."

"It'll happen, all right," Frey said bitterly. "I can see it coming."

Jardinn said: "How about Carren—could *he* see it coming?"

Frey got up from the divan and took a step toward Jardinn. His lean face was twisted. His tongue was working over his lips.

"Now you get out of here, Jardinn!" he mouthed.

"You get out of here! I'm through with you, understand? You can't do this with me. I've been through enough in the last three days. You get out of here—and stay out. I don't want you anymore—you're just a cheap dick—"

Jardinn reached out his left hand and gripped Frey by the shirt. He pulled him in close, said grimly:

"What did you do with Carol Torney, Frey? Better be good."

Frey swore at him and started to bring up his left arm. Jardinn hit with his right fist—he hit hard. Frey cried out, half turned and staggered away from him. He gritted:

"You—bastard!"

Jardinn got both hands around his shoulders as he fell on the divan. He pulled him up close again. He knocked his hands away from his face. His fist had ripped open the cut over Frey's right eye—it looked bad.

Frey said weakly: "You dirty, cheap dick—"

Jardinn hit him again, in the same place. Frey twisted clear and swung wildly. He was cursing in a half whisper. Jardinn caught him by the throat, tightened his grip and dragged him to the divan. He said in a low tone:

"You've lied—from the start. The whole pack of you. There's just one way to get something out of you—"

The phone bell rang. Frey was struggling in the grip of Jardinn's fingers. Jardinn said:

"You didn't hire me—you were working me for protection. Carren squealed on you, before he went up in that ship—"

He relaxed his grip; Frey twisted free. He fumbled for his throat, taking deep breaths of air. His face was a mask of red. Jardinn shoved himself up from the divan, stood looking down at the writer. The phone bell kept on ringing. Frey said weakly:

"I don't know—Carren. I don't know—this woman—Torney. I'll get you for this, Jardinn. I'll get you, sure as—"

Jardinn said: "All right—if you don't know Carol

Torney—they've framed you. That's just as bad. Answer that phone.''

The doorbell rang. Frey said in a voice that held fear: "Don't open—that door!"

Jardinn laughed at him. He turned his back, walked to the door, opened it. Phaley stood in the hall, grinning. Beside him was an officer in uniform.

"Hello, Ben." Phaley grinned and moved past him. "Come on, Ed. What's all the rumpus, Ben? Hello, Frey—hit by a truck?"

Jardinn closed the apartment door and moved into the room behind the officer in uniform. Frey stood with his right forehead covered by a red-stained handkerchief. He said:

"What the hell's this?"

Phaley was a big man with a dark, drooping mustache. His coat was rain soaked and his hat brim dripped rain. He had a cheerful grin on his face. He looked at Jardinn.

"Interrupt something?" he asked.

Jardinn shook his head. The phone had stopped ringing; it started again. Frey answered it. He said in a shaken voice:

"All right—they've come up."

He hung up and Phaley grinned at him. He said pleasantly:

"We didn't wait for the boy to get a rise. We figured you'd be up."

Jardinn said steadily: "Why, Phaley?"

The big plainclothesman shrugged. He grinned at Jardinn:

"Heard you were working for Reiner, Ben. But hell—you shouldn't slam a guy around like this."

Jardinn said: "Sorry—but I just got here. Frey had a fall, if you're talking about that eye."

Phaley said: "What happened—you fall on top of him? Got some red on your knuckles."

Jardinn smiled. He didn't say anything. Frey said in a hard tone:

"That's a lie—a dirty lie. I've retained Jardinn. I paid him five hundred dollars and he took it. Then Reiner came along and he double-crossed me. He got five thousand from Reiner. He's been out to get me, ever since. He came in here and attacked me. He knocked me down. I want to bring charges against him—he can't get away with that. He's trying to frame me—for Reiner."

Phaley whistled softly. His eyes went from Frey to Jardinn. He said:

"Well, well, well!"

Jardinn just smiled. The uniformed officer got out a notebook. Phaley took off his hat and sent a spray of water across the carpet. Frey spoke in a grim voice.

"It's been a put-up job from the beginning. Jardinn's never tried to work the murder. He's been playing around studios, sitting in his office. He's been at stars' houses. He didn't get anything from Carren—but Carren got killed right away. It's damned funny—I'm going to do some talking."

Phaley said: "Well, well!"

The uniformed officer started to scribble on the pages of his notebook. Jardinn said quietly:

"Go ahead, Frey—get rid of it."

Frey stared at him. "I told you I'd get you for what you did tonight," he said.

Jardinn chuckled. Phaley grinned. The uniformed copper said:

"Guess I'll write that down, too."

Jardinn nodded: "Sure," he said. "But now that we've listened to the bedtime story, I'll tell you what happened. I got word that Frey was mixed up in a scrap—came over. The elevator man said he'd just come up and he looked pretty bad. Said his eye was all cut. I said that was too bad and came along. Frey didn't want to let me in. In the fooling around he tripped on a rug or something, and when I put up my right hand to catch him—his right eye touched the knuckles. I came on in—and you fellows came along.''

Phaley said, grinning: ''I don't see any rugs—and you should have opened your hand when you tried to catch him, Ben.''

Jardinn nodded. ''It all happened so suddenly,'' he said cheerfully.

Frey took the handkerchief away from his eyes and said:

''That's a lie.''

Jardinn looked hurt. ''It's the hard words in this business that keep me awake nights,'' he said slowly.

Phaley narrowed his brown eyes on the face of Frey. He said:

''We got a complaint from a guy named Terris. Make-up man over at Warner's. Party at his place and the furniture was wrecked. Seems Frey, here, was thrown out. A fellow named Loomis is at the hospital, still unconscious. He went out of the Terris place with Frey. Just came over to see what it was all about, Frey. Got anything to say?''

Frey shook his head. Jardinn said:

''What time did Frey and Loomis leave the Terris apartment, Phaley? Know?''

The plainclothesman nodded. ''Clock stopped at three-thirty,'' he replied. ''That guy Terris says someone threw it at him, just before Frey and Loomis went out.''

Jardinn grinned. ''Just a nice, sociable affair,'' he said. ''Well—I'm going home and hit the hay.''

Phaley nodded. ''Guess we'll go along down to the station, Frey,'' he said. ''If you want to get a complaint against Ben there—why, that's all right with me.''

Jardinn kept grinning. ''You're in favor of it, Phaley,'' he said. ''But I'll tell you now, it won't be worth a damn.''

Howard Frey smiled bitterly at Jardinn. He said slowly:

"This is just another frame-up. Reiner's back of it all."

Jardinn moved toward the door. Phaley said with interest:

"Well!"

The uniformed cop was still scribbling in his notebook. Phaley looked at Jardinn, grinned.

"Anything new on the Reiner murder, Ben?" he asked pleasantly.

Jardinn let his eyes meet those of Howard Frey. Then he grinned at Phaley.

"Not a thing, Pat," he said. "But I hear you guys have a clue."

Phaley looked serious. "Sure," he said. "We've *got* to have a clue, haven't we?"

Jardinn said to Frey: "If you need bail money—I haven't used all of that five hundred. I'll look you up today, after I get some sleep."

The writer said: "To hell with you, Jardinn—I'm through with you!"

Phaley sprayed more water getting his hat on. He said cheerfully:

"How's that bright kid, Carol Torney, Ben? Always liked her. Getting married?"

Jardinn let his eyes meet Frey's again. Frey was smiling. Jardinn smiled, too.

"Something like that," he replied. "She's fine, Pat. See you again."

"Sure," the plainclothesman replied. "Even if I *do* see you first."

2

It was still dark when Jardinn turned the roadster in at the driveway to the left of his Laurel Canyon bungalow. The rain was letting up, but it was wet enough. He got the car in the garage, but left the doors open. He

was very tired. His key turned in the lock of the rear
door. He went inside. He passed through the kitchen,
went along the hall and got his coat off in the bedroom.
When he got in his pajamas he remembered there was a
light on in the living room.

He smoked a cigarette, sitting with his legs over the
side of the bed. He decided that Howard Frey knew more
than he was willing to tell. He rose, snubbed his cigarette.
The phone beside his bed tinkled—then the bell rang.
He waited a few seconds, got the receiver to his ear.

"Yeah," he said. "Jardinn."

Max Cohn's voice reached him. It sounded distant.
The line wasn't clear.

"They got Howard Frey down at the Hollywood station, Ben—figured you might want to know. Allers tipped
me. He had some sort of a scrap, wrecked an apartment.
He's cut up some. Don't know what the charge is—
disorderly conduct, I suppose. Thought you ought to
know, Ben."

Jardinn got his lips close to the mouthpiece and said:

"I know about it, Max. I've been outside, moving
around. Just got in. Did you stay out late tonight?"

Cohn said: "Not so late. In around two. What are they
doing, framing Frey?"

Jardinn waited a few seconds, and didn't answer the
question.

"See Irish around anywhere?" he asked. "After you
left the office?"

Cohn said that he hadn't. He asked some more questions, and Jardinn answered one of them. He told Cohn
he'd be at the office around ten. After some more talk
he hung up, went into the living room, moved toward
the light switch. The lights had been left burning when
he had hurried out, after Irish had called. His eyes went
toward the divan—his hand came away from the switch.
He said in a whisper:

"Irish!"

She was lying on the divan; her brown dress hung slightly over the front of the piece of furniture. Her hat was on the floor near the divan—her dark hair was loose. She was lying on her left side—her head was turned away from him. He grinned, thought:

When the hell did she get here? How'd she—get in?

He said softly: "Carol—Irish."

She didn't move. He chuckled, spoke in a sharp tone. "Hey, bum—come out of it!"

He started toward her—the phone in his bedroom sent sound into the living room. Jardinn grinned, picked Carol's hat from the floor and placed it on a chair. He went to the bedroom.

It was Cohn again. He spoke in a cheerful tone.

"Just happened to think, Ben—you were asking about Irish. She's got an aunt down at the beach. Santa Monica, I think. She might be down there, if you can't get her uncle at the house."

Jardinn said: "What made you think I wanted to get in touch with her? I just asked you if you'd seen her. That all helps. We've got to keep track of her, Max."

Cohn said: "Well, I didn't figure you were sleeping yet. Just thought I'd let you know that. But she'll be around—she won't go far."

Jardinn swore at him. "You lay off calling me," he said. "I'm all in."

He hung up and frowned at the phone. It was odd—Max calling him back like that. He thought of Carol, on the divan. And then, suddenly, he felt fear run through his body. She was a light sleeper—he had called sharply. Unless she was exhausted—

He moved swiftly toward the living room again. The first light of dawn was showing; it was still raining a little. A machine horn sounded twice, from some spot along the canyon road. He went close to the divan. He said softly:

"Carol."

His hands were on her shoulders. He swung her body around, her face toward him. He said, as he closed his eyes:

"Oh, God!"

He got his right-hand fingers against the skin over her heart. Then he went over to the window that faced down the canyon and stood staring out. His face was colorless; the tears in his eyes made a blur of the canyon road. Several minutes passed.

When he went into the small dining room and poured himself a drink from the decanter he was thinking clearly again. Irish had been scared—there had been reason enough for that. He sat on the edge of a chair and downed the liquor. He felt broken up inside. He said in a puzzled tone:

"Christ—maybe I thought more of her—"

He got up and went back to the living room. But he didn't look at Carol Torney. After a few minutes he banged a clenched right fist into the palm of his left and thought bitterly:

"I'll have to call the police. I kicked her out of the agency—she's dead, in my place. By the time I get things fixed—"

He looked at his watch. It was five-twenty-five. She had talked to him shortly after four. He went over and hated to see the pain in her staring eyes. She'd felt the knife. It would be gone, of course. He had left the house— she had been brought in. He said fiercely:

"Goddam the luck!"

Police investigation, inquest, coroner's jury. Newspaper men.

He touched her gently on a shoulder with the fingers of his right hand and said very softly:

"I'm sorry as hell, Irish."

Then he went to the phone and called the Hollywood police station. When the desk sergeant's voice sounded he waited a second or two, spoke slowly.

"This is Ben Jardinn—at eight six four Laurel Canyon. I got in a few minutes ago and found the body of a woman in my living room. She was dead, apparently stabbed through the heart. Better send someone up here."

There was a clicking over the wire. The desk sergeant said:

"Yeah—will you repeat that now?"

Jardinn closed his eyes and said: "Goddam it—why don't you keep a pencil on your ear?"

He repeated it.

· 11 ·

"POOR, GODDAM KID—"

Phaley came into the living room, followed by a short, chubby-faced man whose eyes glittered on Jardinn's. Phaley looked tired; he grunted at Jardinn, lifted his right-hand fingers to his drooping mustache and stroked the ends of it. His eyes went to the figure on the divan. He said:

"Jardinn—meet Bracker. Cousin of Frey's. He's on the force. Came along with me."

Jardinn nodded to Bracker. The man had a stupid expression in blue eyes. He said thickly:

"Frey never done it."

Jardinn didn't say anything. Phaley went over and looked down at Carol Torney's face. He didn't touch the body. He said:

"Boyce is on his way out—got any ideas, Ben?"

Jardinn lighted a cigarette and shook his head. Phaley went over and sat down on a chair. He faced the body on the divan.

"Poor, goddam kid," he muttered. "You always were hard on women, Jardinn."

Bracker went over and stood staring stupidly down at the dead figure. After a few seconds he turned away, went over and took a chair near the door. Jardinn said:

"Got most of Frey's time accounted for, Phaley? I'd say Irish got that knife about an hour ago. Maybe a little longer back. She talked to me over the phone, just after four."

Phaley turned in his chair and whistled softly. He said:

"Well—she did, eh? Well."

Jardinn said: "How about Frey? Is he all right, pretty well covered?"

Bracker said thickly: "You can't hang *this* one on Frey, Jardinn. He didn't bump Hans Reiner, and he didn't knife this woman."

Jardinn inspected his cigarette critically. He got it between his lips.

"Cousin of yours, isn't he?" he asked quietly.

Bracker got up and started toward Jardinn. Phaley said sharply:

"Sit down, Bracker. I'm running this party. There's a little time of Frey's where he doesn't seem to know just what happened. But that can happen to anybody."

Jardinn said: "Sure. It might even happen to me, eh?"

Phaley said: "It might."

There was the sound of brakes squealing, in front of the bungalow. Phaley got up and went toward the door. He said, as he moved:

"Poor kid—that must've hurt like hell."

His eyes watched Jardinn's as he said it. Jardinn nodded.

"The noose'll hurt, too," he replied. "I swear to Christ it will."

Boyce was a tall, lean man with large, dark eyes and thinning, gray hair. He nodded to Jardinn, smiled at Phaley. He didn't seem to notice Bracker. Phaley said:

"She's on the divan, Doc."

He gestured. Boyce went over and looked at the body. Phaley said to Jardinn:

"You're pretty hard, Ben—you don't seem to mind much."

Jardinn said: "She was mixed up in the Reiner kill, Pat. I kicked her out of the office. She was doing little things that didn't help. I think she reached for gold. She tried to frame Max Cohn, and I caught her at it."

Phaley widened his eyes. "Well!" he said slowly.

Boyce came around and asked where he could wash his hands. Jardinn told him. Phaley asked:

"How long, Doc?"

Boyce shrugged his narrow shoulders. He didn't turn his head as he went from the room.

"Hour or two—hard to say exactly. Long-bladed knife, I'd say. Got the heart—looks like a blow that was driven upward. Take an autopsy to be sure. Very swift death."

Phaley said to Jardinn: "Guess we'd better go down to the station and get your story, Ben. She tried to cross you, eh?"

Jardinn nodded. "I'll give it to you straight, when we get down at the station," he said. "God, I'm tired."

Phaley said: "How about a drink?"

Jardinn pointed toward the dining room and the decanter. Phaley moved away and Bracker said:

"Howard Frey didn't do it, Jardinn."

Jardinn swore. "Who in hell says he *did?*" he replied. "If you keep on yapping that he didn't you'll get him up in the Big House, maybe. You're the hell of a dick."

Phaley said from the dining room: "Now, Ben—now Ben!"

Bracker muttered something that Jardinn didn't get. The medical examiner came out rubbing his palms and fingers together. He yawned mostly. Phaley called:

"How about a drink, Doc?"

Boyce smiled at Jardinn and went into the dining room. He came out dabbing his lips with a blue handkerchief.

"That stuff's good," he said. "Not cut more than twice, I'd say. Can't be local."

Jardinn shook his head. "Brought it up from Caliente," he replied. "It's all right, even if—"

He stopped as a car halted behind the doctor's. Phaley said:

"Coroner's bus, maybe."

Boyce shook his head. "It's the scribble boys," he said. "Well, I'd say it doesn't look like suicide. More like murder."

Phaley swore "Jeez—but you think things out, Doc!" he muttered. His eyes met Ben Jardinn's. "Want to let the boys in?"

Jardinn nodded. "Sure," he said. "Maybe it's a human interest story."

He didn't recognize the first newspaper man to enter the bungalow. Curlew was the second. A photographer came in behind the two.

The first one grinned at Jardinn, said hello to Phaley. His eyes went around the room, rested on the figure of Carol Torney. He went over and looked down at the girl's face. Curlew said:

"Any idea who did the job?"

Phaley said: "I just got here—with Bracker."

The medical examiner said: "Knife wound. Blade reached the heart. Well, so long."

He went out. Curlew looked at Jardinn. He said:

"Miss Torney, wasn't it?"

Jardinn nodded. He said in a flat tone:

"She worked in the agency. I caught her crossing me up. Doing nasty, little things that held me back on the Reiner murder. I kicked her out. She's called me a couple of times, trying to get her job back. I said no. When I got in this morning she was over there, dead."

The reporter that Jardinn didn't know nodded his head. He needed a haircut badly.

"Good story," he said.

Jardinn narrowed his eyes. "I don't know who in hell you are," he said tightly, "but I don't like you. Get the hell out of here!"

Phaley said: "Now, Ben—remember the press. Let's go down and tell it right, to someone that counts."

Jardinn shrugged. He said grimly: "All right, but wait a minute."

He went out and got the liquor, took it to the back of the house. When he reached the living room again Curlew said:

"Was *that* nice?"

Jardinn smiled. The photographer said:

"How about a picture?"

Jardinn made a sweeping gesture. "Go to it," he said. "Sorry I can't produce the knife. If you shoot the house from the outside don't miss that rosebush back of the patio."

Bracker said: "You're hard-boiled, Jardinn."

Jardinn said: "I don't like them when they rat it. That brat was trying to cross me."

Phaley pulled at one end of his mustache and moved toward the door of the house.

"All set, Ben?" he asked.

Jardinn nodded. "Keep your hands off the silver," he said to the newspaper man he didn't know. "I know what's in the place."

The coroner's machine pulled up as they reached the curb. Smith, the assistant, and a suntanned youngster climbed down.

"Boss'll be out pretty quick," Smith said. "We'll just wait around."

Phaley and Bracker went toward their car. Jardinn called after them:

"I'll follow you in."

Phaley just nodded his head. The coroner's assistant lighted a cigarette and said:

"Where's the body, Jardinn?"

Jardinn moved toward the roadster on the driveway at the left of the house.

"Inside," he called back grimly. "It's the one that doesn't move."

2

When Jardinn reached the agency office it was after ten o'clock. He'd had breakfast, but he hadn't had any sleep. He didn't feel much better. At the desk in the outer room Edith Brown was putting powder on her baby face. Her eyes got wide as he went close to her.

"They told me about—"

"All right," he interrupted. "It doesn't affect you in any way. Who's been in?"

She said shakily: "Mr. Cohn is inside. A messenger brought a package. I signed for it. Mr. Ernst Reiner called and said he would be here at eleven. Miss Rand's secretary called and wants you to call the house. She says it is very important. Mr. Howard Frey called and said he would call again later. A reporter from the *Herald* has called twice. Some reporters have been here. That's about all."

Jardinn smiled. "Write what you just told me on a slip of paper. Bring it in after a while, in ten minutes, say. Feel better?"

The girl said: "I didn't sleep much."

Jardinn said: "I didn't sleep at all. It's part of the game. If you sleep too much—you miss things."

He went into the inner office; Max Cohn was standing near the window. He faced Jardinn as he closed the door back of him. His fat face looked sallow; there were little wrinkles at the corners of his eyes. He nodded his head in the quick jerky manner that was habitual in him.

"God—it is pretty bad, Ben," he said thickly.

Jardinn went across the room and dropped heavily into his desk chair. He nodded.

"It's rotten, Max," he said. "But I think I can get clear. May need your help—not right away, but later. Irish is dead—and there was a reason for it. I've got an idea about the reason. She was crossing us, Max."

Cohn wet his thick lips with the tip of a gray coated tongue. His little eyes were blinking. He went around the small table and sat in a chair, facing Jardinn. His stubby fingers played with the chain of his watch.

"They thought she had something—to tell you," he suggested. "Yes?"

Jardinn said: "Something like that. Now, look here—"

He checked himself. The office door opened; Edith came in. She handed him a long envelope; it was sealed. A slip of paper was clipped to it. Jardinn said:

"You've got a funny idea of ten minutes, but it's all right. If anyone comes in—keep them outside and talk to me over the phone."

She went out. Cohn didn't pay any attention to her. Jardinn put the slip of paper in a pocket, opened the envelope. There were notes inside—bank notes. He counted ten fifties, put them back in the envelope, tossed it on his desk.

"For the woman in Glendale," Cohn said, and laughed without mirth. "That was a nice one you pulled, Ben. But hell—if the bulls catch on to it—"

Jardinn relaxed in the chair. He said:

"You got the story across nice, Max. But we're not grabbing the five hundred. I wanted to see if Reiner would lie. He didn't. He told the truth about the actress in Paris. When he comes in I'll tell him we fixed the woman out in Glendale without using the coin, scared her out of it. He gets the money back."

Cohn frowned. "Don't go being too damned honest now, Ben," he said. "Five hundred is five hundred."

Jardinn said: "I've just had a tough session with the police. I'm pretty well fixed with alibis—I was with Phaley at about the time the doc figures Irish was getting

knifed. She called me just after four—and she was scared.
I tried to get to her place in a hurry, but maybe she didn't
call from there. The police are working on the phone
trace now.''

Cohn said. ''God—I'm sorry for her, Ben. Even if
she was crossing us up. She was a good-looking kid.''

Ben Jardinn nodded. His eyes were narrowed on the
wall of the office, beyond Cohn.

''Frey's in bad,'' he said softly. ''Damn bad. He got
tired sitting in his apartment and answering the dicks'
questions. He went out on a party and got in a brawl.
He was thrown out—and there's about an hour of his
time unaccounted for. It's the hour in which we figure
Irish got the knife.''

Cohn sat up straighter in his chair and grunted. He
said:

''He came in here in a hurry, after he knocked Ernst
Reiner down, to get protection. Maybe you made a mistake taking his money, Ben.''

Jardinn frowned at the wall. ''He's all cut up,'' he
said. ''Like he'd been in a fight. Says he fell down. Says
he can't remember where he went after he and some
others were kicked out of the apartment where the party
was being held. Says he just wandered around, he
guesses.''

Cohn muttered: ''He's a killer—or a damned fool,
Ben. He should have stayed at home.''

Ben Jardinn nodded. ''I got this call from Irish, Max—
and she was scared. I didn't get very excited about it.
She said something about having had a couple of phone
calls, gave me the idea that someone was coming after
her. I tried to talk her away from being scared, but it
didn't work. Then something went wrong with the phone.
She called out a name—as though the guy it belonged
to was right in front of her. The connection went bad.''

Cohn's little eyes were wide. ''What name?'' he asked.

Jardinn said harshly: ''Frey.''

Cohn sucked in his breath, made a wheezing sound with his nose, got to his feet. He said:

"I'll be goddamned! Frey!"

Jardinn said quietly: "There was no mistake about you seeing her go into Ernst Reiner's house, the other night?"

Cohn sat down in the chair again. He leaned toward Jardinn and used a stubby finger to accentuate his words.

"Mistake—have I made many since I came into the agency? Don't I know Irish when I see her?"

Jardinn shrugged. "She was crossing us," he said. "I'm damn sure of that, Max. They bought her off, and she got careless. But she kept after me, even when I kicked her out of here. She fooled with that wristwatch of mine, trying to stop me from tracing the right plane. That didn't help things any, because the police grabbed that ship in a hurry. But she was trying—and maybe someone didn't believe that."

Cohn said: "Or maybe they believed she was still working for you, Ben—when she shouldn't have been doing that thing."

Jardinn looked thoughtful. "Yeah," he said. "I saw her last night, talked to her. Down at the beach."

Cohn lighted a small cigar. "I saw her, too," he said. "Tried to tail her, but I couldn't make it. What was the game, Ben?"

Jardinn shrugged. "She wanted to work for me—or maybe she thought she sort of liked me, Max," he said. "Anyway, I played along. Told her to work the Carren end. Wanted her to find out why Carren went out of things. Or to try and trace the ship's passengers. She left first—and next came the phone call. When I got to her place there wasn't a thing mussed up. The phone was all right. Because she'd used Frey's name I looked him up. He'd just come in. I tried to give him a third degree, and in the midst of the party Phaley and a copper arrived. I hadn't got a thing from Frey—and he had been drinking. When I got back to the house—Irish was on the divan,

dead. She talked to me at a few minutes after four. I got
back to the house at about five-fifteen.''

Cohn said: "If Frey did the work on Irish—it's ten to
one he handled the Reiner kill. Maybe she had something
on him. She knew something. He paid enough to stop
her at first. She played along with him, and you got wise.
You kicked her out—and Frey ran low on money. He
was afraid of her, and he got her quiet.''

Jardinn said: "I've got a hunch Frey knifed her. He
didn't do it at her place. He didn't take her out to my
place. She knew things, and he got afraid. A couple of
sharpshooters finished Hans Reiner, out at the Bowl. Frey
didn't do that job. He took care to alibi himself, to be
conspicuous. He called to me, after the Bowl lights went
out. He's got killers working with him. Maybe they were
with him when they walked in on poor Irish—but she
only recognized him. They brought her body out to my
place, just to make things tough. Frey had gone to the
party for an alibi, got into a fight. But he got away in
time. I reached his place thirty minutes after Irish called
me. He had time enough—and he can't account for that
thirty minutes—and another twenty or so, before that.''

Cohn swore. "If they can trace her call to you—" he
breathed softly.

Jardinn said: "They haven't traced it yet—you know
how those things are. No record of a call from Irish's
place, and a lot of others went through at just about two
minutes after four. No Central listening in—that they've
found. A lot of phones are dial system and they're still
making switches. I doubt if they'll trace the call.''

Cohn grunted. "Did you tell the police everything?"
he asked.

Jardinn said: "Sure. I've got to be free. I can't be held
back. Frey denies everything, of course. But they're
holding him inside. I've got a good record, so I can
wander around. Within the state limits. But they're suspicious. And we haven't got enough on Frey, Max.''

Cohn pulled on the cigar and stared blankly toward the office window. He said suddenly:

"What about this Rand woman? Get anything from her?"

Jardinn shook his head. "Just one thing, and I don't think it's worth much. She hadn't heard that Carren was killed in the plane crash. When I gave her the news she fainted. I took her upstairs and when her doctor chased me away he said it was just a case of nerves."

Cohn looked at Jardinn. "And you don't think that faint was worth much," he said. "The hell you don't!"

Jardinn smiled a little. "Supposing you find out what it was worth, Max," he suggested. "You work it from the Carren end."

Cohn nodded. "All right," he said. "What's *your* play?"

Jardinn tapped on the desk surface with his fingers.

"I think I'll stick close to Howard Frey," he said. "But in about a half hour I'm going across to the Christie and catch a few hours' sleep."

Max Cohn got up and shook his head. He said heavily:

"I figured you'd take Irish's going out harder than you are, Ben," he said. "That poor kid."

Ben Jardinn stopped tapping on the desk surface and got to his feet.

"She was crossing us," he said, and there was anger in his voice. "Now you get the hell out of here, Max— you get—"

He saw the surprise in Cohn's eyes, checked himself. Max went toward the door, turned and faced him.

"We're getting in on Frey," he said. "We may be right. There's a motive for the Irish thing—if we can get one for the Bowl death—"

Jardinn sat down again. His lips were twitching.

"You find out about Carren," he said. "The police can't. That'll help. If you should run into Reiner, don't talk about the Glendale woman frame-up. I'll handle that.''

Cohn nodded. ''You better get some sleep,'' he said. ''You tough guys get let down quick, when it comes.''

Jardinn said placidly: ''Now you go right ahead and get the hell out of here, Max.''

· 12 ·

BABY-FACED BRAT

Ernst Reiner's thick, dignified voice reached Jardinn's left ear, over the phone wire. He said:

"It is very terrible, Mr. Jardinn. I am told that Howard Frey—" He stopped; he had uttered Frey's name bitterly. Jardinn said grimly:

"Don't believe half of what you're told. It is terrible, but it gives us more to work on. I'd prefer not to talk over the phone. Everything is being done, Mr. Reiner, and I should like to see you in about two hours. Where—at the studio?"

Reiner said: "I will be in my bungalow. You will be admitted through the gates. At twelve-thirty, perhaps?"

Jardinn said: "Make it one, please. I will want to talk only with you."

"I will be alone," Reiner said.

Jardinn spoke in an irritated tone, as he pressed the button for the stenographer.

"Miss Rand will not be present, I hope."

There was surprise in Ernst Reiner's voice. He replied:

"Miss Rand? She is ill—in her home. She will not be present, of course."

Jardinn smiled. "Good," he said. "I regret to hear she is ill. At one."

He hung up as the baby-faced girl came into the room. He smiled wearily at her.

"I've got to go out and have a chat with a friend," he said. "I'd like you to come along."

Her eyes showed a little fear. He pointed toward the chair opposite the small table.

"Sit down," he said. "You and I are going to put on a little show. Ever act in a show?"

She moved slowly to the chair, seated herself. Her face was pale and her slender fingers twisted around. She shook her head.

"I'm afraid I won't be—very good," she said.

Jardinn smiled with his lips. "Of course you will," he contradicted. "You'll be natural. You'll just be Miss Brown."

She said: "If you don't mind—I'd rather not."

He tapped on the desk with his fingers. He said very softly:

"Can you imagine Carol Torney saying about the same thing? She was a better sport than that."

The girl's eyes were large with fear. She looked away from Jardinn, looked down at her lap. She said:

"It was a terrible thing—"

Jardinn's voice was sharp—very sharp.

"Maya Rand is ill. I want to be very considerate and gentle with her. She is extremely beautiful. If I were to visit her alone I might forget to be considerate. With you along—there will be a reminder."

Her hands started toward her throat, but she checked the motion. She said:

"I'd much rather—not go."

Jardinn got up and stood looking down at her, smiling.

"Just the same," he said, "you're going. I've been over to see D'Este. Know him?"

The fear in her eyes was clear. Her lips trembled. She said:

"He has charge of the Casting Bureau, I—think."

Jardinn nodded. "So many pictures of beautiful women he has over there," he said. "Do you know, there is one that resembles you remarkably?"

She was staring at him. He stopped being pleasant and said nastily:

"Now listen, Doll Crissy—I've got you spotted. You were too frightened when you first came into this office. There was no particular reason for you being frightened, but you were. There was too much 'if you hurt me' stuff. You've scrawled messages for me—and I saw your handwriting on the back of a picture at the Bureau. I lied about the picture—it was taken a few years ago, and you wore your hair differently. It doesn't resemble you too much. But the writing did the trick. You came into this office. Maya Rand put you in here. Why?"

The girl pushed back the chair and got to her feet. She held her right hand, spread fingered, across her lips. Her body was tense with fear.

Jardinn said: "Take it easy—sit down. You won't get hurt. I've got a job for you. Come on—sit down. If you run you won't get beyond the door."

The girl took her fingers away from her lips. Her face was colorless. She sat down in the chair, looked terrible as she started to cry. Jardinn sat down and smiled. He lighted a cigarette.

"You're so goddam feminine I'm getting to like you, Doll," he said. "Now that should make you feel all cheerful again."

2

Maya Rand reclined on the pillowed, wicker divan that had been placed in the sun of the patio, and smiled wanly at Jardinn. He sat in one of the two fan-backed chairs that faced the divan, smiled back at her. She said:

"It was a shock, you see. Mr. Carren had worked in a picture with me, a few months ago. We were merely acquaintances, but I am very sensitive, temperamental."

Jardinn said, still smiling: "What picture did he work in, Maya?"

She said: "He was really a nice boy. It was a great shock. I have not been very well since the affair at—"

She stopped. Jardinn tilted his lean, pale face and let his eyes see the blue of the California sky. He said quietly, almost lazily:

"What picture did Carren work on—with you, Maya?"

He watched anger show in her eyes. She said, with it creeping into her tone:

"Does that matter?"

He nodded. "Lies always matter, Maya," he replied calmly. "Carren never worked in a picture. I've checked him at the field. Even if he had worked in one with you, I doubt if you'd have known it. You're pretty well protected, my dear."

She moved her head on the silk of a pillow, said bitterly:

"What has this all to do with me, anyway? The police do not bother me. Yet you come here—"

Jardinn chuckled. "You're so lovely, Maya," he said. "I'd like to keep you out of San Quentin, if I can."

She sat up, bracing herself with fists buried clenched in the silk coverlet on which she was lying. Her eyes were narrowed on Jardinn's.

"Don't be a fool!" she said sharply. "I don't have to listen to you."

He shrugged. Maya called sharply:

"Carrie—my milk! Be sure it is cool, but not cold."

The dark-colored maid yes-madamed her and moved from the spot almost the length of the patio from them. Her shoes made a slight shuffling sound. Jardinn said:

"Better make it a stiffer drink. I'm going to tell you some bad news."

Maya Rand lowered her head and shoulders to the pillows again. She shrugged.

"Yes?" She said. "I will not need a strong drink. I will not allow you to worry me. I will not be temperamental."

Jardinn said: "Fine. I admire a picture actress who can come down to the level of ordinary folk. You're big, Maya. Christ—but you're big."

Her eyes shot little rages at him, but there was a smile on her lips.

"Christ, but you're hard, Jardinn," she mimicked. "You are so hard with women."

Jardinn let a grim smile stay around his lips. He said:

"Yeah, that's right, of course. Well, I see by the papers that the police say you are not involved in the Bowl murder. And that glass gazer you had over from Pasadena says the murderers are many miles away, seeking to return to the old country."

Maya Rand shrugged again. "I never read the papers," she replied.

Jardinn grinned. "I thought maybe one of your clipping bureaus might have made a mistake and sent you something important about yourself," he said.

Maya laughed nastily. Jardinn said, after a little pause:

"Something like: 'Maya Rand, star of many films, does not believe Howard Frey guilty of murder in the Hollywood Bowl.' "

She sat up, rearranged the pillows, narrowed her eyes on Jardinn's. She said slowly:

"You think Howard Frey did murder Hans Reiner?"

Jardinn smiled. "It begins to look a lot like it," he replied. "Maybe he didn't turn loose the bullets—but he might have bossed the job."

Maya said thoughtfully: "After all, I do not know Frey very well."

The maid came with the cool glass of milk. Maya said:

"Mr. Jardinn will need something. He is giving me a third degree. What will make it easier, Jardinn?"

Jardinn said: "Nothing, thanks."

Maya dismissed the maid with a graceful gesture of her right hand. She sat up and sipped the milk. She was wearing a black something that had a wide trouser effect and a waist that fit her body tightly.

Jardinn smiled sympathetically. "You're lowering the boat, eh, Maya? Getting clear of the sinking ship. By night it will be doubtful if you remember having met Howard Frey, except in a business way."

She smiled. "Yes, I have met him on the lot," she said. "Writer, isn't he?"

Jardinn nodded. "Did the script of *Death Dance*," he reminded mockingly. "Perhaps you remember those lines: 'He's no good—but he can't pull me down. I'll get to him—before he gets—' "

She set down her glass of milk with shaking fingers. She said fiercely:

"Yes—I remember them. They're part of the picture story."

Jardinn said slowly: "Yeah, I know that. Not a bad story, either."

She kept her eyes on his, with her lips pressed tightly together. After a few seconds she commenced to hum. Jardinn sat back, smiling, and listened. She stopped, said in a tone that was intended to be light and wasn't:

"That's the theme song of the picture. 'If It Means You—It Means Love.' "

Jardinn said: "Very catchy, too. Like the rope up in the death house at San Quentin."

He saw her underlip tremble, but she was still smiling.

"If it means *you*—it means *life*," he said slowly. "You're too damned good-looking to hang."

She swung her legs to the side of the wicker divan, leaned forward and said huskily:

"I've played too many trial scenes to let you frighten me, Jardinn. For God's sake cut it out!"

Jardinn said, smiling: "They knifed Carol Torney. You know that, of course. I'd kicked her out of the agency because she'd been bought over. But they got worried. Maybe they didn't believe she was really out. So they knifed her. Not so long before that she spoke to me about you."

Maya Rand widened her eyes a little. She was very pale. She said shakily:

"I'm sorry—about her."

Jardinn nodded. "Don't be," he replied. "She said you wouldn't look so pretty with a rope around your neck."

She rose to her feet, stared down at him, turned away. Almost immediately she faced him again. She said in a tone that was strangely quiet:

"You are lying, Jardinn."

He shrugged. "I might be," he admitted, "but as it happens—I'm not. That's what Irish said. A few hours later she was dead."

Maya dropped on the divan again. She leaned toward him, framing her face in her white hands. She pressed perfect teeth together, smiled.

"Why are you here, Jardinn?" she asked.

He said simply: "I caught that baby-faced brat you got inside the office, Maya. Doll Crissy."

Maya closed her eyes, and swayed a little on the edge of the divan. Jardinn said:

"It was a lucky break. I happened to see handwriting that looked like hers, on the back of a picture at the Casting Bureau. And she was acting scared. She came through, Maya—and that puts it up to you. You paid money to that employment agency, with someone else handling that end, and I took this Crissy kid on. But I was suspicious from the start. I've been having trouble in the agency since the Reiner murder—even before that. You put her inside with me—you wanted to know how we were working things.''

He stopped. Maya opened her eyes and looked toward the goldfish pool beyond him. She said, very faintly:

"It isn't true.''

Jardinn swore. ''You wanted to know how we were working things,'' he repeated. ''Why?''

She shook her head, without speaking. Jardinn turned and called:

''Carrie—there's a Miss Crissy sitting in that roadster, out on the driveway. Ask her to come in, please.''

Maya started to rise and to speak. She changed her mind, sat down again. She said:

''Carrie has good ears—you should be careful.''

Jardinn smiled grimly. *''You* should,'' he corrected. ''Anything I tell you can't hurt me—but it may hurt you. You're lying, Maya—and I haven't time to play that sort of game. The police are working one way—I'm working another. Murder's come right into the agency. Why were you using this Crissy kid?''

The actress shook her head. ''I never heard of her,'' she said.

Jardinn stood up and sighed. ''I'll tell you, then,'' he said. ''You wanted to put up a fight for Frey—but not too much of a fight. You didn't want to get into the thing all the way. Doll Crissy was inside to let you know when we had Frey in a tough spot. Things didn't break so she could help you much. But she got you the stuff about a woman out in Glendale having something on Ernst Reiner.''

He caught the flicker of surprise in Maya's eyes. He said:

''That was all wrong. I had a woman call in—from Glendale. I framed the story with one of my men—and we handed it to Reiner stiff. He came through and told the truth. I'm giving him the five hundred back in an hour or so. It was a play on Reiner—and Doll didn't give you anything that counted."

He watched the actress closely. She kept her eyes half closed and her face was pokered. She wasn't showing a thing.

There was the sound of footfalls; Doll Crissy came up and stood close to Jardinn. She looked frightened. Jardinn tapped her on a shoulder gently, and grinned into her blue eyes. He said:

"Miss Rand—let me present Miss Crissy."

He offered cigarettes to both women—both refused. Maya said coldly, looking Doll Crissy in the eyes:

"You say that you know me—that I hired you to get me information regarding Jardinn's agency?"

Doll nodded her head. Jardinn motioned toward one fan-backed chair, sat in the other. Doll wet her lips, got tears in her eyes and said unsteadily:

"I didn't—want to do it, Maya—"

Jardinn inhaled. "How much did she give you, Doll?" he asked.

The baby-faced girl said in a voice that was very faint: "One thousand—dollars."

Jardinn smiled. "It would have been cheap at that price," he mused.

Maya Rand said contemptuously: "You little liar!"

Jardinn sighed again. "All right, Doll," he said. "You can go out and sit in the Rolls again. I just wanted to hear you say that—and to hear Maya answer it. Don't run away."

The baby-faced girl looked at Maya Rand and said bitterly:

"I didn't want to go there. I was afraid. If you hadn't made me—"

Jardinn waved a hand. "All right—all right," he cut in. "We know all that."

Maya Rand said: "You little liar! I didn't want you to go anywhere!"

Jardinn waved a hand again. Doll Crissy went across the patio tiles and vanished into the living room of the house. Jardinn relaxed in the fan-backed chair and smiled at Maya Rand.

"The last time I came in here," he said slowly, "we both used nice words. But they didn't mean much. This time things are tighter. We forget the words and get across ideas—yes? The first one is this—you put that brat inside my office to see what I was doing. How close I was getting. The girl isn't lying. Carol Torney worked in the office. Now she's dead. If I go to the police with Doll Crissy, money or looks or Maskey or Ernst Reiner won't save you. I can raise so much howl—"

She lifted a hand weakly. He stopped talking and waited. She lay back on the pillows and closed her eyes. She looked very beautiful and very fragile. She said, after a while:

"Ben—Sokolsky's a good publicity man, but I think he's letting me down a little. I pay him ten thousand. You know tricks. I could double that—and it wouldn't take all of your time."

She opened her eyes and Jardinn laughed into them with his.

"God, but you're dumb, Maya," he said placidly. His voice got hard. "To hell with Hans Reiner. That's a job. But—they got Irish. Some dirty, knife sticking, son of—"

He got up from the chair, walked a few feet away from it and watched the fish in the pool. He lighted one cigarette from the stub of the other. Maya's voice reached him. It had almost a bored quality.

"I do believe I have seen that girl somewhere. But then I see so many people. Frightened thing, isn't she? Would she make a good witness in court, I wonder?"

Jardinn forgot about Carol Torney, went close to Maya Rand and stood looking down at her. He smiled, looked away from her with his dark eyes and said softly:

"She'd make a sweet witness, Maya—with a good prosecuting attorney to handle her. The best kind. She's young, and she isn't hard. She's dumb—and she hasn't much of a complicated past. There isn't anything for your defense lawyers to tear down."

Maya kept her eyes closed. Jardinn said in a harsher tone:

"But that's not it. I'm not worrying about that. She's just a good girl to have around."

There was a long silence. Maya broke it. She spoke lazily, huskily.

"I think you could break me, Ben. I think you could."

He said brutally: "You know goddam well I could."

After a few seconds he said: "Don't do that, Maya— it's no good. You're not a child. You've been through a lot. Don't make me smash the decent thing you've done—because you love Frey. Don't—"

He stopped, shrugged his shoulders. She moved her slender body a little, tapped the silk coverlet beside her breasts with fingertips. She called out:

"Carrie—go away, please!"

Jardinn said: "You know something about that pilot, Carren. You know something about the Reiners, both of them. And there's Frey. I don't want to hurt you. By God, I don't, Maya."

She tapped the silk coverlet again. There was exquisite grace in her fingers. Her jet eyes were sleepily watching his; she seemed to be hardly breathing. Her lips, barely bowed, were slightly parted. He thought:

Of them all she is the most beautiful. The most desirable—perhaps the fairest.

She said softly, tapping the coverlet once more:

"Sit here—Ben."

He leaned down, sat on the tiles beside the divan.

The sun was on her face. It was a bright, warm sun. He said:

"God, Maya—you can stand light. When you're not acting—"

She kept her eyes on his. She said very slowly:

"Ben—you've got me. With that girl you can pull me down. I know it. And I never talked with her before."

Jardinn spoke grimly. "It doesn't matter. With that girl—I've got you. I know Hollywood, the part of it that's real. I know the rotten, yellow press. You're at the peak, Maya—but you've got years in the game yet. If you throw them away to protect a killer—killers—"

She shut her eyes. Her lips met in a line that showed hardness. She parted them again.

"You think I know more than anyone else, Ben. So you got that girl. You don't care about Hans Reiner. That's just—a job. But Carol Torney—that hurt you. So badly. And now you're going to hurt me."

He said without looking at her: "The death in the Bowl is the important thing. They've hurt Irish. I didn't love her—but they've hurt her. I'll hurt anyone who stands in the way."

She moved her body a little, so that she was lying on her left side. Her head was close to his.

"And I'm—in the way," she said in a half whisper.

He nodded. "You know things," he said simply.

She closed her eyes, and there was passion in her words.

"Beautiful things," she said. "Beautiful things."

Jardinn said with grimness: "All women know those things. I don't want them—I want the nasty, ugly things."

He got suddenly to his feet. She said in a steady voice:

"You'll say I tried to bribe you—and then to seduce you. You'll say I put a girl inside your agency—to watch you. You'll say I hate one of two brothers, because I was heard to say certain things. You'll say I love Howard Frey—and that I'm protecting him."

Jardinn nodded: "Yes," he said.

She rose slowly, stood facing him. She threw back her head and laughed. It was bitter laughter.

"And *I* will say—that you lie," she said fiercely. "I'll say that, Jardinn. And you know you can't beat it. You know that!"

Jardinn smiled. "May I use your phone?" he asked.

She nodded. Her eyes were filled with fight, dark with suppressed anger. She said:

"The Hollywood police number is Highland Seven thousand. You can get reporters at—"

He grinned at her. "Don't act like a bit player and dramatize everything that happens off the lot," he said quietly. "I want to call a friend and find a nice safe place for your baby-faced brat."

Maya Rand held out a hand, smiling. He took it in both of his.

"She's such a lovely person," she said. "I'm sure she'd be safe—almost anywhere."

Jardinn nodded. "Sure," he said. "Anywhere—*almost.*"

·13·

VERONAL

The roadster rolled toward Famous Studios; Jardinn spoke with his eyes on the boulevard. There was a cheerful expression on his face.

"She's an actress, Doll—that's why she can look you over and say she doesn't know what it's all about. She's an actress."

Doll Crissy said tearfully: "She's in love with—Howard Frey. She did it—for him."

Jardinn frowned. "Yeah?" he said. "Would *you* stay in love with a guy that did the thing Frey did—put me after her by giving me the words she'd used, on the patio that night?"

Doll didn't answer. Jardinn drove the car across Vine Street. He said quietly:

"You're coming in with me—to see Ernst Reiner, Doll. Don't be surprised at anything I say. Just act bored. If I tell him something and then turn to you and ask if that isn't so—you just say it is so. Don't make any mistakes."

The baby-faced girl nodded. She said tremulously:

"Maya may have phoned him."

Jardinn grinned. "Sure," he agreed. "I sort of figured on that. They're all mixed up together, Doll—that's what makes it so tough."

She said: "You'd better let me go away. I'm afraid— of what they might do."

Jardinn swore. "You're safest with me," he told her. "Besides, I like you, Doll."

She said with some spirit: "You like Maya Rand."

He grinned again, pulled the car over near the curb, slid out from behind the wheel. He held her left arm as they crossed to the studio gate.

"Look pretty," he said. "Reiner's an artist first—he may give you a job."

When they reached the elaborate bungalow occupied by Ernst Reiner a chunky woman with a flat face and glasses greeted them. Jardinn said:

"Ben Jardinn—by appointment to his majesty, Herr Reiner."

The chunky woman frowned and left them in a small room. She returned with her hat on straight hair, said:

"Mr. Reiner will see you."

She gestured toward a half-closed door, went out. Jardinn moved to the door, stood aside as he shoved it open. Doll Crissy went through first. Reiner was seated back of a period desk, frowning. Jardinn said:

"Miss Crissy, Mr. Reiner. A valued assistant."

Ernst Reiner bowed without rising. He waved a hand toward chairs that faced the desk. Doll Crissy walked to one and seated herself. Jardinn sat in the other. He took the long envelope from his pocket and tossed it on the desk surface.

"Won't need the five hundred, Mr. Reiner," he said. "There wasn't any woman in Glendale. Wanted to see if you would lie about the Paris meeting with your brother."

Reiner was breathing heavily. He said in an angered tone:

"Me—I do not lie! There was no need for you to do such a thing—"

Jardinn smiled. "That's up to me," he said. "Because you give me five thousand dollars to get a murderer— that doesn't mean that you are not the murderer."

The director rose. His eyes were pinpoints of rage. He said thickly:

"I will not stand such talk! There was more than one person back of the stage in Paris, when I talked with this musical comedy star. There was—"

"Sure," Jardinn agreed. "Don't get excited. You didn't murder your brother. How do you think I know you quarreled with him, in the theater, if there wasn't some-one present? I've told you no threatening woman exists."

Reiner seated himself, still breathing heavily. He glared at Jardinn. He said:

"I come to you—for help. But from the beginning— I have the feeling that you suspect me. I do not like that."

Jardinn said grimly: "You know Carol Torney was murdered. Her body was found in my place. I found it. I have the feeling the police suspect me—and I don't like that. But what can I do about it?"

The director looked at Doll Crissy. He said slowly:

"Howard Frey is under arrest. I have heard he is suspected of something greater than a drunken quarrel."

Jardinn nodded. "I think we're getting close to Hans Reiner's killer," he said in a hard voice. "I begin to think you were right, Mr. Reiner."

The director's small, brown eyes glittered back of the glasses he was wearing. He said thickly:

"It is the proof that I want, Jardinn."

Jardinn smiled. "Maya Rand worked this girl, Miss Crissy, inside the agency," he said. "Maya is in love with Frey, maybe. She wouldn't go the limit for him, though. She had to know when he was getting in very bad. Doll was supposed to tell her, but Doll got frightened—and I got suspicious. Doll knows a few things that sound rather bad for Howard Frey. I'm keeping her near me."

Ernst Reiner widened his eyes on the face of the girl. He said slowly:

"So!"

Doll looked frightened, but did not speak. Jardinn said:

"Frey isn't talking much. He can't remember what he was doing about the time that Carol Torney was knifed to death. He was drunk and he says he had a fall."

Ernst Rainer shook his head and made a clicking sound with his tongue and the roof of his mouth.

"I think I remember Miss Torney," he said slowly. "One day, in your office—"

He let the words die. Jardinn relaxed in the chair and said very quietly:

"Or perhaps at your house, a few mornings ago. She went in the back way, at about three-thirty. She came out at four-ten."

Ernst Reiner stared at him. He got up and walked around the desk. He said stupidly:

"What is that—you say? This woman came into my house?"

Jardinn nodded. "My eyes are excellent. She went in, and she stayed in—about forty minutes. Then she came out and went home."

Reiner stood and looked down at Jardinn. His body swayed a little, from the waist up. Jardinn said:

"So maybe you do remember her, after all."

The director walked slowly around his desk and sat down in the chair. He said in a heavy tone:

"Well—that is so. Yes, it is true. You have found that out. You know that."

Jardinn smiled. Doll Crissy was looking at him with her blue eyes wide. Reiner looked at the girl and said:

"It is perhaps better that we discuss the matter alone."

Jardinn shook his head. "No," he said. "Doll's all right—now."

Reiner frowned. "It was this—" he said slowly—"I knew that Howard Frey had come to you. You are an American—and Frey is one. I am of German descent. I thought: It will be better to know what Mr. Jardinn is doing. I did not think Miss Torney was too wealthy. So I asked her to come and talk with me. And so—"

He spread his hands. Jardinn said in a cold voice:

"And so—she came."

Ernst Reiner nodded. "But she refused to report to me your methods," he said. "I urged her. I wanted to know that I could trust you. I asked her to give me only the truth. She refused. She was not angry—but she refused. She went away. Yes, it was after four. She thought it best to see me at such a time."

Jardinn said quietly: "So you, too, were spying on me. Why in hell did you come to me in the first place?"

Reiner nodded. "You have a fine reputation. I wanted you to protect me—and later, to find my brother's murderer. But I needed to know that you *would* work for me. When I first went to you Frey had not given you money."

Jardinn said: "You quarreled with Hans Reiner, backstage, in a Paris theater. What about?"

Reiner hesitated, shrugged. He said in a precise tone:

"Well, it does not matter. I will tell you. There was an actress I wanted for a picture over here. Sound was coming—and this actress possessed a voice. A very fine voice. My brother was acquainted with her. He was distressed because she had even gone on a Paris stage in a musical comedy. For her he desired concerts. He felt that her voice was very wonderful. We quarreled over—that."

Jardinn said: "There were no blows struck?"

The director said heatedly: "Most certainly not. It was a matter between artists. Hans was the musician—it was my opinion that the woman was a superb actress. I wanted her, perhaps selfishly, and yet not utterly so.''

Jardinn nodded. Reiner leaned forward across his desk and asked:

"How did you learn of—this scene?''

Jardinn spoke simply: "Maya Rand told me.''

The director's voice was a hoarse, grating whisper. He said:

"Maya—Rand?''

Jardinn nodded. Reiner was breathing heavily again. He rose from the chair, paced up and down back of the desk. A voice outside the bungalow called:

"Hey, Shrimp—over to Stage Seven—that lousy bastard McKenna is yellin' for lights!''

The reply was obscene and to the point. Reiner stopped pacing and said to Jardinn:

"I tell you—she is trying to involve me. I tell you, she is doing that. She is in love with this man Frey—you have said that. I think you are right. She put this woman inside your agency, you have said.''

"Yeah," Jardinn replied. "And you tried to get to Carol Torney. You know what that did?''

Reiner looked puzzled. Jardinn said in a grim tone:

"It got her killed—that's what it did. It got her knifed out.''

Doll Crissy covered her face with her hands and started to sob. Jardin turned in his chair and said sharply:

"Damn you—cut that out!''

Ernst Reiner said in a voice that was steady and very gentle:

"That is not good, Miss Crissy. It is all right—it is all right. It is only that Mr. Jardinn thinks I have had my brother killed because of a woman. That is why he shouts at me.''

Jardinn showed his teeth in a swift smile. He rose from the chair.

"That's wrong," he said. "But you're all making it

tough. Frey and Maya Rand. And you, Mr. Reiner. You're all very anxious to turn up the killer of Hans Reiner. But you want it done in this way—or in that. You can't just turn the killer up *any* way. That makes it hard.''

Ernst Reiner looked puzzled. He played with a letter opener he lifted from the surface of his desk with stubby fingers.

''I do not understand,'' he said.

Jardinn looked at Doll Crissy. Her fingers still covered most of her face, but she wasn't making any noise. He said quietly:

''It's all right, Doll. I'm taking care of you. Don't get scared.''

Reiner spoke in a thick voice, his brown eyes half opened on Jardinn's.

''I regret the attempt with Miss Torney. I think that you are right—Frey is the guilty one. He hated me. He was afraid to harm me, because I had gone to you. He knew I loved Hans and—''

Jardinn cut in. ''Yes, you've spoken before of all this. Frey had a motive. But you're holding back something, Mr. Reiner. Something important.''

The director shrugged. ''If you mean the name of the woman we quarreled about—in Paris—''

Jardinn smiled and shook his head. ''No, not that,'' he said. ''I know her name.''

Reiner's face lost color. He leaned back against the desk surface, geting support from it. His lips were twitching. After a few seconds he got a foolish smile on his face and said:

''Yes?''

Jardinn nodded. ''Yeah,'' he replied. ''If she hadn't taken an overdose of veronal it would have been hell for Maya, eh?''

Reiner sucked in deep breaths of air and breathed hoarsely:

''You—you—''

Jardinn said: "Take it easy. Take it easy."

The director took a handkerchief from a pocket and wiped his lips with trembling fingers making the cloth dance. He said hoarsely:

"You know—the name."

Jardinn smiled. "Yeah," he said. "It's an easy one to remember. You just think of grand or sand or land— and then you remember the name. And that woman was coming up, Mr. Reiner. She had looks and a voice, Ollie did."

Reiner started to cough. He held the handkerchief pressed to his lips and bowed his head. Jardinn waited until he straightened up again. He said:

"Olive Rand—Maya's younger sister. All set to come back to the place Maya shipped her away from—and take the play away from a fading star. I doubt that your brother could have prevented her, dangling concert chances. Maybe she *wanted* to come back and shove Maya out of the spotlight. Maybe she didn't love her sister, Mr. Reiner."

The director spoke in a dull voice. He kept his eyes on the surface of the period desk.

"She was so sensitive. Temperamental. And she was working very hard, in London, Paris—the south of France. She could not sleep at night. It was nerves, you see. And there was the accident—she was not too strong. An overdose—"

Jardinn said: "Too bad, too bad. She was pretty young. Young—to die that way."

Reiner said slowly: "You have learned about her. I do not suppose it was difficult. She was well known abroad."

Jardin nodded. "I'm working in Hollywood. There are files I keep—many of them useless things. But events concerning picture people and their relatives interest me. I get clippings from abroad—about them. Olive Rand hasn't been in Hollywood for six years or so. Maya kept her away. A good many people don't even know she has a sister. When she took too much veronal it didn't get into the papers here. She sang under the name of Randling.''

The director said wearily: "Yes, yes. But what has it all to do with my brother's death?''

Jardinn smiled. ''Your brother was questioned by London police, after she died,'' he said simply. ''She died in London—Hans Reiner was there. He was exonerated. He had spent the evening with her in her hotel room, before she took the overdose.''

Doll Crissy was watching Jardinn with her blue eyes wide. Reiner said grimly:

''You mean to tell me, then, that Hans was in some way responsible for her death—and that his murder was a revenge.''

Jardinn shook his head. ''Not exactly,'' he said. ''But perhaps Hans Reiner was in some *sense* responsible for the death of Olive Rand. Perhaps that was the motive for the killing of your brother.''

Reiner said: ''But Howard Frey—''

Jardinn smiled with his eyes on the wall beyond the director.

''Frey and Maya Rand were quite intimate,'' he said. ''Maya, of course, knew conditions as they really existed. Perhaps Frey knew them, too. You were Hans Reiner's brother—and you insulted him. You were powerful enough to break him, at the studio. You are powerful enough to keep him broken.''

Ernst Reiner got to his feet and frowned at Doll Crissy.

''It is not right—talking before this girl,'' he said.

Jardinn smiled. ''It's perfectly right,'' he contradicted. ''I might be hit by a truck—or something. Miss Crissy will remember the conversation, perhaps.''

Reiner said: ''But you have admitted that Maya placed her in your office.''

Jardinn nodded. He said very quietly:

"Remember, the thing you and Maya are trying to do is to get Frey, without injuring your own reputations. You both believe that Frey directed the murder of Hans Reiner. You think he did it because he loved Maya. And because—"

He stopped. The director said bitterly:

"Howard Frey—hated me!"

Jardinn rose and nodded. "I think he did," he agreed. "But he's no weakling. The police won't break him down."

He smiled at Doll Crissy, motioned to her. She got to her feet, her baby face turned toward him. Reiner spoke.

"Jardinn—Maya would never have gone to Frey, told him about that accident abroad. She would never have thought that my brother—"

He stopped. Jardinn said tonelessly, facing the director but not looking at him:

"She didn't have to go to Frey—he came to her. Do you think Maya admires anything in you, other than your art, Mr. Reiner?"

The director's face twisted. He pushed the clenched, stubby fingers of his right hand against material of his suit. He said thickly:

"I do not know—I do not care. I want the murderer of Hans. That is what—I want."

Jardinn said grimly: "Then don't get in my way anymore. Don't mix into agency affairs."

Reiner said: "Publicity—it will finish me. It will finish Maya."

Jardinn moved toward the door. Doll Crissy said insanely:

"I'm glad to have met you, Mr. Reiner."

The director paid no attention to the baby-faced girl. Jardinn said:

"To hell with publicity. It won't break either of you, anyway. Maya Rand's younger sister took too much veronal—and your brother was playing around with her. A few months later your brother comes over here and gets murdered. A select group, connected with both deaths, has a lot of bright ideas. You want something. Maya Rand wants something. Frey wants something. Well, *I* want something, too. I want your brother's murderer, and the one who knifed out Irish. Publicity won't stop *me*."

Ernst Reiner bowed with his eyes half closed. His thick lips were slightly parted. He said grimly:

"I am regretful that I—have interfered."

Jardinn nodded. "You should be," he replied. "By God, you should be."

He shoved Doll Crissy out into the other room. They moved from the studio. When they were inside the roadster, he drove slowly toward Los Angeles. With one hand he got bills from his pocket, handed a roll of them to her.

"Take two hundred," he said. "You're going down to Caliente and just have a good time. Play roulette and things like that. You can come back day after tomorrow."

Her wide eyes showed surprise. Jardinn grinned.

"If you stick around, you're a damn fool," he told her. "This'll be all over by tomorrow night."

She said in a frightened voice. "Howard Frey—killed Reiner?"

Jardinn grunted. "What makes you think that?" he said, getting surprise into his voice. "That talk—at the bungalow?"

She nodded. Jardinn kept the roadster headed toward Los Angeles and made a sound that was almost a chuckle.

"Jeez, Doll—" he said amusedly—"if I told you you weren't dumb—you'd believe me!"

·14·

MERRY-GO-ROUND

Jardinn got back to the agency office at ten minutes after two. He went inside, glanced at the headlines of a paper that lay spread on the stenographer's desk, shook his head grimly and went into his office. Max Cohn was standing near the window, looking out. He turned and grinned at Jardinn.

"They're giving Frey the works," he said. "Phaley and that mutt Donaldson figure he did for Hans Reiner—and knows a lot about Irish getting—"

Cohn stopped and twisted his round face. He said savagely:

"Goddam them for doing that!"

Jardinn squinted his eyes and flexed the fingers of his right hand.

"If I was sure Frey did the job I'd go down and help beat him up," he said. "Sit down, Max. I want to tell you things."

Max Cohn sat down and leaned back in the chair. Jardinn stood on his feet and talked rapidly, without regard for grammar.

"I just sent that baby-faced brat away—up to 'Frisco.

I think she'd been square, but no sense taking chances.
Maya Rand put her in here to watch us. Says she didn't,
but she did. Good actress, the Rand lady. Tough to beat,
on the witness stand. Took the blue-eyed kid over to see
Reiner, before I shipped her out. Talked in front of her—
and so did he. Told him that Maya Rand had put her in
the office, and gave him the news that I knew Carol had
gone in to see him the other night."

Cohn grunted. "Lie out of it?" he asked.

Jardinn shrugged. "Said he was trying to buy her over
to watch me," he replied. "Think that's about right.
Anyway, that stunt had me fooled, Max. I was even
worried about you. Irish had a hunch you were playing
loose with me. But you had it right on her visit to Reiner."

Cohn smiled grimly. "Thanks," he said without humor.

Jardinn lighted a cigarette. "You're such a damn good
dick—did you know that Randling woman who died in
London a few months ago was Maya Rand's sister?"

Cohn sat up and said: "Hell—no?"

Jardinn nodded. "Yeah. Maya shipped her away from
here six years ago, when she started to get too good-
looking. Maya isn't the type to play second—and she could
see that Ollie was going to have plenty. So she got her
going on the idea that a voice counted big. She put the
coin, and Ollie changed her rear name to Randling. That's
my guess, anyway. Ollie was the woman Hans and Ernst
Reiner had the argument about, in the Paris theater. The
maestro wanted her to do concert work. Ernst saw talkies
coming in and figured Ollie was a sweet actress. He
wanted her to come to Hollywood."

Max said grimly: "He had nerve—after Maya had got
her out of the place."

Jardinn pulled on his cigarette, and waved smoke away
from his face with his right hand.

"It meant money," he replied. "Maya can't last much
longer. It isn't that they have to burn her up on the set—
but she's had her time. Ernst was after a new face. To

hell with the old one. Anyway, he came back without her. She played in London, took too much veronal one night, and went out. It happened that Hans Reiner was in London at the time—and he'd spent the evening with her. He was questioned and released. Funny you didn't get that in the morgue stuff, Max.''

Cohn frowned. "They haven't got it," he said. "Randling doesn't mean anything to the Los Angeles papers. Chances are Hans Reiner's name didn't show much. They might not have connected him with Ernst."

Jardinn nodded. "That's right—they slip up a lot on what they clip. Well, I gave the story to Reiner. He was surprised, but when I got all through he gave me the right answer: What of it?''

Cohn slapped the sole of his right shoe against the floor and swore.

"It looks tough for Frey," he said. "But where does he fit in—on this deal?''

Jardinn said: "If Ernst Reiner had tried to bring Ollie back, or had succeeded—and if *he* had been murdered— I could see a nice motive.''

Cohn kept slapping leather against office floor.

"Frey was close with Maya," he said. "If she got the idea that Hans Reiner had something to do with the veronal dose—''

Jardinn said: "Yeah, I can see that, too. And Frey was hating Ernst hard. It was a chance to hurt him—by shooting out Hans. But he didn't do the job himself.''

Cohn said: "Why not go down and shoot the stuff at Frey? He might come through.''

Jardinn shook his head. "We haven't got him tight enough. What the police don't know won't hurt anything. And I want to give Ernst time enough to reach Maya. She may get scared.''

Cohn whistled off key. "Ollie Rand!" he breathed. "With Maya keeping her clear. And the bulls haven't picked up the connection.''

Jardinn said: "It was a quiet affair. They didn't get the name tie-up. I've had the sister tagged for years. Filed away. Even at that, I almost missed it."

"You held back on me, Ben," Max said. "How long have you known it?"

Jardinn grinned. "Since the start of things, Max," he replied. "And I'm not sure yet that it means anything."

Cohn stood up. "Just the same," he said, "you should have put me wise."

Jardinn swore at him. "Where the hell do you get off—telling me what I should do?" he asked. "All right, supposing you'd known this right after Hans Reiner was murdered—what would you have done differently?"

Cohn got a foolish smile on his face. He spread his hands. Jardinn took a sheet of paper from his desk, got a pencil from his pocket. He said:

"Pull a chair up here."

When Cohn was beside him he wrote:

Ernst Reiner was afraid of Howard Frey. Or he was framing Frey. Howard Frey was wise to the fact that Reiner was after him. Ernst Reiner came to me, but he wasn't sure of me. Hans Reiner was murdered in the Bowl. Carol Torney played with my wristwatch. Ernst Reiner says he didn't succeed in buying her, but that's probably a lie. Maya Rand had sent her younger sister to Paris. Ernst and Hans Reiner had quarreled about her. Ernst wanted to bring her back to Hollywood. In London she took an overdose of veronal and died. Hans Reiner had been with her a few hours before. Maya Rand, after Hans Reiner's murder, worked a girl named Doll Crissy into the agency, to see what we were doing. Carol Torney was knifed to death and brought to my house. That was to make it tough for me.

He stopped scrawling. Cohn said: "Phaley's still worried about you—they may pull you down to the station anytime."

Jardinn nodded, smiling a little. He used the pencil again:

Carren, pilot of the plane used in the Bowl kill, got his wind up and took off in a ship with one engine not working—

He looked at Cohn. Cohn nodded. He said in a low tone:

"Can't get a thing on Carren. Someone used him, and they were after him too hard. He got scared, something snapped in his head. He tried to get away. The Bureau of Commerce inspector says the plane was all right inside. But she had a bad engine and had been grounded. Carren just lost his nerve and got foolish."

Jardinn nodded: "Or wise," he said grimly. He scrawled again:

Maya doesn't seem to know Carren. She lies to protect Frey. Frey yelps he's being framed by Reiner. Reiner is sure Frey did the Bowl kill. Police getting nowhere on either murder. Point—has the suicide of Olive Rand in London anything to do with Hans Reiner's murder here? Point—why was Reiner murdered in such a spectacular manner? Point—what was it that Carol Torney knew and because of the knowledge was killed? Point—is the theory of two rifle shots, one at each side of the Bowl, satisfactory? Point—

Jardinn swore and sat back in his chair. Cohn picked up the paper and read what he had written very slowly. He put it down.

"One rifle at each side of the Bowl—that's the way it was done," he said. "Range—about two hundred yards. Maxim silencers to kill the flash. A mob, probably, hemming the riflemen in—and the plane to kill the sound."

Jardinn said nothing. Cohn said slowly:

"I'll tell you, Ben—I think Howard Frey did the job. He did it this way because he was out in the open, had a nice alibi. And he hates Ernst Reiner. He saw Hans Reiner knocked off the conductor's platform by lead—

and he knew that Ernst would see it. He thought he had something like a perfect crime. Maybe the death of Maya's sister had something to do with it—maybe not. Maybe Irish had something—and was holding out for a big price. Frey couldn't pay her—he was almost broke. Irish was clever. So he got her out of the way and tried to stop you at the same time. But he'd come to you first. Another alibi.''

Jardinn nodded. He studied the writing he had scrawled on the paper, then tore it into little bits. He put the bits in a pocket of his suit. Cohn said grimly:

"Irish crossed us, Ben. She got in too deep—and was done in. It's too goddam bad, because she was a good kid, and we'd have got wise to her, anyway. I think you're wrong about Frey—he'll break pretty soon. Maya Rand may not, but Frey will. He's our man.''

Jardinn narrowed his eyes and rubbed his lips with the back of his right hand. Cohn said:

"If they exonerated Hans Reiner, over in London, they didn't have anything on him. But maybe this Olive Rand wrote Maya letters that meant something. Frey was pretty crazy about Maya. He'd have done a lot for her. If Maya thought that Hans Reiner was responsible for her sister's death—''

Jardinn said, frowning: "Hell—Maya sent her away. She's pretty hard, Max. She wouldn't havé sent—''

The phone bell stopped him. He lifted the receiver, listened, said:

"Yeah, Pat—I'm right in the office. Got anything?''

Phaley said: "Frey says you're a dirty liar, and that you and Reiner are framing him. He says you were hired by Reiner to do that. He says Reiner pulled the job on his brother, and if you two don't come down here in a half hour he's going to spill something that'll hurt.''

Jardinn swore into the mouthpiece. "We'll stay away and let him spill it,'' he said. "Did you find the knife he used on Irish, Pat?''

Phaley said they hadn't, but that there were a lot of bulls working on the Torney murder. He said he thought Jardinn had better come down after a while.

Jardinn grinned. "Sure," he agreed. "But we'll let him spill it first, Pat."

When he hung up Cohn said: "What's he got—the sister stuff?"

Jardinn shrugged. "Probably. And it'll mix Ernst Reiner up. And Maya. He's not so dumb, Max."

Cohn grunted. "Still want me to work the Carren angle?" he asked. "It's tough—I doubt if he had any passengers. No books at the field—everything was sloppy out there. He lived alone, and the people at the house didn't know him well. Talked once or twice about getting money for a transatlantic flight. At the field, too."

Jardinn said: "Someone gave him money—enough to make that flight. But he couldn't get clear. No, let him go. See what you can do with the Frey party stuff. Check the police on what happened at the party—and what happened after, before I ran into Frey, just after he'd reached his apartment. I'm going to get some sleep—and then go down and see what Frey let loose. If I don't see you before, I'll drop in here about nine tonight. Be around, Max."

Cohn nodded, and Jardinn got up and stretched. He said:

"I'm tired as hell."

He went out and over to the Christie Hotel. He left a call for five o'clock and told the clerk to be sure they woke him. He fell asleep almost the second he hit the bed. He was so tired he didn't have the dream in which he was falling over the cliff.

2

Maya Rand looked bad. Her eyes had a weary expression, and there were little lines around the corners of her

mouth. She smiled at Jardinn and extended her left hand.
He took it and said:

"It's getting you, Maya. You'd do much better if you
stopped lying to me."

She got angry. "I haven't lied to you," she said, and
went over to the divan near the fireplace.

It had got colder—there was a small fire putting a glow
in the room. It was almost six o'clock. Jardinn said:

"Yes, you have. Frey has done some talking. He's
trying to drag Ernst Reiner into the thing."

Her slender body was taut; she raised fingers to her
lips, said in a muffled voice:

"What did—he say?"

Jardinn smiled gently. He went across the room and
stood looking down at her.

"Just about what I told Reiner a few hours ago—and
what he told you I knew. About your sister and Hans
Reiner. Only he added something. You have letters from
Olive."

Her face was a pale mask. She widened her eyes and
said:

"Of course, Ben. She wrote me from abroad."

Jardinn nodded. "She wrote you that Hans and Ernst
Reiner had quarreled about her—that Ernst wanted her
to come to the States, to Hollywood. She wrote that he
had said he would make her a star—and that she wanted
to return. She disliked her other work. And then she
wrote you again—"

Maya Rand said: "No—no—Howard couldn't have
told—"

She stopped. Jardinn's face was serious.

"He did tell," he said simply. "She wrote you that
Hans Reiner had told her the truth—that you didn't want
her to return, that you were keeping her away. That you
hated her—"

Maya Rand cried out, covered her face with white
hands. When she took them away there was a hard

expression in her eyes. Her lips were pressed into a red, thin line.

Jardinn said: "Hans Reiner wanted her to hate you— he wanted her voice for the concert stage. And perhaps he wanted something else, too. He had argued with his brother; he said Hollywood was a cheap thing for Olive. He accused Ernst Reiner of merely wanting her for money purposes. And it was then that the director told Hans the truth—in order to show him that he wanted Olive for the screen because she was an artist, a fine actress. He wanted her *in spite* of that fact that you had sent her away, that you were afraid of her beauty, ability. He told Hans that because he knew his brother. He knew Hans would tell your sister—and he *thought* she would defy you, come to Hollywood. He was right—Hans Reiner did tell your sister the truth. But he was wrong—she didn't come to Hollywood."

Maya Rand looked at him with dull, hurt eyes. She said, after a long silence, in a voice that was barely a whisper:

"Well?"

Jardinn shrugged. "She knew that you hadn't given her things because you loved her. You were trying to keep her away. You were afraid of her, hated her. So she wrote you that she knew—and a few days later she took veronal—and died. An accident."

Maya Rand said slowly, dully:

"It was—an accident. She couldn't sleep. She was high-strung, sensitive. I am the same way."

Jardinn nodded. "Well, that's what Frey has told. He knew—you showed him the letters. That's all he has told. He's been drinking heavily for months—his heart is bad. He's had an attack, and the doctor won't let them question him more—not just now. They haven't let him sleep—he's sleeping now. But when they wake him—"

Maya said in a hard tone: "What he said is true. But the publicity—"

Jardinn smiled grimly. "Don't be foolish, Maya. Publicity is a small thing. Why do you think Frey told that?"

She closed her eyes, shook her head. A log crackled in the fire and sent sparks to the rug. Jardinn walked over and kicked them away.

"You hated Hans Reiner, when you got that letter from your sister. Because you didn't really hate your sister. You were doing things for her—but you wanted to keep her away. You hated Hans Reiner for telling Olive the truth. That's what Frey says. You are very wealthy, Maya. You hated Hans Reiner—and you hated Ernst Reiner, because he told his brother a truth that could hurt your sister."

Her eyes were little slits looking darkly into his. She said weakly:

"Well?"

Jardinn smiled, shrugged. "Well, the police are very liable to reason that you had a nice chance, Maya. Your money could make that chance. You had a motive. Hans Reiner was killed, while his brother looked down at him. And perhaps that sight of his brother dying—perhaps that will yet break Ernst Reiner. Certainly he will never forget it."

There was a silence. Maya Rand sat stiffly on the divan. She said tonelessly:

"Howard Frey tells a truth—and I am to be suspected of the murder of Hans Reiner."

Jardinn frowned. "I think it can safely be said you had a motive," he stated. "Maya—why did you faint when I told you Carren had crashed and was dead?"

She lifted a hand weakly in defense. Jardinn spoke harshly.

"It was Carren's ambiton to make a transatlantic flight. Did you promise to back him?"

Fear showed in her eyes. She cried out:

"Oh, stop it—please! I had nothing to do with the

murder in the Bowl! I swear to you I hadn't. Nothing, nothing!''

Jardinn made a wide gesture with his hands.

"I think you did, Maya," he said. "But I don't think you planned it. That won't help you any—''

She said with rage in her voice: "Ernst Reiner did not love his brother! He said again and again that he loved him. But he did not. He hated him! He was jealous, just as I was jealous with Olive. Ernst hated Hans that night— the night of the concert. You could feel it. Hans was in the spotlight.''

Jardinn half closed his eyes. "Dog eat dog," he said slowly. "Merry-go-round. Frey loved you, in his manner, Maya. He loved you until things got too tough. While he loved you he did things for you. That makes three. Maya Rand, Ernst Reiner—Howard Frey. All hating the man who died in the Bowl.''

Maya shivered. She rose weakly and went nearer the fire, holding her arms outstretched toward the small flames.

Jardinn said: "Max Cohn tells me that Carren talked of flying the Atlantic. He hadn't much money. I don't think he knew *why* he flew over the Bowl the night of the murder. He only knew that he was to fly at a certain altitude, very low—and reach the spot at an exact minute. Later, when he learned what had happened, he couldn't stand the strain. He took off in a ship that was grounded— and crashed. He was trapped—and I think that means he was handled so cleverly he saw no way out. What he had to tell he knew the police would not believe.''

Maya Rand turned and faced him. She looked older than she had minutes ago, more tired. She spoke in a shaken voice.

"I gave Howard Frey five thousand dollars. I wanted to hurt Hans Reiner. God! how I wanted to hurt him. But not to kill him, Ben. I swear to that. I had the idea one night, when a plane flew low over the house here. A big plane. There was a party and the violinist, Livitski, was playing. He went into a rage—there was so much noise. I told Frey to hire the pilot of a plane with three engines—and to have him fly very low over the Bowl, *each* night that Hans Reiner conducted. It was petty, cheap—but don't you see? I wanted to humiliate him, hurt him. I wanted to smash his music. I gave Frey the money—that much because I knew each night it would be more difficult for the plane to fly over. I wanted to be sure.''

She checked herself, turned toward the fire again. Jardinn said:

"You damn—little fool.''

She went over to the divan and threw herself on it, sobbing. The sounds she made were not pretty. She said in a choked voice:

"Howard—must have—gone crazy!''

Jardinn lighted a cigarette. He shook his head.

"God help you—if he tells the bulls that,'' he muttered. "Maya—I think you're telling the truth. But you're in a bad spot—a terribly bad spot. When Frey came to me and told me he'd heard you using words about 'getting to him through his brother' he dragged you directly into the case. Give me the truth on that—it may help you.''

She turned her head toward him, said brokenly:

"That was—in the script— of *Death Dance*. You know that, Ben. He knew it. Perhaps he didn't remember it—perhaps he thought it would hurt me, to tell you. I wasn't thinking of Ernst or Hans Reiner when I spoke the words. Hans Reiner had had a very formal, cold talk with me. He had tried to tell me that he had nothing to do with Olive's death. I said that I understood. He had been gone almost an hour—I was pacing back and forth in the patio and rehearsing my next scene. The instant I spoke the words the irony of them struck me. I checked myself. But Howard had heard them. He repeated them to you—and I think he knew at the time they were in the script. I think he remembered it.''

Jardinn said: "All right, but *why* did he turn on you? Why did he put you in that position?"

She said: "I was angry with him, because of the fool he had made of himself—knocking Ernst Reiner down. He came to me for money—I refused him. I think he was trying to frighten me—he knew I could explain the lines in the script—but he thought it would frighten me. I would give him money."

Jardinn said slowly: "You're telling the truth this time, Maya—and by God you've got to tell it."

She said: "I'm finished—in pictures. This will finish me."

Jardinn said grimly: "It might do more than finish you in pictures. I'm going to see Frey."

She said weakly: "I've told you—the whole truth, Ben. If you get me out of this—"

Jardinn moved toward the door that led to the driveway.

"If I get you out of *this*," he interrupted, "You'd better start saying your prayers again each night. It'll be something like a miracle."

·15·

TOUGH ONE

Pat Phaley was chewing on a sandwich when Jardinn walked into the anteroom of the Vine Street Emergency Hospital. He was alone. He grinned at Jardinn.

"Hello, Ben," he greeted. "Thought you'd be along."

He took another chew of the sandwich. Jardinn said: "Anything new?"

Phaley finished the sandwich, wiped his lips with a handkerchief and stroked the ends of his drooping mustache. He said:

"Yeah—Frey's dying. Doc gives him an hour or so. Digitalis isn't helping much. He got excited about fifteen minutes ago."

Jardinn smiled grimly. "You mean you got him excited," he said. "Well?"

Phaley said calmly, using a toothpick between words:

"Frey knifed Irish—goddam his soul. He got drunk, ran into her after he left the party. Ran into her coming out of his apartment house. She got away. He called her up and said he was coming over. She hung up—and he went over to her place. She was using the telephone—

he kicked in a window screen and got inside. She let go of the phone and ran to the back of the house. He used a kitchen knife on her, when she tried to get clear. The reason—he'd heard she had been going to Ernst Reiner's place. He says she was framing him. And he was pretty drunk. He says if he'd run into you he'd have done the same thing.''

Jardinn said slowly: "He's lying."

Phaley shook his head. "I don't figure it that way," he said. "He knows he's dying. He says he left the house right away. Carol Torney was lying on her back in the kitchen. There hadn't been much racket. He walked around a while—she'd hit him a few times. Then he went to his apartment and you came along."

Jardinn said: "How'd Irish get out to my place? walk?"

Phaley shrugged. "That's something else again," he said. "I don't think Frey took her there. I do think he killed her. He swears he didn't do the job in the Bowl, and he swears you and Reiner were framing him for it."

Jardinn said coldly: "Come through, Pat. You're lying or holding back on me. He didn't knife Irish just because he was drunk and she was working in the agency."

The plainclothesman said: "I thought you'd fired her, Ben?"

Jardinn smiled a little. "You didn't think anything of the kind, Pat," he said. "And Frey wasn't supposed to have known it."

Phaley went over and sat down on a bench. He spoke with his eyes on the waiting room ceiling.

"I sort of figured you were lying about firing her, Ben. Frey said he caught her hanging around Maya Rand's place twice. Once she was coming out of the house. The Rand woman told him she hadn't seen her, talked with her. Frey figured the two of them were framing him."

Jardinn said: "Why?"

Phaley swore. "Maya Rand was trying to make a fool

of this Hans Reiner—to spoil his concerts with a plane.
She gave Frey money to get the pilot. He used a third
party to make the deal with Carren, and he figured Irish
got wise. He said he was drunk and he was hating you
and Max Cohn—and Irish. He accused Irish of knowing
that he had only handed over the money to have the plane
spoil the concert. He says she told him he was insane—
she didn't know what he was talking about. He thought
she was stalling—and that the agency was going to see
that he got rope, make a reputation and clear up the
murder. He was half crazy—and he grabbed the knife
and did it.''

Jardinn said: ''How'd the body get out to my place?''—

Phaley shook his head. ''Just the same,'' he replied,
''I think Frey was talking straight. He knows he's
going out.''

A short man in a gray suit came out through a doorway
and said:

''He's dead, Phaley. Want to see him?''

Phaley nodded and rose. Jardinn followed the two men
into a small room with a narrow bed. Howard Frey lay
on his back with his eyes opened. The doctor said:

''He didn't speak again, and he went out quietly. I'd
say he's had a rotten heart for years.''

Phaley turned away. Jardinn looked down at the wide
eyes. His voice was low and hard.

''He didn't fix the Reiner kill, Phaley.''

The plainclothesman said: ''I don't think he did—but
if it gets too tough, he'll be good enough for the records.''

Jardinn said bitterly: ''By God, they put him in a tough
spot. But he didn't use too much brains. He got scared—
and drunk.''

Phaley stood in the doorway. ''Come on,'' he said to
Jardinn. ''This looks tough for that Rand lady.''

Jardinn closed his right fist and half raised the arm.
He said grimly:

"Even if he is dead—I'd like to smash him in the face. Dirty woman-knifing bastard!"

Phaley came back and took Jardinn by the raised arm.

"Cut it out," he growled. "They'll raise hell if he's cut up—they always do. We treated him nice. You can't hurt a dead guy."

They went outside and a harness cop came in and handed Phaley something wrapped up in a piece of paper.

"We found it in the lot—like he said," the cop stated. "But without knowing the place it would have been safe for months. A lot of saw grass around—and dead palm stuff."

Phaley unwrapped the knife and stared down at it.

"Jeez," he breathed. "That's the baby, all right."

He wrapped it up again. He got his eyes on Jardinn's.

"I think maybe he got the body out to your place, at that, Ben. If he worked fast, could he have done it?"

Jardinn said: "There's a chance—but he would have had to drive both ways like hell. I came in the shortest way, and I didn't pass any other cars. Someone had to fix the kitchen right again—the house wasn't mussed a bit. He could have done that—but he couldn't have done it and got out to my place and then back to his again— before I got there."

Phaley swore. "The Rand woman is the best bet," he said. "To hell with this using a plane to spoil the concerts—and to get Hans Reiner sore. That's kid stuff."

Jardinn said: "Yeah, but that's on the level. I've just come from Maya's place. The deal got away from her, Pat."

Phaley grunted. "Somebody saw a nice chance to step in and do a neat job," he said grimly. "And they had a couple of goats, eh?"

Jardinn nodded. "That's the way I figure it, Pat," he said. "But who stepped in?"

The plainclothesman swore again. "Well," he said slowly, "there's Reiner's brother. This dope about the Rand woman's sister lets him in. And Maya Rand isn't clear, Bennie. Not by a damn sight."

Jardinn said: "And Howard Frey isn't clear."

Phaley stroked his mustache. "We got something to work on," he muttered.

Jardinn blinked tired eyes and swore toward the hall-way that led to the room in which the dead man lay.

"Did Frey give you the name of the man he used—when he passed the coin to Carren?" he asked.

Phaley nodded. "Got two boys looking him up," he said. "Got his address—but if he's wise he won't be there. His name's Cordova, and he hasn't got a record."

Jardinn said: "What did he tell Carren?"

Phaley grinned. "If you keep asking questions I'll want a split on the five grand Reiner's paying you. Frey said he *was* to tell Carren that a certain picture outfit had it in for the conductor because it was known he was turning down their bid for him—and intended to sign up with another studio. They wanted to make him blow up—on the platform. They wanted to drown the orchestra out, every night."

Jardinn rolled a cigarette between his lips and swore.

"Poor devil Carren," he said. "He fell for it, and he had brains enough to see what a weak story he'd have for the police. Just a guy passing him some money and a bum story."

Phaley said: "He had a crash two months ago—and the field bunch say he was just getting over it. He was planning a transatlantic flight, but he needed coin. The coin he got helped. He probably figured he'd get caught after the second or third night, but he wasn't worried much. He could hand out a line and pay a fine. He was framed right."

The harness copper said: "How about this guy Frey? Is anyone staying with him?"

Phaley shook his head. "We'll take a chance on him sticking around," he said grimly.

2

Maya Rand, her eyes wide with excitement, stood close to Pat Phaley and shook her head from side to side.

"That is a lie!" she kept repeating. "He did not do that—terrible thing. He did not."

Phaley twisted his soft hat in the fingers of his right hand and said in a quiet voice:

"It won't do any good to say that, Miss Rand—we got it all down in writing. Frey admitted the kill, all right."

Maya's eyes went to Jardinn's. She said in a voice that was suddenly grim and calm:

"Ben—is this a trap? I told you the truth—is this a trap?"

Jardinn shook his head. "Phaley's a good fellow, Maya," he said. "What he just told you he told me when I reached the hospital. A cop came in with the knife—said they'd found it where Frey told them to look."

Maya Rand smiled. She said: "You're lying—you're both lying. I've told you everything I know. Howard Frey did not kill the girl. I know that!"

Phaley said: "*How* do you know it?"

Her eyes sought Jardinn's again. He nodded.

"Better come through, if you know something, Maya," he said. "It's a tough spot. If they fasten Irish's knifing on Frey, and don't clear up the Bowl kill, they'll hang that on him, sure as hell. That's the way it's done. And if they get Frey for that—they'll drag you into it with him, Maya."

She said bitterly: "All because I wanted to hurt Hans Reiner! All because I wanted to humiliate him—in the Bowl."

Phaley twisted his head and spoke in a quiet voice:

"The reason we give you a break on this, Miss Rand, is that Frey didn't get the girl's body out to Jardinn's place. We're pretty sure he didn't, anyway. I'm giving it to you straight—he said he knifed Carol Torney."

Maya Rand rose from the divan and stood very straight. Her slender arms were at her sides.

"If he said that—he lied," she said very quietly. "Howard went to a party. You know that. He got in a quarrel and was thrown out. He fell—and he walked the streets for some time after that. But he didn't kill the girl. He was here—with me!"

Phaley swore under his breath. Ben Jardinn said quietly:

"When did he get here, Maya?"

She spoke in a steady voice. "He came here at about twenty minutes of four. I was ill—and Doctor Francis had been called. The doctor was with me. He was instructing Carrie at what hour to give me the next sleeping tablet—when Howard got into the patio. He called my name—and Doctor Francis went to the window."

Jardinn said: "What happened next?"

Maya smiled twistedly, grotesquely. She kept her eyes on Jardinn's.

"Doctor Francis wanted to take him out when he left. He was cut, and the doctor wanted to treat him. But Howard was in a terrible mood. He wouldn't allow the doctor to touch him, and he wouldn't leave. I was very nervous, and Doctor Francis argued with Howard until about ten minutes after four. Then I got him to leave—he went down to the patio and walked around, smoking."

Phaley said: "And Frey stayed with you?"

Maya Rand nodded her head. "For about ten minutes," she said. "He was growing calmer, but he was in a terrible mood. He left very suddenly. It was perhaps a little after four-twenty, because I remember my clock striking the quarter hour—quarter after four—and he swore at it. He kept talking about being framed. He was terribly

angry with me, because of my idea of humiliating Hans
Reiner. Then he left suddenly.''

She sat on the divan and watched Jardinn's face. Phaley
said:

"Was Doctor Francis still on the patio?''

Maya nodded. "After Howard had gone—he came up
and talked with me,'' she said.

Phaley said: "What's his phone number, Miss Rand?''

She gave it to him. Phaley went to the phone and
called the number. Jardinn said grimly:

"If he left here at about four-twenty, he could have
reached his apartment just ahead of me. If he was here
all of the time between twenty minutes of four and twenty
after—he didn't knife Irish. She talked with me a few
minutes after four.''

Phaley said: "Francis has been your doctor for a long
time, Miss Rand?''

Maya smiled coldly. "Yes, but he is a very prominent
California physician. He is worth a great deal of money.
I could not bribe him.''

Phaley nodded, smiled. He got the doctor's secretary,
said:

"Phaley, Hollywood police. Very important that I talk
with the doctor.''

Jardinn offered Maya a cigarette, lighted it for her.
He said:

"I believe you, Maya. The story Frey told was weak.
There wasn't a reason for him knifing Carol Torney. The
body got out to my place—and Frey didn't take it there.''

Maya said: "But why—why didn't he tell the truth?
Doctor Francis, Carrie—myself—we all knew he was
here.''

Jardinn frowned. Phaley talked into the mouthpiece in
a low voice. After a few minutes he hung up. He said
to Maya Rand:

"Francis verifies your time, Miss Rand. He says he

would be willing to testify to such a statement on the witness stand.''

Jardinn smiled grimly: "Francis, Maya and the maid, Carrie. We couldn't beat that combination if we wanted to. Frey lied, just before he went out, Phaley. Why?"

The plainclothesman frowned. "He knew about the knife," he said slowly. "He knew the man who murdered Irish, Ben."

Jardinn looked at Maya Rand. He said very quietly:

"We're getting in close, Maya. Have you told us everything?"

She said firmly: "Howard's dead. Hans Reiner is dead. My sister is—"

She stopped, closed her eyes. She said in a low, hard voice:

"I've told you everything—and I've told you the truth."

Phaley twisted his hat and asked Jardinn for a cigarette. When he had lighted up he said:

"Don't take a sudden trip anywhere, Miss Rand. We don't want anything embarrassing to happen."

There was scorn in Maya's eyes. She said with the same quality in her voice:

"I shall not run away."

Jardinn said suddenly, in a strange voice:

"By God—by God! He *could* think that way—"

He checked himself. Phaley said:

"What's eating you, Ben?"

Jardinn's eyes were little dark slits. He looked at a wall of the living room and didn't reply. Phaley spoke again.

"That's right, Miss Rand—don't run away."

He went toward the door. Jardinn walked over to Maya and touched her gently on the shoulder. She was gazing straight ahead; she didn't appear to feel his touch. He said:

"It's all right, Maya. You just sit tight."

She said with grimness creeping into her words.

"Yes—sit tight—for a long time, Ben."

He smiled down at her, turned and followed Pat Phaley from the house. They got into Jardinn's roadster, and Phaley said:

"I'll go back and see if they grabbed this Cordova bird. Hell—it's a tough one, Ben."

Jardinn nodded. He looked at his wristwatch.

"It's six-fourteen," he said. "We'll ride fast—the way you'd ride around four in the morning. In to the apartment house where Frey lived."

Phaley said: "Sure—no use slipping on a thing. But why did he lie, Ben? And how did he know about the knife?"

Jardinn said: "He was through, and he knew it. If he confessed the murder of Irish—that stopped something."

Phaley grunted. The roadster was rolling fast toward Hollywood. The speedometer showed forty-five. Phaley said:

"If he wanted to protect someone—why in hell didn't he swear he'd done the Bowl job, too?"

Jardinn grunted. "Your brain's not working, Pat. That would have let Maya in for a dose, as an accomplice, maybe. Frey loved her—yes and no like. Loved her and hated her. He went out leaving the Bowl kill up in the air. Maybe he knew you could *think* he ran the job— and the public could think that way, too. But it left Maya Rand pretty safe."

The plainclothesman pulled at his mustache.

"How about the knife?" he asked.

Jardinn missed a slow-moving truck by a foot and took a street crossing at forty. A cop in uniform blew a whistle— and Phaley waved at him. The cop grinned. Jardinn said:

"By God—you've got influence. The knife—that's a tough one."

Phaley grunted. Jardinn said, above the clatter of the ancient roadster's engine:

"You're a good dick, Pat—I'm going to let you in on something. I've got a sawed-off thirty-thirty at the house. Can you get someone at headquarters to rig a Maxim silencer on it?"

Phaley widened his eyes. "Hell, yes," he replied.

Jardinn said: "Good. There's a concert at the Bowl tonight. You and me—we'll go out there. I'll get you the rifle—you have it fixed right. Meet you at the station at eight. Keep it quiet."

Phaley whistled softly: "You've got something, you bum!" he muttered.

Jardinn smiled grimly. "Just an idea," he said. "But it's beginning to look good."

Phaley looked disappointed. "I've had a couple like that—but look what happens to 'em."

Jardinn said: "I can do this job alone, Pat. I won't feel hurt."

Phaley grunted as they swung around a corner and pulled up in front of the Frey apartment.

"Like hell you can!" he gritted. "How long has it taken us?"

The wristwatch showed it was six-twenty-five. Jardinn said:

"Eleven. He could have made better time, at that hour in the morning. He'd have just about got inside the apartment, when I came along."

Phaley swore. "Funny as hell," he muttered. "He tells a nice lie and goes out. The lady he loved comes along and smashes his story all over the place. Is that right?"

Jardinn said grimly: "The way I'm thinking now—it just might be right, Pat. It just might be."

Phaley said: "Yeah—it just *might* be, Ben. You get that rifle. We've got to do a fast job. But we can rig the silencer on it. Can we handle this job all right—just the two of us?"

Jardinn narrowed his eyes. "It's not a pinch," he replied. "I just want to show you something."

Phaley frowned. "I'd like to have a talk with Ernst Reiner," he muttered.

Jardinn looked through the windshield of the roadster and sighed. Phaley said:

"He might be feeling good now—with Frey dead."

Jardinn said tonelessly: "Sure—good and worried, maybe."

·16·

CRESCENDO

Max Cohn was reading a paper in the outer office of the agency, when Jardinn walked in after eating. It was seven-thirty; Jardinn sat on the desk and dug knuckles into his tired eyes. Cohn said:

"You look all in, Ben—get anywhere?"

Jardinn shook his head. "Hear about Frey making a confession?" he asked.

Cohn grunted. "Yeah, and it sounds fishy to me," he replied. "But it might be right, at that."

Jardinn said: "You get anything—on the Carren end?"

Cohn shook his head. "It's tight as a drum out that way," he said. "But I've got a line on a fellow I may be able to see at eight-thirty, out at the field. A pilot who knew Carren."

Jardinn said: "Good—can you get back here around nine?"

Cohn grinned. "Maybe a little late," he replied. "Should make it by nine-thirty, anyway. Something due to break?"

Jardinn swore softly: "There's just a chance. But I'm

all in, Max. And I want to tell you some things before I head for the bungalow and a long nap.''

Cohn said: ''Well, I'll be back at nine-thirty.''

Jardinn looked around the office. He smiled with a hurt expression in his eyes.

''That damn blonde of yours, Irish—and the baby-faced brat. None of them on the level, Max. You can't trust a woman.''

Cohn said: ''Not when other men get a chance to work on them.''

Jardinn shrugged. ''Irish knew something, Max,'' he said. ''I went through her place after I got away from the Christie and that bum nap. Had to work fast. And the bulls had been there, too. But they missed something.''

Cohn's eyes got wide. But he waited for Jardinn to finish.

''Irish knew music,'' Jardinn went on. ''She had a score of that tone poem—the number they were playing when Hans Reiner got hit.''

Cohn said: ''Jeez—trying to figure time, eh? Put someone wise.''

Jardinn nodded. ''Or maybe she wanted to know what the piece was all about,'' he said. ''It's got a lot of noisy music in it. Plenty of horn and tympani stuff. Crescendo after crescendo.''

Cohn said: ''Jeez!''

Jardinn half closed his eyes and looked at the desk. He shook his head slowly.

''She knew things, Max,'' he repeated. ''She wasn't a bad kid. She sort of liked me—but she had an idea I didn't think much of her. I think maybe she wanted to hurt me. She put a fellow next to me that tried to slug me down. Then, after Reiner was out, I think she got scared.''

Cohn screwed up his face and swore. He slapped his foot against the base of the desk.

"It might have been Ernst Reiner," he muttered.

Jardinn said "God knows—but I've got an idea we may get licked, Max. The agency is due for a flop, anyway. We've had luck—good luck. This job needs more than luck."

Cohn said: "We may fool them yet, Bennie. If I can get a lead on Carren—"

Jardinn went toward the office door. He said:

"You'd better get started. I'll be in around nine or nine-thirty. See you then."

Cohn nodded. His chubby face showed a half grin.

"We're ahead of the bulls, anyway, Bennie," he said. "They're running around in circles."

Jardinn said: "Being ahead of them doesn't mean anything," and went outside and down the stairs.

2

It was eight-twenty when Phaley and Jardinn went through the gates of the Bowl. Under the light coat Jardinn was wearing he carried the sawed-off repeating rifle. There was a good crowd in attendance, though the night was cold. Jardinn wore a soft hat pulled low over his eyes, and Phaley kept his head bent forward.

The usher took their tickets and led the way toward the center of the Bowl. The orchestra was tuning as they turned down an aisle, passed the first tier of boxes. The usher stood aside, and pointed out the seats.

"All the way over—next to the rail," he said.

Jardinn nodded, went in first. He took the seat next to the rail. There was no one directly in front of them—behind was a box. It was unoccupied. Phaley leaned forward and looked to the left, beyond the rail. Jardinn said:

"That's the box they use for the radio stuff—Saturday night."

Phaley nodded. "They don't store it there," he said. "It's just in case of rain."

Jardinn smiled a little. They were almost directly in the center of the Bowl, in the eighth row. The rows sloped upward, tier after tier. But the radio box was only slightly raised. Wood planks sloped up from dirt. The box was perhaps five feet above the shell level.

It was as though a section had been cut from the rising tiers of seats, directly in the center. For five feet on either side of the box there were no seats. The roof was almost level with the tier on which their chairs rested. Jardinn said:

"When the lights dim—I'll get up, slide over the rail, drop to the dirt around the box, and get inside. You wait until the maestro comes out—then do the same. Don't hurry."

He saw Phaley's eyes go wide. The plainclothesman started to speak, but checked himself. Jardinn said:

"We'll be crowded, inside the box. It's open at the front end. Just jam in—and don't move around."

The orchestra had hushed—the Bowl lights dimmed as the shell lights grew brighter. Jardinn rose, turned slowly. There was no usher near. He got a leg over the low iron railing on his left, lifted the other. He dropped several feet to the earth, walked around to the front of the box and bent down. He got inside.

There was applause as the local conductor came from the side of the shell. Jardinn moved his body to the left of the box, which was perhaps five feet wide. The maestro mounted the platform and turned the pages of his score. He tapped sharply with his baton. There was the thud of feet striking dirt—the first notes of the piece were crashing, tympanic.

Phaley, breathing hard, was bending over, crawling in beside him. He muttered thickly:

"What in hell's—all this about? I looked this box over—the next day."

Jardinn curved his body and grinned. He said:

"Yeah—so did I."

Minutes passed. The orchestra sent sound into the box; there was an earthy odor inside. It was damp and they were cramped. Jardinn got his head close to Phaley's.

"Two of us got in here—so far it doesn't seem to make any difference. If we were seen—someone thought we had the right to be here. Or they didn't care. Maybe we weren't seen. The Bowl's in a state of confusion, anticipation—when the lights dim."

Phaley said grimly: " All right—we're here. It's damn uncomfortable."

Jardinn grinned. He said: "Light from the shell doesn't hit us directly. The musicians can't see us."

Phaley muttered something he didn't get. The orchestra was working into a crescendo of tone. Jardinn moved his body, unbuttoned his coat. He got the sawed-off thirty-thirty on the earth beside him.

Phaley said: "What the hell—"

Jardinn used an elbow on the plainclothesman's ribs. He gritted:

"This is—my show. Get over against the side, the wood."

Phaley grunted and cramped his body against the right side of the box-like structure. Jardinn rolled on his stomach, raised his legs high from the knee to the foot, shoved back away from the opening. He said in a whisper that reached Phaley above the beat of the symphony:

"This box is well built. It's thick. Any sound that gets out—beats toward the shell. It rolls into the music coming out."

Phaley said: "You goddam fool—those bullets had a penetration from a two hundred yard carry. They went in from opposite sides. One of 'em mushroomed—"

The music was dying—the violins were singing a soft motif. A harp belled an obbligato. Jardinn said softly:

"You goddam dumb dick—you can mark a cross on

the nose of the lead and make it mushroom. You can cut
down the powder in the load and get the same penetration
at fifty yards that you can at two hundred.''

Phaley was breathing heavily. He said grimly, as the
orchestra worked into a movement that brought in section
after section:

"We're fifty yards away—and in dead center. You
can't put bullets in that conductor at different angles—
not from *here*."

Jardinn said: "You watch his back—when you hear
these shots. We haven't got a plane overhead—and we've
got lights. You watch—"

His voice rose as the orchestra sent a fury of sound
into the Bowl. The violins were working in unison; the
horn sections sent a blare of brass noise over the tiers of
seats. Heinrich Bern was moving his body from side to
side; his baton was flashing in the shell light. Jardinn
gritted:

"He's—a target, Pat."

The conductor swung suddenly to the left. There was
a crash of cymbals—a staccato wail from the first violins.
Jardinn said: "Now!"

The box was filled with sound, dulled but still loud.
There was no flame from the rifle—the Maxim silencer
killed it. Bern's body was swinging to the right. He
brought down his baton as the cymbals crashed again.
Jardinn's second "Now!" was almost lost in the tympanic beat. The rifle spoke again—and a short flame
streaked from the barrel.

A wisp of smoke drifted from the opening of the radio
box. Phaley spoke hoarsely.

"God—*one* man—in here! The bullets caught Reiner
as he pivoted to get the first violins—and got him at the
other angle—when he swung to the right!"

Jardinn jerked his head in a half nod. He got the rifle
under his coat again. The music was battering, roaring

up to them. He waited until it quieted. Then he turned
his lips toward Phaley, spoke softly.

"One man—murdered Reiner, Phaley. He had the
plane engines, to kill all sound from his rifle. He might
have had a better silencer than the one I used. What little
flame got loose on the second shot didn't hurt anything.
The audience was watching the ship—he was concealed.
The musicians were all working hard. He caught Reiner
in a swifter pivot than the one Bern just made. Reiner
was a more dynamic maestro. A cut-down powder load
would have stopped the bullets from tearing through
Reiner. If he had been bending forward a little—that
would have made a trajectory guess impossible."

Phaley swore. "Sure as hell—he got the dose from
right here!"

The music was rising to a finale now. Jardinn spoke
in a louder tone.

"When the lights went out the second time he got the
rifle under his coat and cleared out. He got his aim while
the lights were on, and Reiner made a sweet target on
that platform, Pat. A target at fifty yards."

Phaley said grimly: "He had him right."

Jardinn changed his cramped posititon, said: "After
the number—we'll get out. Ten to one we'll be seen.
But that don't count. We've got light on us."

Phaley said grimly: "That smoke—a cigar would let
loose that much. They're smoking all over—the place."

Jardinn nodded. "We didn't have a tri-motored plane,
or anyone to work lights," he said. "Reiner got it—
from right here."

The orchestra crashed into the final bars of the number.
The music ended in a barbaric, discordant note. Heinrich
Bern stood motionless, then faced the tiers of seats. Ap-
plause crackled over the Bowl.

Jardinn rose, bent low, walked out in front of the box.
Phaley was behind him. He turned to the left, followed

a dirt path to a sloping aisle, went up the aisle. A few persons looked at him curiously. An usher came down the aisle and said:

"You can't—cross down there. You should have come up the other way."

Jardinn grinned. "Sorry," he replied. "This looked easier."

The usher frowned at him. They reached an aisle that ran the width of the Bowl, went out through the gates and stood near the big bowl used for coin contributions. Phaley passed the cigarettes and lighted one for Jardinn.

"Christ!" he breathed. "Reiner got it—from that damned box!"

Jardinn kept a hand on the rifle under his coat. He said:

"By God—I thought that sound would get out, without plane engines to drown it. Just luck—hit right on the cymbal crack."

They moved slowly down the sloping path, toward Highland Avenue. Machines were coming up—late for the concert. Phaley said:

"You were sure about that kill from the box. Why?"

Jardinn smiled. "Pretty hard to cover up rifles, on the side paths of the Bowl. Pretty hard to keep people from seeing them raised. And for two humans, even if they were sharpshooters, to hit in the dark at two hundred yards—that would be sweet shooting, Pat."

Phaley nodded. "I never did like the idea," he said. "But it was all we had. I couldn't see the angle shooting from the box, and I missed the cut-down powder charge."

Jardinn said mockingly. "You're one hell of a dick, Pat. But I didn't get the idea that way. I went to the concert master—found out where Reiner was on his score—when the lights went out. He had just turned to the first violins, on his left. But almost in the same motion he swung to the right—and had his baton up for the cello section. The first bullet helped him to swing—the second mushroomed and battered him down off the platform.''

Phaley said grimly: "Well, we know how he was killed—and from where he was killed. But how much does that help us?"

Jardinn said: "I'll tell you, Pat—I think I've got our man."

Phaley stopped walking, sucked in his breath sharply. He muttered:

"The hell you have!"

Jardinn nodded. "Yeah," he said. "I think I've got him. There are a few things I don't know—but I think I've got him, just the same. I'm taking a chance."

Phaley started to walk along beside Jardinn again. He said:

"Is he going to cave in—or be nasty with us?"

Jardinn smiled grimly: "I think he'll be nasty as hell," he said. "We're going to have to do a little work on him, Pat."

Phaley pulled on his mustache and said:

"My hands are in good shape."

Jardinn let his eyes get narrow on the pavement along which they walked toward Hollywood Boulevard. He said:

"We'll go up to the office and get rid of the rifle. The silencer worked nice, Pat."

The plainclothesman swore softly. He said:

"Who's our man, Ben?"

Jardinn shook his head. "I'm not making a fool of myself—give me a chance to handle it my way. But it's a human you never suspected, Pat."

Phaley shot a quick glance at Jardinn, said softly, almost cheerfully:

"My hands are hard enough."

Jardinn said: "Pat—I was cramped, in that box. But if I'd had bullets that counted in this rifle—I think I'd have hit Bern. You don't have to be too much of a shot, lying in a good position, and using a rifle on a fifty yard target.''

Phaley grunted. ''You've got to shoot, just the same,'' he said.

Jardinn tossed aside the butt of his cigarette. He spoke slowly.

''Either bullet would have finished Reiner. That killer got the breaks, too.''

Phaley said: ''Get me close to him—my hands are getting nervous.''

Jardinn smiled grimly. ''It's my party—you let me do the talking.''

Phaley grinned. ''Sure,'' he said in a mild voice. ''You let me do the hitting.''

3

Jardinn and Phaley were sitting in the inner office when Max Cohn came in. He smiled at Jardinn, dropped into the one vacant chair and said:

''Hello, Phaley—you look good. Bennie here—he needs some sleep.''

Phaley grinned. ''The hell he does!'' he said.

Jardinn took his feet off a slide of the desk and said slowly:

''Do any good with your pilot, Max?''

Cohn shook his head. ''He didn't show,'' he replied. ''And I thought I'd better get back here. Had a feeling there might be something doing.''

Jardinn grinned. ''By God, you had it right, Max,'' he said. ''I think we've got our killer.''

Cohn's small eyes got wide. His lips parted a little. He sat up straighter in the chair and said:

''It that right?''

Jardinn nodded. ''It works out something like this, Max,'' he said. ''Maya Rand had a damn good-looking sister. She had a nice voice. Maya's got some brains. You know how women are—once in a while they use brains right, and then the next time they mess things up. They get too emotional.''

Cohn said slowly: ''Sure they do.''

Jardinn lighted a cigarette. Pat Phaley was slumped low in his chair. He grinned.

''Maya is pretty good at the flicker stuff. She's got a few years yet. And she doesn't want to be rushed out of the spotlight. Her sister's name was Olive, and Maya figured Ollie was about ripe to rush her out. Maybe she could stick, but Ollie could take the play away. So Maya planted the idea that her sister had a wonderful voice. She shipped her away—and she kept her away. She gave her plenty of coin, but she didn't let her spend it close to Hollywood. She could see what was coming.''

Cohn puckered his lips and whistled. A streetcar made a lot of noise on Hollywood Boulevard.

''She studied in Paris and London. All right. Hans Reiner was conducting in both cities. He ran into her. And he fell pretty hard. Maybe the kid did have a sweet voice. But she wanted to come back to Hollywood. She kept writing Maya that, and Maya kept writing back that her voice was too good. Not very many people in this town know about Ollie. Maya took care of that. But Ernst Reiner knows. And he knows that Maya is over the peak and slipping, see? And then the talkies come in with a rush. And Ernst thinks about Ollie. He thinks about the picture he's seen of her—and the voice. So he digs up an excuse about looking for material—and heads for Paris. It's between pictures. Ernst Reiner makes big money—but he's got to produce the goods. His idea is that Ollie is the goods. He catches up with her in Paris. Hans Reiner is sore as hell—he hands out a line that's something like the one Maya has been handing out. The voice—too good for Hollywood microphones. Back-stage, in a Paris theater where Ollie is singing some highbrow stuff in a class musical comedy, Hans and Ernst get in an argument. Hans doesn't want to lose her. Maybe he's hit hard—I've got to guess at some of this. If she comes to Hollywood he'll probably lose her. And he wins out. Ernst comes back without her. She doesn't sign up.''

Jardinn tapped cigarette ashes into a tray. Cohn nodded and watched him closely. Pat Phaley looked at the floor and swore.

''But before Ernst left he tried to convince his brother that he didn't just want the girl for money purposes. He said it was for art. He told Hans that Maya didn't love the girl—Maya didn't care about her voice. Maya wanted to keep her sister away. He said that he'd have a tough fight with Olive, here in Hollywood, but he'd take the chance. He really wanted her. I don't know what happened in London, but Maya has a last letter from her sister. Perhaps Olive changed her mind, after Ernst left. She decided to come to this country. Hans Reiner was losing her. So, that last evening he was with her, he told her what Ernst had told him. He told her that Maya really hated her, was selfishly keeping her away. He gave her the truth.''

Phaley stroked his mustache and said: ''Goddam squealer!''

Jardinn shrugged. ''It broke up the girl. It finished her. Maybe she took the overdose of veronal by mistake, maybe not. But she did write Maya one final letter, and in it she let Maya know that she knew the truth. And she wrote that Hans Reiner had told her. Maya started to hate. She hated Ernst for telling his brother, but Hans Reiner was the man she wanted to smash. He came over as guest conductor. And Maya got an idea. She'd hurt him, destroy his prestige. She'd break him, get at his nerves. She'd hire a pilot to wing low over the Bowl. Not one night, but every night. Every night he conducted. He was temperamental—and she'd get at him that way.''

Cohn grunted. Phaley sat up a little. Jardinn smiled.

"It was just a woman's way of hurting. It was damn foolishness. But it might have been effective, at that. It failed, because another human saw a chance. A big chance. If Hans Reiner were murdered as the plane flew over the Bowl—this human had Maya where he wanted her. He could bleed her, again and again. Blackmail her. He could threaten to expose the fact that she had put up money for the ship Carren flew. And if the police knew that, God help Maya Rand. They'd laugh at her truth. They'd believe that she wanted to kill."

Phaley swore grimly. "He had her right," he breathed.

Jardinn nodded slowly. "Maya gave money for the plane pilot—to Howard Frey. He used a third party, to reach Carren. The third party squealed to the one who saw his chance, and took it. Carren didn't know what he was doing. He was trapped. He thought he was just winging a ship low over the Bowl. Spite work. When he realized how completely he was trapped, he nearly went mad. The police were hounding him—I was after him. He made a break for the ship—a plane that was grounded and had only two engines in working order. He crashed and was killed."

Phaley said slowly: "And that was a break for the Rand woman."

Jardinn looked at the ceiling. "But she was pretty worried. She had to know what was going on in the agency. She worked that dumb Crissy brat inside. And the baby-faced kid was so scared she gave things away. Ernst Reiner and Frey had fought. They were afraid of each other. The kill gave Reiner a chance to get at Frey. He didn't lose any bets. Or maybe he really thought Frey did the job."

Cohn said thickly: "It wasn't Frey, Bennie?"

Jardinn shook his head. "It wasn't Frey," he replied. "But the murderer of Reiner and Carol Torney—" Jardinn's voice was suddenly hard—"wanted me to *think*

it was Frey. It was important to keep the chase away
from Maya Rand. She could be suspected, questioned—
but not too much. She mustn't come through with the
truth. That was the thing he would use for blackmail.
She hired the plane that flew over the Bowl as Hans
Reiner died.''

Jardinn got up and went over to the window. He faced
Cohn and Phaley, lowered his voice a little.

''Frey wouldn't talk—the killer was sure of that. At
first he was. Frey loved Maya. But then, something
happened. There was a leak in the agency and the killer
learned that Frey had said something that dragged Maya
into the case. And I knew that things weren't going
right in the agency. Reiner had tried to bribe Irish. My
wristwatch had been fixed, I pretended to kick Carol
out, but she wasn't out. We met, away from the office.
The killer got scared—and then Irish got scared. And
then the killer closed in and knifed her. She was getting
too close. And if he could get her to my place, mix me
up in a murder—''

Jardinn stopped. Cohn's sallow face was turned toward
him. There was a stupid expression in his little eyes.
Moisture glittered on his thick lips.

''You had—Irish working—all the time—''

His voice was strained, husky. Jardinn said quietly:

''Hans Reiner was shot to death from that radio store-
house box, Max. One man did the job. With a Maxim
silenced rifle. He had the score of that tone poem. He
knew it had fireworks in it, noise. He knew that Reiner
would work over the orchestra, swing from side to side.
He used the gun—got clear. It was for money, Max—
big money. Maya has it. He could bleed her again and
again. Maybe he could get a hundred thousand, before
he was through.''

Max Cohn swore hoarsely. Phaley got up, stroking his
mustache, and went toward the door that led to the outer
office. He closed it, stood with his back to it.

"Christ—it's getting cold in here," he said in a strange voice. "Getting slimy like."

Jardinn looked down at Cohn and spoke with lips almost pressed together.

"You dirty bastard—we've got you, Cohn!"

Cohn's little eyes got big. His tongue came out and flicked an upper lip. He got a smile on his face.

"Cut the goddam—kidding, Bennie," he said. "It's a hell of a time—"

Jardinn said: "You planted a man next to me, at the concert, to knock me out. You wanted to get rid of that rifle and reach the platform before me. It didn't work. You're a short man, Cohn—and you're a killer. You killed two men. You can shoot. Inside that radio box you had room. You don't make a lot of money in the agency—and you've got a shrewd brain. It was a sweet chance—and you took it. You figured the police would give the theory of two rifles a play—and that might mean a mob. And there was Frey. And Reiner. The two of them at each other's throat. Irish got in the way—and you finished her. You had to—you were in deep. Frey went out, but before he died you got to him. I've talked to Barrett, the copper you bribed to get inside the hospital room. He thought it was just an agency job, and he let you in. I don't know what you told Frey, but I can guess. You told him they were giving Maya Rand the works. He knew he was finished. You said that Maya had gone crazy and knifed Carol Torney, because Carol was wise to the plane hiring. You said if he confessed to that murder the police would lay off. You said she'd told you where the knife had been thrown—"

Cohn cut in grimly: "That's a lie—they're all lies! All of them!"

Phaley said softly: "Jeez—my hands are starting to get nervous."

Jardinn said grimly, looking down at Max Cohn:

"Frey was too sick to figure how Irish's body got out

to my place. He thought you were all right. He loved
Maya. He came through with the confession—and right
away Maya smashed it all to hell with a perfect alibi for
him. You slipped up there, Cohn. You slipped up in
other ways. *You* fixed my wristwatch—not Irish. I fed
stuff into the wastepaper basket—and *you* grabbed it.
I've suspected you from the start, Cohn—but I told you
things. I played ball with you. You weren't in sight of
anybody when Hans Reiner died—and you weren't in
sight of anybody when Carol Torney got knifed. You
had a damn good reason to get her to my place. Then
you'd run the agency, with me fighting for a murder
charge. But you called up twice before I found her lying
on the divan. You didn't want me to suspect, so you
talked as though she was alive. You dirty, woman-kill-
ing—rat!"

Jardinn took a step forward, reached out his left hand
and dragged Cohn from the chair. He hit with his right.
Cohn fell heavily, near Phaley. Phaley kicked him savagely.

Cohn pulled himself to his knees. He said thickly,
twistedly:

"It's all a—goddam lie!"

Jardinn stood swaying a little. After a few seconds he
stopped swaying and smiled. The knuckles of his right
hand stood out redly.

He spoke in a flat, unemotional tone. "Tell me this
is a lie: You've always said you don't know anything
about music. You had Irish believing it. She used to joke
about your low taste. But a half dozen times I've had
reports that you were at the Bowl. You stayed high up—
in the highest tiers. You didn't want to be seen, but you
were seen. Two weeks ago Billy Long came in and said
he'd seen you, spoken to you. You hadn't answered him.
He wanted to know what the hell was wrong. And you
could get at the office files, Cohn. You knew the reports

I got from abroad. You knew about Maya's sister. You knew about the quarrel between Hans and Ernst Reiner.''

Cohn was on his feet, leaning heavily against the office wall, pressing a shaking palm against the left side of his face. Phaley took a step toward him, but Jardinn said sharply: "No, Pat—wait."

Cohn said in a hoarse tone: "You've got it wrong—I'm telling you—"

Jardinn nodded to Phaley. The big plainclothesman stepped in close to Cohn, smothered his protecting, up-flung hand. He drew his right fist back and struck three times. Cohn made no sound, but when Phaley stepped away he slipped to the floor of the office, covered his face with stubby fingers.

Jardinn said: "What in hell's the use, Pat? We've got him. We're up here alone. He isn't yellow, like a cheap crook. He's a dirty killer. But, by God—he's got guts. We can't beat it out of him."

Phaley swore. "Irish was—a good kid," he said bitterly.

Jardinn closed his eyes, swayed again. When he opened them Cohn was propped up against the wall, his face a half-red mask.

Jardinn said: "You had that blonde on the outside, Cohn. The one I kicked out. She was costing you money. You don't make too much in here. Maybe she was after you all the time, like a lot of women. They've got to have things. You saw a chance to pick up a lot of money, Cohn. You took it."

Cohn stared at him dully, shook his head. Jardinn opened the drawer of his desk and took out an automatic. He said softly:

"Get his gun, Pat. We'll save the state some trouble. The way I told you."

Phaley reached down and got Cohn's gun. Jardinn spoke in a toneless voice.

"He confessed, Pat—and then he made a break for it. You pulled your rod, and you both let loose at the same time. He missed you. You got him. I let go and got two hunks of lead inside. He was trying to make a break for it—and we stopped him."

Phaley said grimly: "Sure—that was the way it went, Ben. I'll put a bullet over there—from his gun."

He gestured toward the wall opposite from Cohn. He walked a few feet away.

"Then we'll just—let him have it," he said quietly.

Jardinn nodded. He said: "Start it right, Pat—knock over a chair."

Phaley raised Cohn's gun a little, reached for the nearest chair with his left hand. Cohn said in a flat, dead voice:

"That goddam—woman. Wait—I'll talk."

Phaley dropped his left hand. Jardinn stood motionless. Cohn wiped red from his swollen lips, spoke slowly in a thick, dull tone.

"That blonde—she had me licked, Ben. She was always wanting something. Once in a while I got a little graft money. But that wasn't enough. She had me licked a lot of ways. I owed money. She was always—going to leave me. And I—didn't want—that."

Jardinn said slowly: "Reiner—and Irish—all for a rotten woman—"

Cohn cut in bitterly. "Hans Reiner—he wasn't any good. I could read between the lines—in those reports. He drove Olive Rand—to suicide—"

Jardinn said: "You're looking for an out, now. You don't know what he did. Never mind that—what did *you* do?"

Cohn stared at Jardinn. His voice was low and husky.

"It looked like—a perfect kill. And I could get the money I needed. Maya Rand has plenty—and with Hans Reiner dead as the ship flew over the Bowl—I had her nice. I could bleed her. More than once. I got him from the radio box. The rifle's buried—on the hillside, at the left.''

He paused, wiped his lips again. Pat Phaley was staring at him, breathing heavily. Jardinn stood motionless, his face expressionless.

"Things didn't break right, after the kill. The goddam blonde—she was wise. I got afraid of Irish. I couldn't be sure of her. I was afraid she'd get to—"

He checked himself. Jardinn said:

"Yeah—your woman. You were afraid she'd rat it and squeal, to save herself. So you—finished Irish."

Cohn said hoarsely: "Christ—I was in a tough spot. I went to Irish's place. We started to talk—and her eyes looked wise. I grabbed her. I got a gun out and made her call you, Ben—and use Frey's name. She did it—she was scared. Then she ran for the kitchen. I was afraid to shoot. I caught her, near the door. She didn't yell. There was—a knife—on a table—"

Jardinn said: "God—what a deal!"

Cohn said grimly: "I drove her—out to your place—went back home."

Phaley's big fingers were twisting. He didn't speak. Cohn said:

"You had it right—about the way I got to Howard Frey. It was Carren who put me wise. He wanted to know what sort of a dose he'd get, if they caught him winging low over the Bowl. He didn't know what it was all about. Frey used a man named Cordova as a go-between. But Cordova described Frey to Carren. The pilot gave me the description. And I knew it was Maya Rand's game. I was watching Frey. And he didn't have money—not enough money. Maya Rand wanted to *hurt* Hans Reiner. I saw—the big chance."

Cohn's thickset body shivered a little. Jardinn said slowly:

"Ernst Reiner and Frey were hating each other. You thought that would be a cover-up. You wanted the police to get Frey. You knew he wouldn't squeal on Maya. But when he weakened a little—you got scared."

Cohn didn't speak. Jardinn said bitterly:

"I wasn't sure—until I crawled into that radio box. You're a short man, Cohn—you would fit in there nice. I didn't. And you've—killed before. You're greedy. That blond woman—"

Cohn said bitterly: "Goddam her."

Phaley drew a deep breath. "Cordova—where's he? Who worked with you—on the lights?"

Cohn said harshly: "I don't squeal. They've both skipped. They didn't know it was to be a kill—just a concert smash. A dirty, Hollywood trick."

Jardinn turned away, went over and looked down on Hollywood Boulevard. He said softly:

"That poor, damn kid—Irish—"

Phaley said: "I'll take Cohn down to the station, Ben. You coming?"

Jardinn didn't reply. Phaley said slowly:

"Come down later, Ben."

Jardinn said: "Yeah—later."

He heard them moving toward the door. He turned, and said in a hard, low voice:

"I'm going to put you—on the trap for this, Cohn. I'll watch it sprung—"

Cohn's eyes seemed to be looking beyond him. He turned away, stared out of the window again. He could hear their footfalls on the stairs beyond the office. After a while the janitress came in. She smiled at him.

"Can I clean up, mister?" she asked.

Jardinn said heavily: "If there's anything left—to clean up."

When he reached the street a kid with eyes that were so much like Carol Torney's they hurt shoved a paper in front of him.

"Latest, Mister!" he said. "All about the Bowl murder!"

Jardinn said: "Sure." He took the paper, gave the kid a quarter. He didn't look at it. A half square away he tossed it into a refuse can. When he reached the police station Brenniger grabbed him by an arm and said grimly:

"Hell, Ben—you did it again."

Jardinn squeezed his tired eyes closed. He said in a bitter tone:

"Yeah—swell, isn't it?"

He went slowly toward the sergeant's desk.

Also Available in Quill Mysterious Classics: